Paper Trail

By
Arlene Brathwaite

BRATHWAITE PUBLISHING
www.brathwaitepublishing.com

Books by Arlene Brathwaite are published by

Brathwaite Publishing
P.O. Box 38205
Albany, New York 12203

Copyright © 2010 by Arlene Brathwaite

Library of Congress Number:

ISBN: (10 Digit) # 0-9797462-3-x
ISBN: (13 Digit) # 978-0-9797462-3-9

This book was printed in the United States of America.

Acknowledgments

An author's success is never the result of just their dedication and hard work. It is the consorted effort of the many men and women working behind the scenes who are just as dedicated and hard working.

Brathwaite Publishing continues to grow because of its team of talented professionals and our commitment to readers all over who have come to expect nothing but our best.

Special thanks go out to my content editor Olivia Haynes (Locksie of ARC Book Club Inc.). Your suggestions were right on the money. To my proof readers, Tamicka Ramey , Andrea Anthony, Abdul-Aziz aka R. Fason, Derrick Ackerman, Leon Infinite Law, Linden Boule aka "L". Thank you for your honesty and constructive criticism.

I can't forget the man who put the dollar sign in the word hu$tle, Maxwell Penn, Author extraordinaire. Thank you for opening up doors for me and putting my books where they needed to be. To Keith of Marion Designs. As always, you never cease to amaze me with your cover designs.

A special thanks to Curtis Witters of LilVillaPub and to his music group CLASHY, for the theme song for *In The Cut*. You were with me when *Music Meets Literature* was just an idea knocking around in my head. You helped make that part of Brathwaite Publishing a reality.

A special thanks to the newest member of the team Mr. Lee*G (Leroy Griffith Jr.) of Oonlah Records. Who would've thought that once you came on board to do the theme song to *Paper Trail* that you would also end up being on the cover?

A special thanks to Multimedia Specialist, Jamel Mosely for the sound effects on the audio excerpt for *Paper Trail*, your work was priceless.

And last but not least, thank you to all the supporters of Brathwaite Publishing. You are the engine of this machine. You drive us to give you nothing but the best.

To The Readers

First off, thank you, thank you, thank you, for your love, support, letters, e-mails, and suggestions. It is your words of encouragement, inspiration and criticism that make every book I write better than the last.

To the first time readers: I was at a loss for words when I got e-mails from people who never read a book in its entirety until they read Youngin'. And now they can't stop reading. I am honored that Youngin' opened the door for so many first time readers. And I hope you keep on reading, because I'm going to keep on putting out hit after hit.

After I put out Youngin' and Ol'Timer, I got crazy e-mails telling me that I had to write a book about Devon. A lot of people were feeling his character for their own different reasons and they had to know what happened to him while Brian was doing time. So, my way of showing my appreciation to the fans of Youngin' and Ol'Timer, I made it my business to hunt Devon down. After six months of nagging him, he finally caved in and agreed to meet with me. He said he would tell me exactly what happened to him, from a fictional point of view, of course.

For those of you who read Ol'Timer, you got the idea that Devon was doing it big. Well, nothing's changed. When I got to the airport, there was a pilot waiting for me at the gate.

"Good morning, Mrs. Brathwaite, my name is Walter. I'll be flying you to London."

"Me and who else?" I asked, as I looked at that big ass jet.

"Just you, ma'am."

I'm not going to bore you with the details of the flight. I basically talked to my husband on the Jet's phone the whole time. Devon's doing it big; he can afford it, right?

When we landed in London, Devon blew me away. Right there, on the runway, was a beige Rolls-Royce awaiting my arrival. I took my cell phone out and began taking pictures of it to send to Brian.

A woman with a bob-style hair cut stepped out of the back of the Rolls and approached me.

"Mrs. Brathwaite, it's a pleasure to finally meet you." She extended her hand.

I shook it. She looked to be about thirty years old and athletic looking.

"My name is Ginja."

"Nice to meet you, Ginja."

We climbed into the back of the Rolls-Royce and it pulled off.

"So, what do you do?" I asked her. I wasn't wasting any time.

"I'm one of Devon's personal assistants."

"How many personal assistants does he have?"

She smiled. "I think I'll let him answer your questions."

I could tell I was making her nervous. She kept fidgeting with her diamond bracelet.

The Rolls pulled up to a brownstone. Ginja escorted me up the stairs and towards an elevator. We took it to the top floor. The brownstone was decked out to say the least. Wall to wall carpeting, plush sofas, crystal chandeliers, oil paintings, the whole nine. We walked to the end of the hall to an office. Ginja knocked once and then opened it. She allowed me to walk in first.

"The girl from the park," Devon said, as he got out of his chair and walked over to hug me.

"How have you been?" I asked.

"Fine. How's my boy?"

"Brian's doing well. His home repair business is picking up." I could tell by the look on his face he hated the fact that Brian was doing manual labor when he knew all he had to do was give him the word. Devon was ready to give my baby half of his corporation just on the strength. After seeing what he was working with, I was tempted to go back and convince my baby to stop playing with that hammer and come on over here and claim his. After all, none of this would have been possible if Devon didn't have those bricks of coke to start out with. I looked around the office and smiled at the other people who were sitting there.

Devon first introduced me to the four men sitting together. "Arlene, this is my cousin Recker, the gentleman next to him is the General, and the men next to him are Knots and Porter."

"Nice to meet you," I said.

"Ya' came 'ere to do a story, huh?" The General asked in his native patoi.

"Yes."

"Yeah," the General said, nodding his head. "Me remember back in '83 when a news reporter did a story on me. Hey did I ever tell y'all about the time when…"

"Yes!" everyone in the room shouted.

"At least fifty times," Recker said.

"Well, all me saying is if she came for a story, me got some stories."

"Some? Ya' ave story fa eeeverytin."

I looked at the white woman sitting on the other side of the room who just spoke. I tried to hide my amazement, but I was never too good at hiding my emotions.

"Don't worry, sweetheart," she said to me. "A lot of people look 'pon me like that when they first hear me speak."

"Wow, I'm sorry. It's just that I've never…"

"Heard a white girl with a thick Jamaican accent?"

"Yes." I looked at her amazed. Everyone else had a Jamaican accent, but hearing hers just blew me away.

"It's not uncommon in Jamaica," she said. "Me name's Ivory."

"It's a pleasure to meet you," I said.

"The pleasure's all mine, darling."

"You must be tired," Devon stated.

"Actually, no; I got a lot of rest on the plane." I sat down and opened up my laptop. "I'm ready."

"Ready?" Devon asked.

"Me like her style," the General said. "No nonsense, straight for 'de jugular."

I arched an eyebrow at that comment and then looked at Devon.

"Well," Devon said. "I guess we can start. We have about an hour or so."

"What's happening in an hour?" I asked.

"I'm taking you out to see London."

"Nah, this is fine."

"I know you didn't think I was going to sit in some stuffy office and tell you my story just like that, did you?"

"I'm okay with that," I said.

"But I'm not. I can't have you go back and tell my boy that I had you cooped up in the house the whole time you were here."

"Besides, the sights are beautiful and I know where all the best boutiques are," Ginja chimed in.

"I didn't bring money to shop."

"We're going to spend his money," she said, pointing to Devon.

"Well, I guess we can do a little sightseeing."

"And a lot of shopping." Ginja and I started laughing. I was beginning to like her.

"Well, where do I start?" Devon asked.

I put my glasses on. "Start from…. when you first found out Brian got arrested."

"Umm, okay, here we go."

Prelude

Devon crept down Quana's street in his truck, eyes peeled. It was three in the morning and so quiet, that he could hear his heart pounding in his chest. Sonia called him earlier that evening in a frenzy. The Atlanta police came to the house and had taken Brian to the precinct. When he got there, two detectives from New York were there waiting for him.

"They arrested him, Devon, and they're taking him back to New York. What the hell is going on?" Sonia asked.

"I don't know."

"What do you mean you don't know? You're like his second skin. He doesn't do anything without telling you."

Devon made a U-turn and headed to Andrea's house. "Let me make a couple calls and then call you back in a few."

"No, tell me what the hell is going on, right now. I'm two weeks away from having this baby and Brian swore to me that he wasn't doing anymore crime."

"Sonia, please let me make a couple calls. I swear I'm going to get back to you."

"I'll be right here, sitting by the phone."

"All right, bye."

Brian drove up to Queens a couple days ago to grab two more kilos of the coke they had stolen from the stash house in

Long Island. It had been his third trip that month. Instead of just letting Devon transport all 88 kilos to Atlanta in one shot, Brian decided to let Andrea hold on to the money and the coke. He trusted her enough to know that she wouldn't dare tap either one. But now that he was in custody, Devon wasn't taking any chances. He cursed under his breath when he pulled up in front of her house and saw her mother's car parked in the driveway. Fuck it, he thought. The police could be on their way here for all I know. As he headed to the front door, he was surprised to see Andrea standing behind the screen door with her arms folded. He looked in all directions to make sure he didn't walk into a trap. Andrea read his body language and answered the question he didn't get a chance to ask.

"I saw you drive past three times. What were you doing, making sure the coast was clear?"

"Something like that," Devon answered.

"What's up?"

"I know this is not the best time to do this, but I'm going to need everything you're holding onto for me and Brian."

"You mean everything I'm holding onto for Brian."

"Whatever. I need to come inside and collect all of it."

Andrea pulled out her cell phone and dialed Brian's number.

"He's not going to answer."

"Why not?"

"He's in jail."

"What?"

"The police in Atlanta came to the house and arrested him. Detectives from New York are bringing him back here."

"Oh my God! How much trouble is he in?"

"Right now, I don't know. But I have a feeling that Jason ratted us out. If he did, he most likely gave the police your name."

Andrea folded her phone shut when she got Brian's voice mail and bit her bottom lip as she stared at the ground.

Devon snapped his fingers. "I need that stuff now."

"I can't just give it to you."

"What?"

"I'm not giving you anything until I hear from Brian."

"Andrea, don't do this." Devon looked past her into the house.

Andrea looked over her shoulder and caught a glimpse of her mother going into the kitchen. "My mother's home, so even if I wanted to give you Brian's things I couldn't do it now."

"Andrea, either you're going to let me in so I can grab what I need or—"

"Or what?" Andrea said with attitude.

Devon reached around into the back of his waistband and whipped out his .45 caliber. He shoved Andrea back and walked into the house toward the kitchen.

"Andrea, what's going on out there?" her mother asked, hearing the commotion.

Andrea ran in front of Devon and stood in front of the small cannon in his hand. "Okay, I'll give it to you. Please put that away."

"Andrea?" her mother called out again.

Devon stared at her for a moment and then stuffed the .45 back against the small of his back.

Andrea's mother walked out of the kitchen. "Is everything okay?"

"Yes mommy. This is Devon, one of my friends. Uh... he had a big fight with his parents a couple nights ago, and they kicked him out.

"Oh my."

"He didn't have anywhere to put his belongings, so, I took some of his stuff and held it in the basement for him until he was able to go back home. He just came by to pick them up."

"Sure, honey. Would you like something to eat, Devon?"

"No, Ma'am, but thanks for asking. I'm kind of in a hurry."

"Okay, I'll let you two go on and get your things."

Without a word or help, Andrea watched Devon carry the garbage bags of coke and money to his truck. The last thing he loaded into the back was the chest of guns and money Brian had in Andrea's closet. He slammed the door and wiped the sweat from his brow.

Andrea gave him the evil eye. "If I find out that you played me, I'll kill you." Devon tried walking past her, but she shoved him in the chest. "Remember what I said."

"You don't have a clue who you're threatening, do you?"

"I don't give a fuck who you think you are. You bleed just like the next man."

They stared at each other, neither refusing to break eye contact first.

Andrea's mother interrupted the stare down. "Andrea, get in here and help me program this DVR to record my show while I'm at work."

Andrea stared at Devon for a couple more seconds before heading back inside.

* * *

It was hard for the cops to go unnoticed staking out a house at three in the morning. But the ever paranoid Devon, coasted down the block. If there was a car on the block he didn't recognize, he was going to keep it moving. He breathed easy when he recognized every vehicle. He put his truck in reverse and parked in front of Quana's house. He pulled out his cell phone and dialed her number.

"You better be calling me because you died and went to hell, because if you're calling for any other reason, at three in the morning—"

"Brian's in jail."

"What?"

"Detectives from New York went to Atlanta to bring him back."

"God, no."

"I'm in front of your house; I need to see you now."

"Come around back."

Five minutes later, she slid the patio door open and stepped outside. She looked at the garbage bags at Devon's feet.

"What's in the bags?"

"Money."

"How much money?"

"A lot." Devon stepped away from the bags as she approached them. She stooped down and looked inside one of them and gasped.

"That's a whole lot of money." She backed away. "Under normal circumstances I would be happy to see that amount of cash, but right now, I'm scared to death. What's going on?"

"I think Jason gave me and Brian up."

"That rat motherfucker. Y'all grew up together. I can't believe he would flip on y'all like that." She watched Devon pull out his phone and look at the caller ID.

"It's my grandmother. She told me the police came by the house earlier wanting to speak with me. She's been blowing up my cell ever since."

"What did y'all get yourselves into?" Quana asked.

"That's not important, right now. What's important is getting Brian a damn good lawyer. I know he's going to call you. I need you to hold this money for him."

"Are you insane? I can't hold on to all this. I'm shaking as we speak. I can't—"

"If there was ever a time that Brian needed you, it's right now. You're a strong woman, you can do this."

"I can't go to jail, Devon."

"And you're not. Trust me. No one can trace this money to you."

"Why can't you give it to Sonia?"

"Brian would want me to give it to you."

She looked at the ground.

"Quana, look at me. I would never put you in any kind of danger. You know that, right?"

"Yes."

"Get our boy out of prison. Can you do that?"

"I'll do whatever I got to do."

"Thank you." He hugged her and started to walk away.

"What about you? What are you going to do?"

"Tell Brian I left you the money and that I took everything else."

"Everything else? You mean there's more?"

"Just give him the message. He'll know what you're talking about."

"Watch your back, Devon."

"That's what I do best."

Chapter 1

Rosedale train station. The police most likely had an APB out on him and his truck, so he had to dump it and find a temporary ride. He drove through the parking lot until he came across the perfect vehicle. It was a brown Chrysler caravan. He jimmied the lock and let himself in. He had the vehicle running in under a minute. He quickly transferred the coke and Brian's chest into the back of the caravan. He hopped in and drove onto Sunrise Highway. Before he knew it, he was on the I-95 heading south. He was now a fugitive with a carful of drugs and guns. There was no turning back. Either he was going to make it to Florida or die trying.

He made three pit stops; one to piss and get something to eat, one to shoot the chest open. The chest contained five thousand in cash, two 9mm guns, and a bullet proof vest. His last stop was a parking lot in Richmond Virginia to steal another vehicle. If the police located his truck, they were going to do two things. First, they were going to show his picture to the clerk at the train station to see if he purchased a ticket. Second, they were going to check with the Nassau County police to see if any cars were reported stolen from the parking lot in the past couple days. He doubted if New York's finest

worked that efficiently, but he was never the type to underes-
timate anyone.

Florida was his only way out of the country. His uncle
owned an import/export company in Fort Lauderdale. His
business was about as legit as liquor in the prohibition days,
but his connections in commerce could care less as long as he
kept their deep pockets filled to the brim with Jacksons,
Grants, and Benjamin's. His phone rang for the umpteenth
time. His grandmother and Sonia were tag teaming his cell.
When he finally shut it off, he felt like he severed the last line
to his life in Queens. His heart was colder than Jack Frost's
breathe, but he knew that if he was going to survive the plan
that was brewing in his head, his heart was going to have to get
a whole lot colder.

* * *

Devon pulled up to his uncle's warehouse the next day. He
stepped out of the car and did a full body stretch before
heading inside. He took one sweeping look at the interior
before laying eyes on the female who was looking at him like
he was lost.

"Can I help you?" she asked with a deep country accent.

"I'm looking for Clifford."

"Who you?"

"I'm his nephew."

"Nephew? How come I ain't never seen you before then?"

"I'm from out of town."

The female curled up her lip and looked at him like he just
passed gas. "Clifford!"

Devon winced as his eardrums vibrated.

"Cliffor—"

"Hey, hey, hey, girl," Clifford said, coming around the corner. "Why don't you use the PA system?"

"I don't like how my voice be sounding on that thing.
Your nephew is here." She cut her eyes at Devon.

Clifford spun around, oblivious that Devon was standing there. He squinted. "Devon?"

"What's up?"

"Boy, as God is my witness, I wouldn't have recognized you if Fredricka didn't say nephew. The last time I saw you, you were 13, 14 years old?"

"Something like that," Devon said as the two men hugged.

"Skinny as a handrail back then, too." Clifford's eyes quickly looked Devon over.

"You got someplace where we can talk in private?" Devon asked, cutting his eyes at Fredricka.

She sucked her teeth. "Ain't nobody want to be listening to y'all conversation."

"C'mon," Clifford said, putting his arm around him. "We can talk in my office." Clifford walked him outside the warehouse and around to the side where there was an office annexed to the building. As they entered, Clifford went straight to the minibar and poured himself a glass of Absolute. "You want a shot?"

Devon shook his head. "I don't drink."

"Good for you. This shit'll rot your liver." Clifford gulped down the 100 proof Vodka and then poured himself another. "So what brings you all the way down here to Fort Lauderdale?"

"I'm on my way to Disney World and decided to make a pit stop to visit my favorite uncle."

"Bullshit," Clifford said sitting down behind his desk. "Something tells me I better be sitting down when you lay it on me."

Devon remained standing. "I got into a little bit of trouble in New York."

"What's a little?"

"A lot."

"You killed someone?"

"I need to get out of the country, Unc."

"Jesus Devon!"

"Can you get me to Jamaica?"

"You know I can."

"I also have a few things I need for you to ship there for me."

"What's a few things?"

"82 bricks of coke."

"What the f—" Clifford jumped out of his chair like a volt of electricity just shot through his body. "Boy, are you out of your mind? Me can't do nothing like that."

"Sure you can, Unc. I know you still got your connections in Customs."

"And how do you know that?" Clifford arched his brow.

"You may be a lot of things, but a fool isn't one of them. You would never shut that lucrative backdoor."

A smile crept across Clifford's face. "How's my mama doing?"

"Grandma is doing well, but she could be doing much better."

"How so?"

"Hearing from you other than Mother's Day would be much better. And moving her out of that house she's been living in for the past fifteen years would be nice."

"There's nothing wrong with that house," Clifford said defensively.

"It's not the house, it's the neighborhood. Laurelton isn't the nice suburban community it used to be."

"Mama hasn't complained."

"And she won't you know that."

"I'll give her a call and tell her to start looking for another house."

Devon clasped his hands behind his back. "So… about my problem."

"Yes, all 82 bricks of it. I'm going to be up front with you, Nephew. If I can get this shipment into Jamaica, and that's a big if, it's not going to be cheap."

"How much are we talking?"

"I can't give you a price, not until I talk to some people."

"And when will that be?"

"Three, maybe four days."

"I hoped to be in Jamaica by then."

"And you can. It will just be a little more time to get your product there."

"Why am I getting this feeling like you're trying to fuck me?"

Clifford finished the rest of his drink. "Before you throw that word around so loosely, think about what you're asking me to do, and think of what can happen to me and all those involved if your shipment gets caught in transit. We'll be the ones fucked. Besides, what am I going to do with all that stuff? I don't know the first thing about selling drugs, and the last thing I'm going to do is attract attention to myself by trying to sell that shit."

Devon smiled. "You got a point there. Plus, I know you wouldn't want to be the cause of bad blood between the family."

"As I'm sure you wouldn't want to be either when it's time for you to pay up."

Devon nodded.

"Did you tell anyone you were coming here?"

"No."

"Did you bring everything with you?"

"It's in the car outside."

"Whose car is it?"

"I stole it in Richmond."

"Let's go on out here, so you can show me what you got."

Devon took him to the car and opened the trunk.

Clifford peeked inside one of the bags. "That's a lot of shit."

"But you can get it to Jamaica, right?"

"Would you be here if you thought I couldn't?"

Devon smiled.

"First things first." Clifford pulled out his cell phone. "Chopper, how goes it? Come and check me, I have one for you. It's on the house… yeah come as soon as you can." He hung up. "That was my man Chopper. He owns a junkyard not too far from here. He's going to come by and get rid of this piece of crap." He reached into the trunk and grabbed one of the bags. "For the time being, we can put everything in my office."

Devon grabbed the chest and followed him.

"Your Auntie Lorraine and Uncle Junior are going to be happy to see you. I'll give them a call and let them know you're coming."

"Nah, don't do that. I don't want them going out of their way."

"Nonsense you're family. They're going to take care of you."

"I don't want them involved with what I'm doing."

"How do you expect to get rid of this stuff?"

"Recker has to know some people who will be interested."

"Recker? You mean your cousin Derrick? Humph, if anyone knows where you can get rid of this shit, it's him. How much did you say you had all together?"

"82 bricks."

"How much can you get for each one?"

"I'm trying to get them off as fast as I can so I'm not asking the going price."

"But you don't want to sell them too cheap, because buyers will become suspicious."

"Which is why I'm going to let them go for 15 thou a piece."

"That's… a little over one million two hundred thousand." Clifford had a calculator for a brain. "Damn, I'm in the wrong business."

"Trust me, Unc, you don't want to be in this business. If I'm lucky, I'll probably clear a million. You know dudes are going to want deals."

"What are you going to do with a million dollars?"

"I don't make plans with money I don't have in my hands."

Clifford shook his head. "I hope you know what you're doing."

"Outside of you, I will be the only one who knows where I'm at and what I'm doing."

Clifford nodded, letting Devon know he read between the lines.

* * *

Two days later, Devon entered the terminal at Ft. Lauderdale International Airport. It was 89 degrees, but he was as cool as ice as he got on line to pick up his ticket. Two women were working. He got on the line of the heavy-set one. She looked exactly the way Clifford had described, all the way down to the gold front tooth.

"Next," she said, waiting for him to step up.

"I made reservations over the phone yesterday," Devon said, as he pulled out his fake credentials and handed them to her.

She looked at the picture and then cut her eyes at him.

Devon took a deep breath and held it. What if Clifford got greedy and decided to keep the coke for himself. Devon looked toward the exit, deciding whether or not to take off.

She handed him back his ID and printed up his ticket. "Your plane will be boarding in fifteen minutes. Enjoy your flight."

"Thank you." Devon headed to the waiting area and sat down before his legs gave out. One thing he couldn't stand was not having control of a situation. Right now, he was naked, meaning, he didn't have a gun in case anything was to pop off. The only thing he had with him was a carry-on bag containing a couple shirts and shorts he brought at a thrift shop. He looked at his watch and perked up. It was boarding time.

* * *

Devon was born in Queens, New York. His mother was African-American, his father was full-blooded Jamaican. At the age of three, his father decided to move back to Jamaica, West Indies. He snatched Devon up and took him with him. He lived in Jamaica for seven years. Two months out of each year, his father would send him up to New York to spend time with his mother and grandmother. At the age of eleven, his father got into a shoot out with some dreads who ambushed his truck. He was able to ram his truck through the roadblock and kill three of them before going out in a hail of gunfire. Devon's uncle and aunt sent him back to New York to be raised by his mother. She immediately put him in private school. But Devon purposely flunked out of private school, wanting to be like his rude boy father, who ran the streets of Jamaica. It was then that his mother enrolled him in PS 30, where he met Brian and Jason.

When the airplane landed in Kingston, Devon immediately noticed two things. One, the translucent waves of heat rising from the runway told him it was hot as hell, and two, it had been almost ten years since he'd last been here. After going through customs, with his carry-on bag slung across his shoulder, he exited the terminal, heading out into the blazing sun.

"Dev!" A thin youth in his early twenties was sitting on the hood of a Nissan Sentra. His head was crystal ball smooth and peach fuzz spotted the underside of his chin. "Long time no see, Cuz."

"It hasn't been that long, has it?" Devon asked, as he walked toward the car.

Recker hopped off the hood and met him halfway. Devon slapped him five. Just as Recker was about to pull his hand back, Devon grabbed it and looked at it. Recker's right index finger was missing.

"What the hell?"

"Me and another dread had some heavy beef. When our paths crossed, we had a shoot out. One of his punk faggot boys snuck me from behind, hitting me in the back of the head. His crew held me down while the dread pulled out his ratchet knife and—"

"All right," Devon said, shaking his head. "I can imagine what came next."

"I still have a trigger finger." Recker made an imaginary gun with his right hand and then started pulling an imaginary trigger with his middle finger.

"Is your aim still accurate?"

"With my Uzi, all I have to do is aim in the general direction. A one second burst is sending 15 bullets at you. If I can't hit you with 15 shots, then it ain't meant for me to hit you."

Devon put his arm around him and punched him in the chest. "So young and so violent."

They climbed into the Nissan and drove off.

Devon sat back and took in the beautiful scenery.

"So talk to me, Cuz," Recker said, "What am I getting myself into?"

"What makes you think you're getting into something?"

"The fact that you called out of the blue and told me to meet you at the airport, and you didn't want me to take you to my parents' house. You know they're going to kill me if they find out you're here and I didn't tell them."

"Auntie Lorraine and Uncle Junior aren't going to know I'm here if you don't say anything."

"So talk to me, what's the deal?"

Devon studied the foam dice bouncing on the rearview mirror for a moment before he spoke. "Some shit went down in New York. Me and my boys, Brian and Jason, were doing a routine snatch and grab. Only, we were caught by surprise. The dude's chick was in the truck. She pulled out and started shooting."

"My kind of woman."Recker smiled.

"Shit got hectic and we started shooting back. When the smoke cleared, dude and his woman were dead."

"You got the money, of course."

"Of course."

"Mission accomplished. Shit happens."

"That was only the beginning." Devon continued. "The kid we stole the money from found out that we were behind it. The guy we were working for had a little sister. Come to find out, this sick motherfucker was molesting her from when she was old enough to walk."

Recker screwed up his face. "I know you put him out of his misery."

"Of course. Anyway, his sister, wanting to get back at him, ratted him out. What she didn't know was ratting on him would point the finger at us. So to make a long story short, we had to put in some work. Jason got arrested. I don't know what the police told him at the precinct, but he snitched us out. My other partner, Brian, was already in Atlanta starting a new life with wifey and their soon-to-be-born child. I get a call from her a few days ago, telling me that New York Detectives came down to Atlanta and brought him back to New York. I don't have to tell you the rest, right?"

"You got your ass on the next thing smoking."

Devon nodded.

"Damn, Cuz, what type of dudes were you messing with? One molesting his sister, another one snitching."

"Enough about me and my hood tales. You still running crazy in the streets?"

"Cuz, I be running the streets."

"Oh here we go, just what I need, another wannabe boss man."

"I'm not a boss man, I'm a soldier." Recker puffed up his chest.

"A soldier?"

"Yeah, and I got my own team."

"A team, huh?"

"Totally thorough."

"Well, I may have some work for y'all."

"We don't work for no one but ourselves."

"I don't want you to work for me. I want you to work with me. Partners, fifty-fifty."

"And what do you have that I might possibly want half of?"

"A million dollars."

Recker swerved off the road.

* * *

"Devon don't play with me."

"Have you ever known me to play?"

Recker's eyes narrowed as he tried reading Devon's non-expressive face. He sucked his teeth and stomped on the gas pedal. The Nissan's tires spun in the dirt a good three seconds before shooting back onto the road.

Devon was far from the trusting type, family or not. But he knew that if he wasn't up front with Recker from the get-go, it would come back to bite him in the ass. He needed absolute loyalty and a team that would have his back. The only way to get that was to show trust, even if it was only an illusion.

"I'm going to need some guns."

"Guns are not a problem, but check it. You can't come down here on that New York rah-rah shit. The rude boys down here don't play."

"I don't plan on starting any trouble. I just like to be prepared for whatever may come my way."

"As long as everyone knows you're rolling with me, you're not going to have any problems."

"That may be the case, but I still prefer to have it and not need it than to need it and not have it."

"Can't argue with you there."

Recker turned down a side street. Houses lined one side of the block. The other side was a gigantic plot of un-kept land. Wet paper, torn open trash bags, and old car tires were scattered all over. Devon could see the beach just beyond the mound of trash.

"Who owns that land over there?"

"Damn, your money long like that?"

"Nah, my money ain't long like that. I was just asking."

"You had to be asking for a reason."

"No reason."

"Whatever you say Mr. asking-for-no-reason." Recker pulled into his driveway. "It's not much, but it beats staying with my moms and pops."

They got out and headed inside.

Recker gave Devon a tour, which took all of fifteen seconds. The biggest rooms were the three bedrooms.

"This room is yours," Recker said.

Devon threw his bag on the bed and started stripping.

Recker was about to close the door to give him some privacy, but froze when Devon stripped down to his shorts. "I was wondering why you were wearing that hot ass velour sweat suit," he said, staring at the money taped to Devon's chest, stomach, back, and legs.

Devon convinced good ol' Uncle Clifford to loan him ten thousand to put with the five he found in Brian's chest.

"You going to just stand there or are you going to help me get this shit off of me?"

"Let me go get a knife."

Chapter 2

Devon got caught up staring at the moon. He had forgotten just how beautiful it looked without having to gaze at it through the glare of city lights and smog. It hung in the night sky, while stars glittered in the backdrop.

The smooth breeze swirled the ocean's scent all around him. Damn it was peaceful on the beach. The white sand, clear water, and the tide rushed to the shore and covered his bare feet in sand before slipping back into the ocean. He inhaled the crisp Jamaican air and held it. Recker was standing next to him. He took a deep breath, as well, and held it. He held it until his head felt like it was going to burst and then he exhaled the weed smoke in Devon's direction.

"I was having a moment," Devon said, cutting his eyes at him.

"Fuck having a moment. Have some of this." He held the blunt out to him.

Devon walked closer to the water to get away from the weed smoke.

Recker took two more pulls. As he exhaled, he started to sway. "Ah, that's my shit."

"What's that?" Devon asked.

"Ahh, yeah." Recker started dancing. "I said giiirl, it's been so long, since you sit down on this john, make you hold my hand, make you moan in pain…"

Devon was about to tell Recker that, that weed was frying his brain, but then he heard a faint beat. About a quarter of mile down the beach, he saw a pair of headlights bouncing toward them. "Unbelievable. I can't believe you can hear that shit from way down here."

Recker took another pull and exhaled. "I'm telling you, Cuz, weed gives you super powers. You need to stop playing and hit this shit. Get your Superman on, my dude."

"I can get my Superman on just fine with this, right here." He patted the 17 shot, pearl handle, 9mm Beretta Recker gave him earlier.

"Whatever you say, Gunslinger."

Devon could really hear the music thumping out of the black Ford F-150 pickup heading their way. As the truck got closer, he saw two guys standing in the flatbed, holding onto the chrome roll bar. They both threw a fist in the air to Recker. He did the same. The truck stopped by a rusted 55 gallon oil drum. Devon raised an eyebrow when two women jumped out of the truck's cab.

"Recker what's good?"

The first female Devon laid eyes on had a brownish red complexion. She was about 5' 6". She wore her reddish brown hair in a bob-style cut. The second female was bone white. She was an inch taller than her partner. Her hair color was bleach blonde and it tumbled to her shoulders. Her green eyes twinkled in the moonlight. Both women had small waists, big busts, and big butts. They were both wearing bikini tops and airtight jeans.

"Y'all know what it is," Recker said, passing the blunt to the white girl. She took it and filled her lungs to their capacity and then passed it to her partner. She closed her eyes and pulled on the blunt. She shuddered as she held her breath. When she exhaled, she sighed as if she just had an orgasm.

"What's good?" the white girl asked Devon. Her Jamaican accent was strong.

"The name's Devon."

"I'm Ivory." She walked up to him and hugged him like he was her boyfriend.

"Heard a lot about you," the other woman said. "I'm Ginja." She hugged him harder than Ivory did.

"He's family," Recker said.

Neither woman responded.

"Repeat after me... Devon's family."

"We heard you the first time," Ginja said, as she let Devon go.

"I want to make sure that both of you understand."

"We ain't retarded, Recker," Ivory said.

Instead of trying to understand the point Recker was trying to make, Devon looked past them to the two guys jumping out the back, and the driver climbing out of the cab. The driver was wearing dark shades, jeans, and a tank top. He had that light skinned, pretty boy look.

The two that jumped out of the flatbed were both dark skinned and wearing faded blue jeans and bare-chested. One had shoulder-length dreads, like Devon, and the other had on a fitted cap turned backwards on his bald head.

Recker did the intros as they approached. "This is my cousin, Devon, from New York, but he was raised right here in Kingston."

The driver spoke. "The Gunslinger from New York. They call me the Great Dane, but the fam just calls me Dane." He tapped his fist against Devon's.

"Stripes," the dread said, shaking Devon's hand and then hugging him roughly.

"Rippa," the bald headed one said.

"Ginja!" Stripes called out. "Bring the cooler from out the back of the truck."

"Me look like your bitch?" Get dat shit your motherfucking self." Ginja's Jamaican accent was always thick when she got angry.

"That's why we can't take you nasty mouth bitches anywhere."

"Your mother's a nasty bitch," Ivory said, getting up in his face.

"Why don't y'all chill the fuck out?" Rippa said.

Ginja turned to spew a few choice words at him, but closed her mouth when Dane looked at her.

"Chill," he said. "Go grab the cooler," he said to Rippa.

Rippa nodded and headed back to the truck. Ivory and Ginja unbuttoned their jeans and slid out of them. Devon couldn't help but stare at them.

"You know where we'll be," Ginja said. "Give us a holla when y'all are done bonding." Both women sashayed off to the water.

"Don't worry, you'll get used to it," Stripes said to Devon. "They know we ain't trying to fuck 'em, so they parade around us like we're blind."

"Even a blind man can see that they're holding," Devon said, licking his lips.

Dane looked at Recker. "You didn't tell him?"

"Tell me what?" Devon said.

"I didn't get a chance to tell him," Recker said.

"Tell me what?"

"Them bitches is dangerous and trifling. Never be alone with them," Recker said.

"Get the fuck out of here," Devon said, waving him off.

"I'm serious. We always make sure that none of us are alone with them. Every man that gets involved with them disappears."

"You can't be serious."

"I'm dead serious. Am I lying, Stripes?"

"Hell nah."

"I don't know any females in the world who are as ruthless as they are," Recker said.

Devon thought of the twins, Jennifer and Paula. He snapped out of it when Rippa dropped the cooler in front of him and opened it. He pulled out five Coronas and started passing them around. Devon grabbed the one he handed to him, but he had no intentions on cracking it. Everyone else cracked theirs and chugged down at least half the bottle.

Recker dug in the pocket of his cargo shorts and pulled out another blunt. "Put some fire to that."

Dane took it from him and lit it up. Stripes ran to the truck and turned up the music. Dane took two pulls and then offered it to Devon.

"I don't smoke."

"What? Stop playing."

"I don't play either."

Recker reached past him and grabbed the blunt. "He don't smoke or drink. The man don't know what he's missing."

"Damn," Dane said. "Don't smoke, don't drink. Do you fuck?"

"Pass that," Stripes said when he got back from the truck.

"The Gunslinger don't smoke or drink," Dane said to Stripes.

"Get the fuck out of here."

Devon shrugged.

Stripes looked at him like he was crazy. "Do you fuck?"

Devon let his bottle fall to the sand.

"All right, knock it off," Recker said, knowing what Devon's next move was going to be. He knew he shouldn't have given him that gun so soon. "Y'all know why we're here. My cousin got some shit he wants to get rid of, and we're going to help him move it."

"What's our cut?" Dane asked.

"I already told you," Recker said.

"I want to hear it from him." Dane looked Devon in the eyes.

"There's five of y'all. I'm giving up half a mil, American, you do the math."

Dane turned up the rest of his Corona and finished it off. He tossed the bottle into the 55 gallon drum and grabbed another one out the cooler. "I just needed to hear you say it."

"There's a dude in St. Catherine that I can convince to cop from us," Rippa said.

"What about you?" Recker asked Stripes.

"I know a few, but they're not going to fuck with it if it's not better than what they're getting now."

Recker looked at Dane.

"Dillard and Sterling will definitely be interested."

"The two dreads who claim that they got it going on in Europe? You think they would be interested?" Recker said.

"They're always looking for some good shit. As a matter of fact, they're in Jamaica for the next two weeks."

"Get in touch with them and see what's up."

Dane gave the thumbs up and cracked open the bottle he was holding.

"I'm not going to sit here and lie to you," Recker said to Devon, "this isn't something we're used to doing, so it's going to take some time to get rid of what you got. Besides, we don't want to make too much of a noticeable dent in someone's pocket. All that's going to do is bring unnecessary heat to us."

"I'm not in a rush. I'm not going anywhere."

Each man, except Devon, polished off four bottles as they tried coming up with more people they could get to take a few bricks off their hands. Devon stole a glance at his watch. It was 10:30pm. He blinked long and hard. Being around all the weed smoke was giving him a contact high. "I got to go for a walk."

"Don't wander off too far," Recker said, pulling out another Corona.

Devon gave him half a wave and walked off. He took a deep breath and then yawned. "Shit," he said as he wandered too close to the water. He jumped away as the tide rushed in and hit him just below the knees. He looked over his shoulder and was surprised to see Ginja and Ivory walking up on him. He waited for them to catch up. Their bikinis were wet and clinging to their bodies.

"You can't walk around here by yourself," Ivory said.

"I can handle myself."

"I bet you can," Ginja said, as she stood on his right. Ivory grabbed his hand from his left and they started walking.

"We got to protect our investment," Ginja said.

"Is that what I am to you?"

"And you're family."

"So tell me a little something about yourself," Ivory said, holding his gaze with her green eyes.

"Like?"

"Like, is it true that you killed a lot of people?"

"Is that what Recker told you?"

"Umm hmm."

"What else did he say?"

"He said that your solution to everything is violence," Ginja said.

"No it's not. I'm going to kick his ass for lying on me."

"I think he knows you better than you think," Ivory said.

"I noticed you didn't touch the blunt or beer," Ginja said.

"You were watching me?"

"Most definitely," both women said.

"What's up with that?" Ginja asked. "You don't get high?"

"I don't drink or smoke."

Both women looked at each other.

"What?" Devon said.

"Down here, the only ones who don't smoke or drink are squares and... the constables," Ivory said.

"I look like the police to you?"

"Undercover don't look like police."

Devon snatched his hand out of hers.

Ginja took his right hand in hers. "Whoa, Gunslinger, she didn't mean anything by that."

Devon wanted to snatch his hand out of Ginja's but a sudden calmness overtook him.

Ivory took his left hand back into hers. "Your cousin has no reason not to trust you, but Dane, Rippa, and Stripes are another story. They don't trust anyone who doesn't get high with them."

"You two trust me?"

"As long as we don't betray you, we don't have anything to worry about."

"And how do you know that?"

"We just know certain things," Ginja said, giving his hand a gentle squeeze.

Devon snatched his hands out of theirs. Every man that gets involved with them disappears. Recker's words echoed in his head. "I think we better get back."

"You sure?" Ivory asked in a sultry voice.

Devon looked at Ginja and could see the lust in her eyes, as she slightly stuck her chest out.

"Yeah, I'm positive."

* * *

Recker was the first one to see Devon and the girls walking back. "We were just about to get in the truck and come looking for you. Where you been?"

"I told you I was going for a walk."

"For two fucking hours?"

Devon looked at his watch. It was 12:30am. When he looked at Ginja, she winked at him.

She got on her tiptoes and whispered in his ear. "Time flies when you're having fun."

Devon didn't know what to say.

"We about to head back to the house," Recker said, as he approached him. He put his arm around Devon and pulled him away from Ginja and Ivory. "Go put some clothes on," he said to them. They sucked their teeth and walked to where they left their jeans. Devon couldn't help but watch them squeeze back into them.

"What the fuck did I tell you about them bitches, Cuz?" Recker whispered to him.

"I'm cool."

"No, you're not. You disappear for two fucking hours and didn't even realize you were gone for two hours?"

Devon looked over at Ginja and Ivory. They were leaning on Dane's truck, smoking a blunt and downing Coronas like bottled water. Ginja looked right at him and blew a cloud of smoke his way. Ivory turned up her bottle and guzzled it down. She flashed him a devilish grin and then burped long and loud.

"That's exactly what I'm talking about," Stripes said, shaking his head. "Can't take you disrespectful bitches anywhere."

Ginja stuck her middle finger up at him.

* * *

Over the next few days, Recker took Devon shopping for some clothes and a set of wheels. Devon copped a 1995 Jeep wrangler. It wasn't the prettiest, but it would do. It was green with black trimming. Buying the jeep put a dent in the 15Gs he came down with, but if everything went as planned, he should be hearing some good news in a few moments. He pulled up to a pay phone and dialed his uncle's number.

"Trans Import/Export, how may I help you?" Fredricka said.

"I'd like to speak with Clifford."

"May I ask who's calling?"

"His nephew," Devon answered.

"Please hold." Fredricka transferred the call to Clifford's office.

"How's the weather?" Clifford asked when he picked up the line.

"Hot and humid."

"Sounds about right for this time of year."

"You got some good news for me?"

"Sure do. Your refrigerator and stove have been shipped and will be there in two days. Got a pen so I can give you the address?"

"Go ahead."

Clifford read the address off to him. Devon repeated it to make sure he memorized it correctly.

"It's the biggest warehouse on the block."

"And when am I supposed to pick up my appliances?"

"Thursday anytime after 3:00pm. And the invoice is taped inside the refrigerator door."

"I hope you didn't charge me an arm and a leg."

"And then some," Clifford said with a chuckle.

"Well, you know I'm going to get it to you as soon as possible."

"Please do that."

"Take care."

* * *

Recker was standing on the porch, talking on his cell phone when Devon pulled into the driveway. He threw up the peace sign as Devon got out of his jeep. He hung up and stuck his phone back in his pocket.

"How's the rust bucket holding up?"

"It gets me where I need to go." Devon slammed the truck door.

"It ain't going to get you any chicks, though."

"I don't need a ride to get chicks."

"You're going to use that slick New York game on them?"

Devon changed the subject. "Who were you talking to?"

"That was a potential custy. He wanted to check out the merchandise, but being that we don't have any—"

"It'll be here Thursday."

"Okay." Recker pulled his cell phone back out and hit redial. "Yeah, it's me. I'll have a sample for you Friday night... yeah at the Square. Peace."

"What's happening on Friday night?" Devon asked.

"What's happening on Friday night? If you're going to be living here, you got to get up on what's happening around here. Fridays are Dutty Fridaze. This Friday we're going to be at Fletcher's Land Square. The way the women be grinding and winding up on a brother, you don't know if y'all are dancing or fucking."

"The team's going to be there, right?"

"Of course."

"Let's go," Devon said, heading back to the jeep.

"Where we going?"

"You're taking me to the Square."

"Now? What for?"

"Come Friday night, I want to know that place like the back of my hand."

Chapter 3

Thursday afternoon at 3:15, Recker pulled up to the warehouse in Dane's pickup. "This is it."

Devon looked at the warehouse, and for a brief second, he thought maybe his uncle was setting him up. The warehouse looked like a spot you took a person to kill and leave there for the rats. "You ever been here?"

"Nope."

"I don't like it."

"I told you we all should've come," Recker said.

"Nah, I didn't want everybody in my business." Devon pulled the Beretta out of his waistband and chambered a round. "Sit tight, I'll be right back."

He approached the warehouse, senses on high alert. When he got to the entrance, he pulled on the door. It didn't budge. The windows on the door were painted, so he couldn't peek inside. He knocked and took a step back. After a minute, he knocked again.

"What do you want?"

Devon looked up and saw a woman's head sticking out one of the second story windows. "I'm here to pick up a package."

"What kind of package?"

"A refrigerator and a stove."

"Who it came from?"

"Clifford."

The door swung open. The beefy man standing in front of him stared at him through slitted eyes.

"No one followed them," the woman yelled down to the man.

"Who's that in the truck?" the man asked.

"A mover."

"Tell him to pull around back." He slammed the door in Devon's face. Devon looked up at the window. The woman was gone.

"Go around back," Devon said when he got to the truck. The man was waiting at the gate. He pointed the two boxes out, and disappeared back into the warehouse.

"C'mon," Devon said to Recker.

"They're supposed to load that shit onto the truck. That's what shipping and handling is for."

"Get your lazy ass out the truck. I'm not trying to be here all day."

"Recker kicked the truck door open and jumped out with a huff. They loaded the refrigerator box onto the truck and then the stove.

"That shit was heavier than a motherfucker," Recker said, breathing hard.

"You should've smoked some of your super weed."

"I would've if I had known I was going to be lifting refrigerators and stoves."

Devon shut the flatbed door. "Let's go."

* * *

Devon and Recker carried the refrigerator and stove into the living room. Recker collapsed on the couch, while Devon went into the kitchen to grab a knife. He cut through the plastic strips running up and down the boxes and lifted the box off the refrigerator. He opened the door and snatched the invoice taped on the inside of it. The bill was for 30Gs, and that didn't include the 15Gs he owed for the loan. He crumpled it up and threw it at Recker.

"How much he asking for?" Recker asked, while opening the crumpled invoice.

"30Gs."

"What?" Recker jumped off the couch and stared at the invoice. "How's he going to charge family like that? Fuck that, we ain't giving him shit."

"I got 82 bricks. I sell three, that's the money I owe all together. We still got 79 left. 79x15 is a mill one eighty five."

"I got to go smoke something. I'll be in my room. We ain't paying him 45Gs, fuck that."

Devon didn't pay him any mind. The money from the first three bricks was going to his uncle. He couldn't afford to betray the only man in the States who knew where he was. What if the police paid him a visit? It would be nothing for him to point them in his direction. He doubted if he would, but he wasn't going to test him to find out. He opened the fridge and counted the stacks of coke on the racks. Then he counted the stacks in the freezer. He lifted the box off the stove and counted the stacks in the oven. All 82 bricks were accounted for.

* * *

Devon and Recker arrived at Fletcher's Square at midnight. Dane, Rippa, and Stripes came strolling through a half hour later. When they met up, Dane told them that Ginja and Ivory would be along soon. The Square was packed and popping. Devon could tell from the energy level of the crowd that this party wasn't ending until sunrise. The air was thick with weed smoke and musk. Devon was tempted to tell Recker to open a window, only, how can you open a window when you're outdoors?

"See y'all in an hour," Recker said, as he strolled off to find a dance partner.

Devon grabbed him by the arm. "We're not here to have a good time."

"Relax, Cuz, I told you Sparks wasn't showing up til 1:00. You're the one who wanted to be here an hour early. I'm just not going to stand here holding my dick when one of these gorgeous women can do that for me. I'm out."

Dane, Rippa, and Stripes scattered into the crowd, as well.

Scanning the faces, Devon could tell that most of the people here were interested in four things: dancing, getting drunk, getting high, and fucking. Besides the weed and alcohol, he peeped several people popping X like it was candy. He spotted the DJ standing under a tent working his magic. As much as he tried to focus, even his colder-than-ice demeanor couldn't resist the temperature rising, bass line thumping out of the six-foot speakers. His pulse quickened when he saw a woman sandwiched between two men and loving it. Directly in front of him were two women taking turns winding and grinding on one guy. The guy was bulging in his pants, but he didn't seem to care, neither did the women.

He swallowed hard when he saw a woman make a beeline for him. She walked right up on him until her pointy breasts were poking him in the sternum. She locked eyes with him. He flinched as she thrusted her pelvis into his and started winding. She was so high out of her mind that she was oblivious to the fact that he wasn't moving. She continued to grind on him and stare him in the eyes. She slid her hands under his tank top and traced the deep creases of his six-pack. She smiled to let him know she liked what she was feeling.

Devon rested his hands on her shoulders and took a step back. She turned around and mesmerized him by rotating her hips like a belly dancer. She slowly bent at the waist and grabbed her ankles. With her butt in the air, she looked back at him, giving him the okay to grind on it. Devon was a butt man, and the butt in front of him was round, firm, and his if he wanted it. Just as he was about to give in, he felt an icy hand grip his shoulder from behind. He turned and there was Ivory staring at him with those intoxicating green eyes.

"How do I look?" She slowly turned around, modeling for him. His eyes fell to her breasts that were threatening to bust out of the tight vest she was wearing. Then he got an eyeful of her thick thighs spilling out of her tight shorts.

He nodded and cracked a smile when he felt a pair of arms slither around his waist from behind. He had totally forgotten about the butt he was about to park up on. As he turned around, Ivory walked around him and hit the female with a look that froze her in mid grind.

"Find someone else to dance with." She grabbed Devon by the arm and pulled him toward her. When the female refused to move on, Ivory bared her teeth and stood in between her and Devon. "I said go find another dick to dangle off of."

"What did you just say?" The women said with an attitude.

"You heard what I said. You running around here smelling like a musk rat. That smell is not cool at all."

The female turned blood red. Her nostrils flared as she subtly tried to smell her aroma. She cut her eyes at Devon and then at Ivory before scurrying off.

Ivory shook her head. "Some bitches are just so skanky. And you were about to dance with that cunt-bleeding bitch."

Devon opened his mouth to speak.

"I dare you to lie to me and tell me you weren't about to grab her by the waist and grind up on her. You were probably thinking about leaving here with her."

Devon didn't respond.

Ivory looked into his eyes and smiled. "And like the man that you are, once you would've found out she was on her period, you would've talked her into giving you some head. Tell me I'm lying."

"You got a keen sense of smell I see."

"I'm part bloodhound." She grabbed the bottom of his tank top and raised it to her nose. She closed her eyes and took a whiff. "I got you. No matter where you are on this island, I will be able to sniff you out."

"You do know that men aren't attracted to crazy women, right?"

"You are."

"No, I'm not."

"Yes, you are."

"Where's Ginja?"

"She's around." She interlaced her fingers behind his head and whispered in his ear. "I'll be more then willing to give you some head, right now." She ran her tongue around the outside of his ear.

He grabbed her by the wrists and pulled her hands from behind his head. "I think the shorty you chased away has a better head game than you. She had juicier lips."

"Let me go find her and bring her back and let's see who has the better head game."

"I think you're playing head games with me, right now."

"I'm dead serious."

Devon looked up and saw Recker waving at him. Sparks had just entered the Square.

"It's showtime," Devon said.

"Wait." Ivory put her hands on his chest and looked over his shoulder. Devon turned around and saw Ginja. She had on a red halter top and a pair of red, hip hugging jeans. She blew Devon a kiss and then walked up on a dread who couldn't take his eyes off her bouncing breasts.

"Ginja counted three men in the crowd that's going to have their eyes on you the whole time."

"Three men? Sparks just arrived, how does she know about the three men?"

"He made eye contact with each one the moment he entered the Square. Chances are they're strapped and ready for whatever."

"Which ones are they?"

"Ginja is approaching one now. I'll be sliding up on one in a moment. And the third one is rocking a platinum colored skin fade. You can't miss him. Keep one eye on me. If I blow you a kiss, grab Recker and walk away."

"Nah, this isn't how I work."

"I don't give a damn how you work. This is how we work."

"Cuz!" Recker called out, looking impatient. Devon pointed his finger at her. Without a word, he headed toward Recker and Sparks.

* * *

Sparks made himself at home on one of the benches near the DJ tent. He was both pudgy and stubby, like a spark plug. He rested his hands on his protruding stomach and kept eye contact with Recker until he sat next to him.

"How goes it?" Sparks asked.

"So far, everything's going just fine. This is my cousin, Dev."

"How you doing, Dev?"

"I'm cool."

"On a hot night like this, it's pretty hard to stay cool; you know what I'm saying?"

Devon hit him with the stone face.

Sparks smiled and then turned his attention back to Recker. "You have something for me?"

Recker handed him the sample of coke. While Sparks rubbed the coke on his gums, Devon casually looked around the Square. He spotted Ginja with the dread. He was so wrapped up in watching her lick her lips that he wasn't paying Sparks any mind. Ivory was grinding on a wiry fellow with glasses. Although he was into her, he kept a watchful eye on the bench. Mr. Platinum colored fade had moseyed his way into the DJ tent and was holding a conversation with the promoter. Ivory made brief eye contact with Devon, but she didn't blow him a kiss. What did she mean by that's not how we work? It was obvious Recker didn't know about the three henchmen.

"Yes, me brother," Sparks said with numb gums. "We are definitely going to do some business together." He shook Recker's hand. He turned to Devon. "How much do you have?"

"How much you buying?"

"What's the discounted rate for five?"

"15 thou a piece."

"Bring them by my restaurant tomorrow night at 10:00. Recker knows where it is."

"You'll have 75Gs by tomorrow night?"

Sparks laughed so hard that his belly jiggled. "He's funny," he said to Recker. He stood and patted Devon on the shoulder. "See you tomorrow night."

Devon didn't respond. He watched him leave. A few seconds later, his henchmen exited the Square as well.

"It's that easy," Recker said. "I'm going to go celebrate."

"What's going on?" Devon was looking over Recker's shoulder.

Recker turned around and saw 3 constables making their way through the crowd. They were heading for the tent. When the DJ saw them, he cut the music off and said something to the promoter. Devon was about to grab Recker and breeze, but that thought quickly left his mind as he saw 5 more constables armed with high powered rifles walking down one of the roads that converged on the Square.

One of the constables entered the tent and started speaking with the promoter. The crowd stood around talking and sucking their teeth. The longer the conversation between the constable and the promoter went on, the louder the crowd's grumbling became. Finally, the officer exited the tent and gave his men the signal to move out.

"You no have nutten fi do?" Recker said in his hard Jamaican accent.

"What the fuck are you doing?" Devon mumbled. "You know we packing."

"Fuck dem."

The DJ hurried up and turned the music back on to drown out any other sudden outbursts.

Recker was about to yell something else, but Devon grabbed him by the collar. "Shut the fuck up and let them leave so we can leave."

"I can't stand them. They always come around here, flashing their guns like they the only ones with guns." Recker stood up on the bench and yelled. "We got guns too!"

Devon snatched him off the bench and mushed him in the face. Recker fell back on the bench, his lip began to quiver.

"Don't even think about it," Devon said, reading his body language. "I'll embarrass you."

Recker jumped up and brushed past him. Dane, Rippa, and Stripes walked up on Devon.

"Everything all right?" Dane asked.

"No, everything isn't all right. Recker is reckless."

"The music was on full blast, the police couldn't hear him."

"That's not the point. We don't need any kind of attention drawn to us."

"I agree," Dane said, "but mushing him in the face isn't going to solve anything."

"It shut him up."

"I just don't want you two bumping heads and fucking up what we're trying to do here."

Devon patted him on the shoulder. "Don't worry about me and Recker."

Rippa and Stripes were standing behind Dane, trying not to show Devon that they weren't feeling the way he had punked Recker. If they weren't open on getting a hundred thousand a piece, they probably would've smoked Devon right then and there.

"I'm out," Devon said.

"So what happened with Sparks?" Dane asked.

"We're on for tomorrow night."

Rippa and Stripes nodded and then cracked smiles.

"Where you heading?" Rippa asked Devon.

"Home."

"It's still early. We usually head out to the beach after this."

"Y'all can go to the beach. I'm going to sleep."

Devon pulled up to the house, not surprised that Recker wasn't home, yet. He cut his jeep off and drummed his thumbs against the steering wheel as he listened to the clicking of his engine cooling down. He knew he had to patch things up with Recker in front of the team. He started his jeep and headed to the beach.

* * *

Devon turned onto the boardwalk and drove down the ramp onto the sand. In the distance, he could see a fire blazing out of the rusty 55 gallon drum. He spotted Dane's truck parked a few yards away from the fire. The team huddled around the truck listening to Reggae. They watched him drive up. Recker grabbed a Corona out the cooler and headed toward the water.

Dane waited for Devon to walk up on them before he turned down the music and spoke. "Thought you were going home?"

"I was, but then I thought of all the fun y'all might be having without me."

"Shit," Stripes said. "The fun part is smoking this fat blunt and polishing off the rest of this 360."

Devon eyed the bottle of 360 vodka in Stripe's hand. "That looks like some hard shit."

"I'm a hard motherfucker." Stripes took a swig and then ran his forearm across his mouth. "Hit this one time," he said, holding the bottle out to Devon.

"I'm cool."

"That's your motherfucking problem. You're too cool." Stripes shoved the bottle against Devon's chest.

"He said he's cool," Ginja said.

"What are you, his fucking mother?"

"Keep talking to me like I won't take that bottle and crack it over your big ass head."

Stripes sucked his teeth. He cut his eyes at Ivory, and as always, she was ready to go out for her homegirl. "Yeah, whatever," he said, turning up the bottle and sucking down the vodka.

"So what do you do for fun?" Dane asked, as he took a pull off the blunt.

"I workout," Devon said.

"Workout? What's fun about working out?" Rippa asked.

"My workout partners."

It took him a minute, but Rippa finally got it. "Oh... workout, workout." He slapped Devon five. "Hell yeah, I'm down with that kind of sexercise."

"So, the Gunslinger does have a sense of humor," Dane said.

"What's up with y'all calling me Gunslinger?"

"Recker said you know everything there is to know about guns."

"Yeah, aim and pull the trigger."

"How's your aim?"

"Not too good, but better than most."

Ginja and Ivory stifled their laughs.

Dane cut his eyes at them and headed to his truck. He returned with a machine gun. "You know what this is?" He tossed it to Devon.

Devon tried not to let on his surprise. He inspected it and weighed it in his hands. "It's a M-16. Lighter than the ones I'm used to."

"I'm impressed that you noticed the weight difference. I modified the muzzle, making it perfect for urban warfare."

"Actually, I was referring to the missing clip."

"Yeah, that would definitely make it lighter."

"Where is it?" Devon asked.

"In my pocket."

"Let me see it."

"Yeah right," Dane chuckled.

"What, you don't trust me?"

"Not with a loaded machine gun."

"You're hurting my feelings."

"Give him the clip," Ginja said.

Dane looked at her like he wanted to take her head off. Devon tossed the gun back. He pulled the bottom of his tank top out of his jeans and let it hang. He bent down and took a Corona out of the cooler and cracked it. He winked at Dane and then turned it up. He downed it without batting an eye. He let the empty bottle fall to the sand and then grabbed another one. He cracked it and guzzled it down like he did the first one. He let it fall to the sand. He hiccupped and burped long and loud. Ginja and Ivory looked like they were creaming in their pants. He bent down and picked up a third bottle.

"I thought you didn't drink," Dane said.

Devon twisted the cap off the bottle. "I don't." He held it up to Stripes, who then held up his bottle of 360. Devon gave Rippa a nod and headed toward the water to have a man-to-man with his cousin.

Recker just finished his beer when Devon walked up on him. Devon offered his to him.

Recker knocked the bottle out his hand and got in his face. "We ain't kids anymore. If it was anyone else who pulled that stunt in the Square, I would've emptied my gun in his face."

Spittle landed on Devon's lip. He pushed Recker back. "Listen—"

Recker punched him in the face. Devon staggered back. Before he had a chance to retaliate, Recker was already in motion. He pulled his .38 snub nose out the front of his pants and clocked him in the head. Devon fell to one knee.

"What?" Recker screamed, as he shoved the gun against Devon's head. "You think I won't dump off in you?"

"Yo, Cuz—"

"Now it's yo, Cuz, huh?"

Devon looked toward the truck. The team had their eyes glued to them like they were watching a movie.

"Put the gun away." Devon looked up at him.

"Or what?" Recker pressed the gun harder against his head.

"If you want to get this off your chest, we can do that, right here, right now. You said we ain't kids anymore, right? So let's handle this like men." Devon slowly reached behind his back and pulled out the Beretta and tossed it. "What do you say, Cuz? You man enough?"

Recker gritted his teeth. He kneed Devon in the head and then tossed his gun in the same direction Devon tossed his. Devon was on his hands and knees when Recker jumped on him. They wrestled around in the sand, dragging one another closer and closer to the water.

Recker threw a wild punch that Devon easily slipped past and then threw a punch, hitting Recker on the temple. Recker stumbled back into the water. Devon jumped on him. Recker shoved him off and kicked him in the groin. Devon went down. Recker seized the opportunity. He stood up and kicked Devon like a soccer ball. He tried covering up, but Recker didn't let up. His shin connected with Devon's forehead, snapping his head back. The next kick caught him behind the ear. Devon fell face first onto the wet sand.

Recker grabbed him by the dreads and pressed his face into the shallow water. Devon thrashed as he clawed at Recker's fingers, but they were like ice picks digging into his skull.

Recker could feel Devon's grip on his hands loosening. Ten seconds later, Devon stopped moving. Recker yanked his head out of the water and flung him to the sand. Devon fell on his back with a thud and didn't move.

"I'm the motherfucking man!" Recker said, pointing at him.

Ginja and Ivory ran toward them.

"What the fuck is wrong with you?" Ivory screamed at Recker, shoving him away from Devon. Ginja kneeled down beside Devon and felt for his pulse. She held his nose and blew into his mouth. She put one hand on top of the other and pumped his chest. When he didn't respond, Recker's eyebrows crinkled. He was about to push her out the way and try to save his cousin himself, but he heard him cough.

Ginja rolled Devon on his side as he threw up the water he swallowed. She rubbed his back as he started to dry heave.

"You could've killed him!" Ivory said, shoving Recker again. He pushed past her. Devon got on his hands and knees and attempted to stand. Ginja allowed him to put his arms around her as he struggled to hold his wobbly knees still.

"Damn, Cuz," Devon said in between coughs. "How your scrawny ass get so strong?"

Recker's snarl slowly turned to a smile. "I told you. Weed gives you super powers."

Devon bent down and picked up their guns. He stuck his in his waist and handed Recker his. "We cool?"

Recker picked up the Corona he slapped out of Devon's hand earlier and downed half the bottle. "We were always cool."

Devon looked up by the truck. Dane, Rippa, and Stripes looked on as they passed a blunt among themselves. Rippa and Stripes nodded at Devon. He nodded back. He locked eyes with Dane and nodded. Dane took a long pull off the blunt and turned his head.

Chapter 4

Waking out of a deep sleep, Devon heard the floor boards of his bedroom creak as someone walked across them. He opened his eyes only to have them nearly seared by the sunlight shining through his bedroom window. He hissed as he pulled the sheet over his head. Last night's events came back to him in fragments. After making up with Recker, they drank more beer, and then everyone came back to the house where they continued to drink more beer. Then he remembered getting up to use the bathroom and seeing everyone laid out in the living room.

"You're finally up," Ginja said, placing the breakfast tray down on the night stand.

"What are you still doing here?"

"Fixing you breakfast."

Devon slid the covers down to the bridge of his nose and peeked up at her. "Is that one of my tank tops?" His eyes fell to the pinstriped boxers hanging loosely on her hips. "And those look like my boxers."

"I couldn't fit into any of Recker's bony-ass underwear, so I had to put on a pair of yours."

Devon stared at the ceiling as he massaged his temples.

Ginja sat next to him on the bed and grabbed the glass of green muck off the breakfast tray. "Drink this." She held it an inch from his lips.

Devon turned his head. "My head is pounding too hard to drink anything."

"This'll make the headache go away."

He eyed the green liquid.

"Trust me."

"I'm definitely not drinking it now."

"You owe me a hundred thou, so logic should tell you that I'm one of the last people who would want to do anything to you." She put the glass back on his lips. He sat up on his elbows and allowed her to feed him the green concoction. It tasted better than it looked. It was sweet and ice cold. After drinking half the glass, she pulled it away.

"What is that?" he asked, licking his lips.

"You don't want to know." She finished off the rest of it and then placed the glass back on the tray. Devon followed her eyes to his morning hard-on that was making a tent out of the sheet.

"I can take care of that for you," she said, licking the green froth off her upper lip.

"What if Ivory walks in?"

Ginja looked back at the doorway, and then turned back around with a sly grin. "She'll probably drop to her knees and join me." Her hand glided down the sheet until it brushed against his solid mass. Devon didn't move. He wanted to see how far she would go. Locking eyes with him, she ran her forefinger slowly up the underside of his shaft. The longer it took to reach the top, the wider her smile got. She pouted when he grabbed her hand and put it on her lap. Refusing to give up easily, she nibbled on his neck.

Devon grabbed her by the back of her neck and yanked her head back. She moaned keeping her eyes fixated on the bulge under the sheet. He tightened his grip on her neck to get her attention.

"Why do men disappear around you?"

"What?"

"You heard what I said." He squeezed her neck harder.

"You're hurting me." She slapped his hand off her neck and pulled away from him.

"You like it rough."

"No, I don't."

"Yes, you do."

"And what would make you think that?"

"Well, you're still sitting next to me."

Ginja's scowl softened. "It seems like you got me figured out, almost as well as I got you."

"You don't know anything about me."

"I know that stunt you pulled last night was all a front for Recker to save face in front of us."

"And how would you know that?"

"When I started to give you mouth-to-mouth, I stuck my tongue in your mouth and you moved your tongue away from mine."

"You and Ivory are dangerous."

"We would never hurt you."

Devon grabbed her by the wrist as she stroked his shaft. He bent her wrist back, threatening to snap it. Ginja winced, but the lust welling in her eyes told him that she loved every bit of the pain. He let her go.

"Move," he said, shoving her away from him. He swung his feet onto the floor and sat on the edge of the bed. "Get out."

She stared at him for a few seconds before heading out. She stopped at the doorway and took one last look at his hard-on. "Last chance."

"Shut the door behind you."

She shrugged and closed the door. Devon exhaled. The precum in his drawers was causing them to stick to his legs. He closed his eyes and shuddered as he realized how close he had come to giving in. He reached for a piece of toast and scooped some eggs on it before stuffing it into his mouth. He looked at his watch. It was 10:30. He wolfed down the rest of the breakfast and started to get dressed. It was time to wake the team and prepare for their first sale.

* * *

Recker and the team arrived at Sparks' restaurant at 9:30 that night. Recker pulled up in his Nissan. Rippa, Stripes, and Dane pulled up in Dane's F-150. Ginja rode up on her triple black Yamaha Raptor four-wheeler. Ivory pulled up alongside her on her black and yellow Suzuki Quadracer. Ginja wore a pair of vacuum-tight black leather pants with a vacuum-tight black vest. Ivory's black and yellow leather suit matched the design of her ATV. Rippa went with the baggy look, a Phat Farm two piece denim outfit. Stripes donned an urban yet sleek Rocawear get-up. The Great Dane was dipped in Louis Vuitton, all the way down to his driving gloves. The team huddled by Recker's car for a few seconds before going inside.

In an alley facing the restaurant, Devon stood in the shadows listening, watching.

The team was greeted at the door by one of Sparks's men. He led them through the restaurant, across a busy kitchen, and up a set of stairs. He knocked on the door and then left them on the landing. A moment later, the door opened and out stepped another one of Sparks's men with a wand in his hand.

"Hands up," he commanded. He ran the hand-held metal detector over their bodies. He had Recker pop open his briefcase. The man nodded when he saw the 5 kilos of coke and stepped back into the room. He allowed them to enter. The room was filled with men with an assortment of guns. They all stopped what they were doing when Ginja and Ivory strutted in. They quickly lost interest when Recker and his boys stepped in.

The man led them down a hallway that opened up into another room that was furnished with five card tables. Recker eyed the stacks of chips on the table. He recognized a couple of the gamblers. Most of them owned businesses on the island. After walking through another hallway, they finally came upon Sparks's office. Their escort knocked on the door once before turning the knob.

Sparks was sitting behind his desk, puffing a cigar. "Make yourselves comfortable." His eyes were glued to Ginja and Ivory.

Recker sat in the wing-back chair in front of Sparks' desk while the rest of the team posted themselves around the spacious office.

"I don't see your cousin. What's his name again?"

"Devon, and no, he didn't come. He doesn't go anywhere where he can't bring his hardware."

"Is that so?"

"Yeah, he's paranoid like that."

"I guess he doesn't have to be present as long as you have what we agreed to."

"I have it as long as you have the money we agreed to."

Sparks reached under his desk and pulled out a briefcase and placed it on his desk. He snapped it open and allowed Recker to look inside. Recker could see stacks of hundreds. Sparks slammed it shut when Recker attempted to reach in and count the money.

"Ivory," Recker called out to her without bothering to turn around.

"Talk to me, baby," she replied. Her thick Jamaican accent made Sparks do a double take.

"Did that look like 75Gs?"

"Hardly," she responded, not taking her eyes off her freshly done manicure.

"What kind of game is this?" Sparks asked.

"Ivory's my accountant. She counts money in her sleep."

Sparks clenched his jaw. Then he looked around his office. Dane, Rippa, and Stripes looked bored. Ginja was at the minibar fixing herself a drink. None of them looked to be over 25. "There's 75 thousand in this briefcase."

"That's not what Ivory says." Recker leaned back in the chair.

"Are you sitting in my office and calling me a liar?" The anger in Sparks' voice caused his man at the door to perk up. Sparks put the suitcase back under his desk and leaned back in his chair. He directed his question to the man at the door. "Did you check his briefcase?"

"Yes, he has the product with him."

Sparks studied Recker for a moment. "There's 60 thousand in the briefcase, take it or leave it."

Recker leaned forward in the chair. "I came here to get paid, not bloody."

Sparks rested his hands on his belly. "What's to stop me from just taking those 5 kilos from you and having you thrown out of here on your asses?"

"Ginja," Recker called out, just as calmly as he called out to Ivory earlier.

With drink in hand, she walked toward Recker. She took the briefcase off of his lap and sat it on the floor. She gave him her drink to hold as she sat on his lap and began to address Sparks. "I heard you're quite the gambler."

"I win my share of bets."

"Do you?" Ginja picked the briefcase up and opened it. She pulled out the 5 bricks and lined them up neatly on his desk. "I'm willing to let you have these 5 bricks for free if I lose the bet."

"What bet?"

"I'll bet you that this little game that you're playing is just to test my man. And to prove that I'm right, I'll bet that the rest of the money that's supposed to be in that briefcase is right there in your desk drawer."

Sparks looked at Recker. "You're sanctioning this bet?"

"If the rest of my cash isn't where she says it is, the coke is yours."

Sparks tried reading through Ginja's flirty smile. "And who the fuck is she?" he asked Recker.

"She's my analyst, and she's never wrong."

"An accountant who counts money without counting the money and an analyst who is never wrong." He stubbed out his cigar in the ashtray. "And what if the money is where she says it is?"

"Then you will stop wasting our fucking time," Ginja said, not bothering to hide her annoyance.

Sparks kept his eyes on her as he opened his drawer and pulled out four stacks of bills. He lifted his briefcase off the floor and placed the bills inside with the rest of the money.

"How we looking?" Recker said to Ivory.

She glanced at the money and nodded. "That's more like it."

Sparks snapped the briefcase shut and slid it across his desk. "Don't take my little test personal. I had to—"

"See if he would fold under pressure?" Ginja said. "If he would've folded, no telling what he would tell the police if he ever got popped for something, huh?"

"I like you," Sparks said.

Ginja got off Recker's lap, grabbed her drink, and grabbed the briefcase. Recker stood up and smoothed out his shirt. "We have a lot more whenever you're interested."

"I'll be in touch."

Recker shook Sparks' hand and headed toward the door. One by one, his team filed out after him. Sparks couldn't take his eyes off Ginja. She made it her business to be the last one out. She put an extra switch in her walk as she exited the office.

Recker hopped into his car with the briefcase and called Devon on his cell phone. "Everything went smooth, Cuz."

Devon hung around for a half-hour after the team drove off before deciding to leave.

* * *

Recker and the team were sitting around the kitchen table dividing the money up when Devon walked in.

"Hey, Gunslinger," Ginja said, winking at him.

"It's all here," Recker said.

Devon looked at the two stacks of money. He pointed to the biggest one. "That's the 45Gs?"

"Yeah, I still don't see why you're giving unc all that fucking money for something he should've done on the strength."

Devon stacked the bills in the briefcase and closed it. "You know what to do with the rest," he said disappearing into his room.

Recker divided the rest of the money into five stacks and wrapped a rubber band around each one. Then he tossed a stack to each of the team.

Chapter 5

Two months later, things were still running smooth. In that time frame, Sparks brought 15 more bricks. In addition, 10 more were sold to various people Recker and his team had connections with. Recker upgraded his Nissan Sentra to a Nissan Ultima. Rippa and Stripes graduated from riding shotgun in Dane's truck to street bikes. Rippa copped a black and silver Yamaha. Stripes spent a large chunk of his money on a candy apple red Ducati.

As for Ivory, she spent her money on eight hundred dollar pairs of jeans and six hundred dollar pairs of stilettos. Ginja spent a little of her money getting things in her house repaired that had been broken for years. Devon didn't go on shopping sprees or spending binges. He stacked his paper, knowing he would need it when he stepped his game up to the next level.

He pulled up to the house. He grabbed his take-out plate of grilled hot wings and headed inside. Recker was sitting in the living room, staring wide-eyed at his 42 inch HD plasma screen TV. He was playing his favorite game, *Metal Gear Solid 3*.

"Give that shit a break," Devon said, as he walked past him and into the kitchen. "I left you on that thing seven this morning and it's almost two o'clock."

"This is my stress release."

"Stress release?"

"You take morning drives, I play my PS3."

Unbeknown to Recker, Devon's morning drives weren't to relieve stress. He wanted to learn every road and street in Kingston. Soon, he would know every nook and cranny in the city the same way he knew the streets of Queens.

"Fuck!" Recker threw the controller on the couch. "I can't get past this fucking stage."

Devon took the aluminum foil off his plate and started busting down his hot wings.

Recker stretched and went to the bathroom. He came out a minute later. "I held that since seven this morning."

"You need to go to Play Station Anonymous or something."

"The only things I'm addicted to is money and pussy."

"Well, pull yourself away from that game long enough to make some calls."

"Calls to who?"

"Here." Devon gave him a piece of paper.

Recker read the list of guns, ammo, and holsters. "Are you serious?"

"Is that a trick question?"

"Who are we going to war with?"

"I don't know yet."

Recker looked at the list again. "We're down to 52 bricks and we got a buy lined up for this weekend. Everything is going smooth."

"It's going smooth because we haven't put a big enough dent in anyone's pocket yet. As soon as someone realizes that their pockets are kind of light, they're going to come looking for us."

"You give the word paranoid a whole new meaning, Cuz."

"Can you get the guns or not?"

"Everything looks attainable, except for the full body armor."

"But everything else should be easy to get?"

"Let me make my calls. You should have your arsenal in a few days."

Devon finished off his wings and washed his hands. "Aside from the disappearing men, what else do you know about Ginja and Ivory?"

"Not much."

"Do they have any family on the island?"

"Not that I know of."

"Do they talk about their pasts at all?"

"No. Why, what's up? You found something out I should know about?"

"Nah, you know me, I'm just being thorough." Devon plopped down on the couch.

"Paranoid's more like it. They won't dare cross us."

"And why is that?"

"They had plenty of opportunities to and they didn't."

"Maybe they're waiting for the right one."

Recker sucked his teeth. "You need to go to Paranoid Anonymous or something."

"I'm only addicted to one thing."

"And what's that?"

"Staying alive."

* * *

On East Street, in downtown Kingston, two dreads wearing tailor made suits entered a clothing store. They walked through the aisles checking out what was on the racks, but the last thing they were interested in was clothes.

Dane stepped out the back and got their attention. The dread with the block head, Dillard, tapped his man, Sterling. They followed Dane to the back.

"What's up Great Dane?" Dillard said, as he gave him a pound.

"You tell me," he responded, inviting them into the office. "Have a seat."

Rippa, Stripes, Ginja, and Ivory walked in and took seats around the room.

"I see the whole gang is here," Sterling said.

"Everybody except the one Dane has been telling us about," Dillard said.

"He'll be here shortly," Recker said. "So talk to me, how much you looking to buy?"

"If your shit is better than what we're getting now, we're looking to be regular customers," Dillard said.

"Our shit is the real deal," Recker said, pulling out a sample bag and tossing it to Dillard.

Dillard passed it to Sterling. He took out a testing kit and opened it up. He sprinkled a little bit of the coke in the solution and stirred it up. After thirty seconds, Sterling nodded. "Yeah, this is what's up."

"Let me hear a number," Recker said.

"I like the number 6."

"6 is my lucky number," Recker said.

"6 it is," Sterling said.

"Dane will call you with the time and place where we're going to make the exchange," Recker said.

"No problem." Dillard sat up on the edge of the chair. "You know my other offer still stands," he said to Recker.

"We're fine right here in Jamaica."

"But you will be better in Europe. Do you know how many people would kill for an opportunity like the one I'm offering you and your crew?"

"Why don't you hire one of them to be your regulators, then?"

"Because with the type of clientele we cater to, we need regulators who are young, suave, and know how to move in silence."

"Sounds like you're talking about me," Devon said, as he walked into the office.

"You must be Devon," Dillard said.

"Yeah."

"I'm Dillard and this is Sterling."

Devon nodded.

"Well, we better be heading out," Dillard said, as him and Sterling stood.

"We'll be in touch," Recker said.

"We'll be waiting for your call," Dillard said.

Dane escorted them out of the store.

"So those are the dreads from Europe, huh?" Devon asked.

"Yeah, the so called balling out of control ballers," Recker said.

"What do you think, Ginja?" Devon asked. "You're the analyst. Are they balling?"

"I would say they're making money, but balling out of control, no," Ginja said.

"And what is it about them that would give you that impression?" Devon asked.

"First, whenever they come to Jamaica, their clothes and shoes are always spanking brand-new."

"Shit. That would tell me that they are balling out of control," Rippa said.

Ginja acted like she didn't hear him and continued. "Then Dane contacts them about some bricks, and they're eager to see what we got. Then, they want 6 right off the bat."

"Okay, I'm definitely not following your logic," Recker said. "Everything you just mentioned is what ballers do."

"True, they're doing what ballers do, but they don't look natural doing it. Their whole flow just seems forced."

"I think you're just as sick in the head as my cousin."

"When I was on my way in, I heard them talking about you regulating for them in Europe. How many times have they offered you that proposition?" Devon asked.

"Every time they come to town. They're beginning to sound like a broken record."

"I agree with Ginja," Devon said. "I picked up on the brand-new clothes, too. But what sticks out at me is the fact that they're begging you to come to Europe."

"Begging?" Recker looked confused.

"Offer a job once, it's a proposition. Offer it more than twice, it's a plea. Offer it repeatedly, you're begging. And why would they be begging?"

"Money," Ivory said. "No one can make a substantial amount of money in the game and not be tested."

"So, you think someone is pressing them?" Devon asked.

"It's one of the laws of the game."

"What do you think Stripes?" Recker asked.

"I think we should stop wasting time hypothesizing about them dudes and what their motives may be and focus on moving the rest of these bricks."

"I agree," Recker said.

"Amen," Rippa cosigned.

Dane walked back into the office. "What did I miss?"

"Nothing," Recker said.

"Now, to our next order of business," Devon said.

"We got to go," Ginja and Ivory said, heading toward the door.

"Yeah we got something to do, as well," Rippa said, as him and Stripes grabbed their helmets and took off.

"I got to stay here and help my uncle out with the store," Dane said.

"What's up?" Devon asked. "No one wants to come with us?"

"Ah… no," Recker said.

"This guy's the real deal, right?"

"He's one of the last of a dying breed, and he's probably the only one on this island who loves guns just as much as you do."

"So, how come nobody wants to come with us?"

"Remember that cartoon character *Colonel McBragg*?"

"The old dude who used to spin the globe and wherever his finger landed, he had a war story to tell?"

"That's the one. In a few hours, you're going to meet the Jamaican version."

* * *

It didn't take Devon long to figure out why Recker insisted they take the jeep. It had been forty minutes since they turned onto the dirt path, where there were no street signs.

Fifteen minutes later, there was no path.

"This is the back country, for real," Devon said, keeping his jeep at a snail's pace as he crept up the steep slope of grass and rocks.

"Pull over by that wire fence," Recker said. "We're going to have to go the rest of the way on foot."

"You're joking right?"

"You want your guns or not?"

Devon pulled over and shut the engine off. He hopped out of his jeep and grabbed the backpack of money. The fifteen minute walk wasn't as bad as he thought. It was worst. He almost sprained his ankle twice. In the clearing he spotted a weather-worn shack. "Please tell me that's where we're going."

"That's it."

A man wearing nothing but a pair of shorts sat in front of the shack in a rusted lawn chair. He looked like he was sun-bathing. Devon noticed that the old man's skin was tough and scaly.

He must've sensed them coming because he cracked an eyelid and then stood up. His dreads were thick and fell all the way down to the bottom of his calves. His knotty beard stopped at the middle of his chest.

"Greetings!" His voice was vibrant.

"Greetings, General," Recker said. "This is my cousin, Devon."

The General studied him closely. "You and ya' father could pass fo' twins, mon."

The General's accent was so thick, Devon barely understood him.

"What did you say?"

"Me seh, you and ya' father, you two look so much alike."

"You didn't know my father."

"Curry wasn't ya' father?"

Devon hadn't heard anyone say his father's nickname since he was sent back to the States to live with his mother. "How do you know him?"

"He was a good man. An honest man, but he was not someone to play wit."

"I didn't know you knew my uncle," Recker said.

"Wha you need all these guns for?" the General asked Devon.

"I like to be prepared."

"Fo' wha'?"

"For whatever."

The General grabbed the lemon off the lawn chair's armrest and bit into it. He eyed the backpack on Devon's shoulder. "Dat be fo' me?"

Devon swung the bag off his shoulder and handed it to him. "It's all here."

The General dug into the bag and pulled out a couple stacks of twenty dollar bills which totaled four thousand dollars, and then handed the backpack back to Devon.

"What's this about?" Devon asked.

The General's smile was toothless. "Family discount, mon."

"I'm family, too, so I get a discount from now on too, right?" Recker asked.

The General made a fist and shook it at him. "Me got ya' discount right 'ere." He disappeared into the shack and came back dragging a suitcase. He stepped away from it and let Devon inspect the contents.

The first gun Devon pulled out was the Block Buster. A semi-automatic shotgun. Its pistol grip and semi-auto feature would come in handy if he had to fire a second round single-handedly. The barrel was eighteen inches, but he planned on shaving it down to twelve for better concealment and maneuverability. He placed the Block Buster on the ground and reached in the suitcase for the .45 automatic. The fo'fif reminded him of Brian. He placed it next to the shotgun and reached in for the P89s. They felt feather-light in his hands. He put them down and pulled out the holsters for each weapon.

"Where's the ammo?" Devon asked, looking through the suitcase.

"First tell me wha' the guns are for."

"Do you ask everyone that question?"

"Me asking you."

Devon put the guns back into the suitcase and zipped it up. He threw the backpack at the General's feet. "I don't need any discounts, and I'm sure I can get ammo from someone else without the 20 questions." He picked up the suitcase and started to walk off.

"Wait." The General went inside and came out with another suitcase filled with ammo. Recker grabbed the suitcase.

Devon nodded and turned to leave.

The General grabbed him by the shoulder and turned him around. "If you go after dem, you'll start a war you can't win."

"Go after who?"

"The ones who killed your father."

* * *

Recker focused on trying to keep the jeep from rolling on its side as he hung a turn on the steep hill. Devon was too distraught to drive. In all the years Recker knew his cousin, he never saw him cry until the moment the General sat him down and told him who killed his father. Recker could see Devon out the corner of his eye still wiping tears from his eyes. He took a chance and asked a question.

"Are you going to take the General's advice and leave the situation alone?"

"You think I'm going to let Irons get away with gunning my pops down? I'm going to kill him, it's that simple."

"That simple? I never thought I would say this, but I need for you to run this situation through your paranoid head, because it's not that simple." Recker looked over at him. "Are you listening to me?"

Devon didn't respond.

When Recker turned onto the main road, he pulled out his blunt and lit it. He knew Devon was in the deepest recesses of his mind, laying out a plan that he would have to be high as a kite to listen to.

Chapter 6

When Recker pulled up to the house, Devon grabbed both suitcases and headed inside. Recker walked in just in time to see Devon enter his room and slam the door. He blinked when he heard him lock it.

He thought about knocking, but figured Devon needed time to sort things out.

Devon lay on his bed and tried to process what the General just related to him. His father's truck was hijacked by a gang of miscreants called *Villainy*. Their leader, Irons, had itchy fingers and two Colt. 45s with hairpin triggers. Irons fancied himself to be some kind of Jamaican cowboy. The General told him that instead of Irons killing his father out right, he gave him a chance to save his own life. Irons tossed him a gun and told him to hold it at his side, while his hands hovered over his pistols, holstered at his sides. As soon as Devon's father raised his gun, Irons had both of his out, blasting. Devon's father was dead before he hit the dirt.

Devon snapped out of his daze and opened the suitcases. He pulled out the guns and lined them up on his bed, along with their respective ammo. He started with the P89 9mms. With a flick of his pinky fingers, both clips dropped out of the guns and landed on the bed. He held each gun on either side of his face. The metal was cool against his cheeks. He laid them on the bed and began loading the clips with gold-tipped bullets. Once both clips were filled, he slid them into the guns and chambered a round into each one. He grabbed the double holster and slid one into each. He stood up, loosened his belt and strung it through the double holster. The holster was designed to fit snug against the small of his back. He practiced reaching around his back and drawing the pistols. It felt awkward, but with practice, his movements would become fluid.

He moved to the .45 automatic. He ejected the clip and loaded it with hollow points. After chambering a round, he shoved it in its shoulder holster. He then picked up the two Heckler and Koch MP5 machine guns and pointed them in different directions. He did the same with the pair of Uzis.

He put the guns back into the suitcase and shoved it under his bed. He went into the bathroom and splashed some water on his face and then headed to the living room.

"Where's my keys?"

Recker tossed them to him. "Where are you going?"

"For a drive."

* * *

Devon pulled up to the pay phone. He kept one eye on his surroundings as he dialed the number.

"Hello?"

"Quana, it's me."

"Oh my God! What happened to you?"

"I figured the way things were going down, I needed to keep a low profile."

"You did the right thing. The police are looking every-where for you. They're arresting dudes off the corners and willing to let them go if they tell them where you are."

Devon shook his head. "What's up with Brian?"

"I spoke with his lawyer. The D.A. charged him with the same murders he charged Jason with."

"How's that?"

"Snitch-ass Jason told him that Brian was the trigger man." Devon closed his eyes. "Are you there, Devon?"

"Yes, I'm here. What's the chance of Brian beating this?"

"The lawyer says that he has a chance, but it's a slim one," Quana said.

"How's Sonia?"

"Devastated."

"Brian has to beat this rap, Quana."

"I got him the best homicide lawyer money can buy. I don't know what else to do."

"You're doing just fine."

"Devon, you need to call me more often so—"

"I can't, Quana."

"Devon, I can't do this on my own. You're the only one left. The only one I can talk to. I'm trying to be strong for Brian and Sonia, but I'm cracking."

Devon leaned against the wall and sighed. "I tell you what; I'll call twice a week to check on you."

"Thank you." Quana sighed.

"I have to go. You need anything?"

"I should be asking you that."

"I'm good. I'll call you in a few days, okay?"

"Okay."

Devon hung up and clunked himself in the head with the telephone receiver.

* * *

Devon wasn't surprised to come back to the house and find Recker on his Play Station.

"So what's the game plan, Cuz?" Recker asked.

"It's business as usual."

Recker ice grilled him. "So that's how you going to do me, just shut me out?"

Devon gave Recker a serious look. "I'm not shutting you out. We have to focus on getting the rest of this coke off. Once that's done, then I can focus on other things. So, for now, the shit that the General dropped on us stays between us."

"Of course."

"I don't care how cool you and the team is, my personal business is my personal business," Devon stated.

"Family business stays between family. I got you, Cuz."

"What was your beef with Irons?"

Recker leaned back on the sofa and ran his hands over his bald head before answering. "I used to run with Villainy."

"You were down with this dude?"

"I was 14 and wanted to be down with something, anything. Irons welcomed me into the family. I was wild so I rose quickly through the ranks. He took a liking to me, started to refer to me as his son."

"What happened?"

"I was drunk one night and talking reckless to Grim, his second in charge. Irons used to brag about being the fastest gun in the West Indies. I told Grim that I was faster than him on any given day. This motherfucker goes back and tells him what I said."

"He couldn't resist those brownie points, huh?"

"I think he was scared that Irons was going to demote him and give me his spot. So Irons confronted me and I confessed that I was drunk and I said that. He went crazy. He challenged me to a gunfight, right then and there."

"Like the wild wild west?"

"Yeah. Of course I tried to apologize, but that only made him angrier. No matter how much he taunted me, I refused to shoot it out with him. After calling me every degrading name he could think of, he said being that I wasn't man enough to face him in a gunfight, I didn't deserve to have a trigger finger. He had the crew hold me down and you know the rest."

"And in all these years, you never tried to kill him?"

"There have been those who tried. When they failed, Irons killed them, after he killed their families in front of them. If I fail—"

"He'll kill Uncle Junior and Aunt Lorraine in front of you before taking you out."

"That's how he gets down."

"I think we should take Dillard and Sterling up on their offer."

"Go to Europe and work for them? Hell no."

Devon had to break it down. "What are your options stay here in Jamaica? And do what? You know what I see? I see two businessmen who have a gold mine in Europe but don't know how to mine it. Then, I see a young man who has a team who is loyal and sharp, but he doesn't know how to use them. How long do you think your team is going to stay around you when they realize that you're not willing to take them to the next level?"

"The next level?" Recker looked puzzled.

"Before I came on the scene, y'all were shaking down drug dealers on the corner for beer and weed money. Open your eyes, Recker. Your team is open off the money we're making right now. Once the bricks are sold, do you think they're going to want to go back to beer and weed money?"

"But we don't know the first thing about Amsterdam."

"We're quick learners and the rules are the same wherever you go: fall back, see who's who and then get in where you fit in."

"And it's that easy, huh?" Recker was not convinced.

"It's even easier when you got a way in. Dillard and Sterling are our way in." Devon said.

"And you're sure?"

"When a paranoid man says he's sure about something, you best believe you can bet the house, car, kids, and the wife on it."

"I'll tell Dane to set the meet up with them tomorrow night. And being that this is your idea, I'm going to let you run it by the team and I'm going to let you spell out our terms to Dillard and Sterling."

Devon nodded. "Cool."

* * *

On the outskirts of Kingston, Dillard and Sterling pulled into the parking lot shared by a diner and a ten room motel. Sterling grabbed the brown paper bag of money from the backseat as Dillard shut the car off. They got out and headed to the motel. They climbed the stairs to the third floor and looked at the numbers on the doors.

"It should be the last room," Dillard said.

When they got there, Sterling knocked and stepped back.

Ginja opened the door with an inviting smile. "Right on time, fellas." She stepped to the side to let them in.

Recker was sitting in the kitchen eating waffles. "Have a seat," he said, pointing to the sofa.

"Where is everybody?" Dillard asked.

"They're packing," Devon said, walking out of the back room.

"Packing?" Sterling said.

"We're coming to Amsterdam."

Dillard looked at Recker. "Is he serious?"

"We've decided to take you up on your offer," Recker said.

"I'm glad to hear that."

"Of course, we have some stipulations," Devon said.

"Like what?" Dillard arched an eyebrow.

"First, our coke is our coke. If you choose to buy from us, the price remains the same, and we can continue selling to individuals we were already dealing with."

Dillard looked at Sterling. They both nodded.

"Second, if we're coming on board, we will need to know the locations of all your businesses and who's in charge of running each one."

Both men were silent, but Devon kept on going.

"And last, if we have to collect on any outstanding debts, we keep twenty-five percent of what we collect."

"Some people owe us four to five thousand. You want twenty-five percent of that?"

"Look at it this way. If a person owes you four thousand you're paying us a thousand to get you three. So it's up to you. Do you want three thousand or do you want someone owing you four thousand for God knows how long?" Devon looked at them waiting for an answer.

Dillard shook his head. "We're going to need some time to think… can we think about this?"

"No." Devon finalized.

A half-hour later, Dillard and Sterling left the motel with their six bricks, while Devon, Recker, and Ginja left with ninety thousand in a brown paper bag.

"I got to give it to you," Recker said to Devon, as he opened his car door and threw the brown paper bag in his backseat. "You impressed me back there."

"I told you them dudes were desperate. They're probably laughing their asses off, thinking that they bought us for next to nothing."

"Little do they know," Recker said.

"Little do they know," Devon repeated as he opened his jeep door and climbed in. He unlocked the passenger side for Ginja. "I'm going to drop Ginja off at her crib," he said to Recker.

"I'll be at the house counting this loot."

Devon nodded and shut the door.

"You okay?" Ginja asked.

"Sure, why, what's up?"

"I don't know, you just don't seem yourself. You seem like you got something on your mind."

Devon reclined his seat and closed his eyes. "I am stressing like hell. My boy, Brian…"

"What about him?"

He let his seat back up. "Nothing." He started his jeep and pulled off.

When Devon pulled up to her house, she got out of the jeep and held the door open. "I want to show you something."

"What is it?"

"C'mon."

He watched her walk up her driveway and into her garage. He got out and followed her. He stopped halfway when the garage door opened. Ginja sprung out on her four-wheeler. Devon moved to the side when she skidded in front of him.

"Hop on," she said, tossing him a helmet.

"Where are we going?"

"I told you, I want to show you something."

Devon didn't take his eyes off of her as he slid the helmet down on his head. He climbed on the back and with a sharp twist of the throttle, Ginja shot out of the driveway. Devon tried not to wrap his arms around her waist, but the way she was cutting corners and swerving in between cars, he gave in and held on for dear life.

Fifteen minutes into the ride, she turned off the road onto a stretch of dirt so camouflaged that only those who traveled it knew it existed. The bumpy terrain forced Ginja to keep the ATV between fifteen and twenty miles per hour. Devon felt like he was riding a bucking bronco. Slowly, the trees started to thin out and the ground leveled off. Up ahead, he could see a clearing. He took a chance and looked back the way they came. All he could see was foliage.

Ginja throttled into the clearing that was unlike any he ever saw. They were in a bowl-shaped valley surrounded by spire-like hills. He hopped off the ATV and removed his helmet. "Where are we?"

"We are in uncharted territory." Ginja grabbed him by the hand and led him on a short climb up a steep hill.

Devon stopped in his tracks when he spotted the mouth of a cave.

"You can't see what I want to show you from out here."

"Why don't you just describe it to me?"

"Because it's beyond description."

Devon didn't move.

"You're not afraid of the dark are you?" Ginja smirked.

"I'm just not trying to be one of those men who disappeared."

Ginja put her hands on her hips and stared him down. "Do you really believe everything Recker tells you?"

"You didn't deny it."

"All the violence you've been around and you're afraid to go into a cave with a woman?"

Devon sucked his teeth, while studying the cave's entrance. "Ladies first."

Devon ran his fingers along the jagged walls as they walked down the cave's steep slope. He looked up at the ceiling, imagining the world of trouble they would be in if the icicle-shaped rocks hanging above were to rain down on them. Ginja stopped short, putting him on high alert. She made a sharp right and stopped by a crack in the wall.

She looked back at him with a smile. "We're almost there." She turned sideways and slid through the narrow opening. Devon shook his head and slithered through. When he came out on the other end, he saw her reach behind a rock and pick up a flashlight. She turned it on. The light lit up the lip of the sixty foot high cliff they were standing on.

Devon looked around in awe.

"I told you it was beyond description." She led him down a rugged path around stone columns.

On their way down, Devon examined the ancient symbols on the walls. "This is incredible."

"You haven't seen anything yet," She said, leading him by the hand deeper into the bowels of the earth.

After five minutes of hearing nothing, but his footsteps and his heartbeat, Devon cocked his head when he heard the faint sound of running water. He felt a cool breeze on his face and he smelt... flowers? A few moments later, they were in a chamber that was a hundred times awe-inspiring than the last. This one had flowers of all different colors hanging from its roof. Thirty feet below them, he could see the underground river. Ginja handed him the flashlight and pulled a lighter out of her pocket. She walked to a torch set into the wall and lit it. She walked to four more and lit them as well.

"You like?" She asked.

"I've never seen anything like this in my life."

"There's much more to life than what you're used to seeing, Gunslinger."

Devon looked at her. "I really don't like that name."

"That's what you are, right? I bet you got a gun on you right now."

"Two, actually." She hit him on the arm. "I'm assuming you set these torches up."

"I replaced them."

"Replaced them?"

"When Ivory and I first came across this place, the torches were rotted. Back in the day, runaway slaves used these caverns and the rough terrain to fight off being recaptured. These caves number in the thousands."

"And how do you know this?"

"By the writing on the walls. Ivory and I took pictures of it and compared it to languages on the internet. It's a Niger-Congo language called Fulani." Ginja sat on the ledge and looked down at the river below. Devon sat next to her.

"What do you know about the Great Slave Trade?" Ginja asked.

"Africans were brought over here by the Europeans as slaves."

"How were the Europeans able to get into Africa, raid villages, enslave the people, and ship them to America with hardly any resistance?"

"I never really thought about it."

"Think about it."

"Now?"

"Right now," Ginja said.

"Okay, the Europeans had to have help."

"Help from who?"

"Help from the inside, help from other Africans."

"And why would Africans help them enslave other Africans?"

"The same reasons anyone else would sell their own people out: Greed or to save their own ass. In this case, I would say it was greed."

"Do you think the Africans who worked with the Europeans knew that the Europeans were going to double cross them and enslave them as well?"

"Of course not, greed is blind."

"What about you, Devon? Are you blinded by greed?"

"Why, you want to make me an offer?"

"No, I just want you to remember that greed has been responsible for destroying the greatest of people."

"Greed didn't destroy them."

"What was it?" Ginja asked.

"Trust."

"Trust?"

"The Africans trusted the Europeans to be true to their word. And the downfall of some of the greatest men in history had been by betrayal from their most trusted advisers."

"So you don't trust anyone?"

"If I had to trust someone, it would be my boy, Brian." Devon nodded. "We're like brothers."

"So you do trust someone."

"I said if I *had* to trust someone."

"I would love to meet the only person in the world you would trust if you had to trust someone. Why don't you invite him down?"

"He's in prison right now."

"What did he do?"

"I don't want to talk about it." Devon looked away from her.

"I was just asking."

"Well, don't ask ever again."

"Damn, I'm sorry."

"Yeah, whatever." Devon stood up. "I'm ready to go."

"I said I was sorry."

Devon picked up a rock and tossed it down into the river. "There's nothing to be sorry about. I just don't like people in my business."

Ginja stood up and walked up to him. She caressed his neck. Her fingers looped around his platinum chain. She pulled it up til the platinum cross popped over his shirt. "You're religious?"

"No, I wear it as a reminder."

"A reminder of what?"

"Jesus's downfall."

Ginja shook her head. "I'm almost afraid to ask. What was his downfall?"

"Trust, of course. He was betrayed by Judas, one of his own."

"For a man who doesn't trust anyone, you sure do expect everyone to trust you. None of us have ever been to Amsterdam, hell, we never been out of the Caribbean. And you want us to just trust that you're going to take care of us."

"See, that's the irony of it. A man who doesn't trust anyone is a man who can be trusted."

"Oh really?" Ginja placed her hands on her hips.

"One thing that I can't stand is a backstabbing snake. Why would I become the very thing that I hate? My word is my bond, and I will die before I fail my word."

"Promise me that you won't let anything happen to me or Ivory when we get to Amsterdam."

"Nothing's going to happen to you that won't happen to me first." Devon sat on a rock and looked around the cavern again. "I see why you come here when you're stressed. This place is peaceful. So how many other men have you brought here?"

"You're my first." She walked in between his legs.

Devon looked up at her. "What's up?"

"You." She squatted and rested her hand on the bulge in his pants.

"It's time for us to go," Devon said, starting to stand.

She refused to let him get up. "I see the way you stare at me when you think I'm not looking."

"You've lost your mind."

"I can read people, remember?"

"And what are you reading in me?"

"You want to bust a nut so bad, but you haven't found a woman you trust enough to allow yourself to be vulnerable."

Devon started laughing. "Woman, please, you don't know me." He stopped laughing when she unzipped his pants and snaked her hand into his boxers. She pulled him out and wrapped her hand around his shaft. She messaged it as she stared into his eyes. "It's time for you to bust that nut."

Devon looked down at his shaft throbbing in her hand. He looked around the cavern.

"Time to let it go," she said, before lowering her head.

Devon stiffened as her hot lips slid down his shaft. His eyelids closed half-way as his body relaxed. Ginja bobbed her head up and down, pausing every now and then to flick the head of his manhood with her tongue. Devon palmed the back of her head and made her deep throat him over and over until he felt himself swelling. "I'm about to…" He tried pulling her away as he felt his juices coming down the pipe, but her lips were like suction cups. Tasting the first drops of his nectar made her bob up and down faster. He clenched his jaw and his head rolled back. Every time he squirted, his body jerked. When the spasms stopped, Ginja stood up and walked to the wall. She spat his juices out and then wiped her mouth with the bottom of her shirt. He stood and zipped up his pants when she started walking back.

"Just busting a nut, right?" she asked.

"Yeah, one that needed to be cracked a long time ago." He stared at her while he caressed her cheek. "I hope you don't catch feelings for me."

She pulled away from his touch. "Feelings? I sucked your dick and then hawked-spit your cum against the wall."

Devon nodded. "And that shit turned me on."

"Humph, I hope you don't catch feelings for me."

"This relationship is going to work just fine."

Chapter 7

"This is some bullshit," Recker said, looking out the flat's window. "This weather is the worst. It's always raining and it's always cold. I need to find something to do, shit I miss Jamaica!"

"Play your PS3," Devon said. He was online gathering information on the names Dillard had given him a few weeks back.

The team had been in Amsterdam for three weeks. They decided to follow Devon's lead and fall back. They observed Dillard and Sterling's operations.

A good chunk of their money came from gambling spots tucked away in the back rooms of cafes, boutiques, and showrooms. Another sizable income came from the nightclub they owned in the Docklands. It was a three story warehouse that they had converted into a three floor nightclub. The first floor catered to the techno dancers, the second floor was for the reggae and hip hop heads, and the third floor was R&B.

"I can't believe this," Devon said, staring at the screen. "This guy David Hagen is a private consultant for an international corporation that offers consulting to American companies operating overseas."

"How much does he owe?"

"Three Gs. Five out of the seven on this list that Dillard gave me are making six figures a year, easy."

"So how come they're not paying?"

Devon ignored him and punched in the next name. "Unbelievable. James Bechman used to be the Dean at the University."

"Which University?" Recker turned to look at Devon.

"The University of Amsterdam."

"How much he owe?"

"Five hundred."

Recker walked away from the window and plopped down on the couch. "I say we go after the ones who owe the most first. And I say we start this weekend. We've been playing low-key long enough. It's time to flex our muscle, let these bitches know we're in the country."

"Be easy."

"Fuck being easy. I'm tired of being easy. Motherfuckers owe. They got to pay."

"You don't think anything through, do you?"

"There's nothing to think about." Recker shook his head stubbornly.

"We're not going to start collecting for another four weeks."

"So, it's going to take you four more weeks to think things through?"

"I've already thought everything through. Dillard and Sterling have no credit limit with their clients. So, the retired dean who owes a measly five hundred, in four more weeks, will owe around two thousand. Twenty five percent of two thousand is a hell of a lot more than twenty five percent of five hundred."

"That sounds good, but do you have a plan for those who can't pay?"

"Everyone's going to pay, one way or another."

Someone from the team knocked on the door. Three knocks followed by two, and then one.

Devon looked at Recker. "You're not going to answer that?"

"Why can't you answer it?"

"Because I'm working," Devon replied.

Recker huffed and got off the couch. He peeked through the peephole before opening the door.

Ginja and Ivory walked in and removed their wet coats and boots.

"Talk to me," Devon said, and looked up another name.

"Where do we start?" Ginja said.

"With the money," Recker said.

"Well," Ivory began. "Devon's right. These guys are sitting on a gold mine. I looked at their books for all their establishments and then Ginja and I went to one each night and the books don't match."

"So, their accountant is skimming?" Devon asked.

"Maybe, but that's not where it starts," Ivory said.

"Ivory calculated the winnings of each table we sat at, and at the end of the night not one table turned in the figure she came up with in her head," Ginja said.

"And of course the overseers have to be down with it," Recker said.

"Of course," Ivory said.

"Okay." Devon looked up. "We're going to have to make some adjustments in the way money is being monitored."

"That's not all," Ginja said.

"What else," Devon said.

"The club is caking. Crazy money is being made, but Dillard and Sterling are only getting the crumbs."

"Explain," Recker said.

"Most of the money is being made by the dealers pedaling pills and the girls prostituting in the bathrooms."

"Pills and prostitution," Devon said, shaking his head.

"Let me guess, Cuz," Recker said twisting up his face. "We're going to track down the motherfuckers pushing the pills and pussy and put a stop to it."

"Yes, we are definitely going to find the motherfuckers pushing the pills and pussy, and no, we're not putting a stop to it. Not a pill or piece of pussy is going to be sold in that club without us getting a percentage."

"We're here, Cuz," Recker said, pointing two fingers back and forth between their eyes.

"And how long do you think the pills and prostitution is going to last?" Ivory asked. "All it takes is for one person to overdose or for someone to find a prostitute in one of the stalls with her throat slit, and its curtains."

"We'll make a shit load of money by then," Devon said. "And if the club does get shut down, we haven't lost anything."

The team looked at Devon.

"Hey, we're taking this team to the next level, remember? Some toes are going to get stepped on and some heads are going to get bashed in. Speaking of bashing, where's Dane, Rippa, and Stripes?"

"You know where they are," Ginja said.

"Recker, you got to talk to them," Devon said. "This is getting ridiculous."

"They're doing them." Recker grinned.

"They're fucking up our flow. They're in the Red Light District, tricking on them hoes every night. Then they wobble back to their flat and sleep the whole day away."

"They're just waiting for something to do. Like collecting some money or bashing some heads," Recker said.

"Bashing heads, huh? Okay," Devon said.

"Okay, what?"

"Call them and tell them to get their asses over here, now."

"Why what's up?"

"We're going to put in some work."

Recker balled up his right fist and slammed it into his left palm. "Finally! Who's first?"

"The motherfucking pill and pussy man," Devon said.

"You know who it is?" Ginja asked.

"After Dane, Rippa, and Stripes stomp some people out we'll know, right Recker?"

Recker headed to his room.

"Where you going?" Devon asked.

"To go put on my ass-kicking boots."

* * *

Club Insomnia was jumping on each floor. Ginja and Ivory were on the first floor, Recker and Stripes were on the second, and Dane and Rippa were on the third. Devon was sitting in Dillard and Sterling's office staring at the TV monitors. Dillard and Sterling had cameras everywhere, including the bathrooms. "Freak ass dudes." Devon directed his attention to camera number seven. "Men's bathroom on the south side, second floor," he said into his headset to Recker.

Recker tapped his earplug twice to let him know he was on it.

"The third stall," Devon continued. He watched Recker and Stripes walk through the bathroom door and kick the stall in. Dane yanked the woman out by her hair while Recker held the trick at bay with his 9mm.

"We're heading up," Recker said into his transmitter.

Devon kept his eyes on the screens. A muscle-bound white guy slid up on Ivory and grabbed her hands. Devon could see that he was trying to get her to join him on the dance floor. She tried to ease away from him, but he wasn't taking no for an answer. That is, until Ginja rolled up and stuck her tongue down Ivory's throat. The white guy backed up and looked like he was apologizing. Devon looked up when he heard the three knocks, then two, then one.

Dane walked in pulling the woman by her hair. Recker walked in behind them.

"Get the fuck off me," the woman kept saying.

"Have a seat," Dane said, shoving her to the couch. She started to stand. Dane shoved her back on the couch. She started to get up again.

Recker stepped in. "My boy is asking you nice. If I have to ask, you're going to be missing some teeth."

The woman sat in silence.

Devon got up from the desk and walked up to her. "Who do you work for?"

"I don't know what you're talking about."

"Take her back to the bathroom," Devon said to Recker. "Make it look like an accident."

"No problem," Recker said.

The woman watched Devon walk back to the desk and sit down. Then she watched Recker retrieve a needle out of the cabinet.

"Wait a minute," she said.

"Don't worry, baby," Recker said. "You won't have to feel pain ever again."

"No, wait."

Dane grabbed her from behind and held her down as Recker removed the sheath off of the needle.

"Cabrini," she shouted. "His name is Cabrini."

"Wait," Devon said to Recker. "Is he in the club?"

"Yes." The woman was shaking.

"Where?" Devon asked.

"First floor. The booth by the bar."

Devon looked at the monitors. "Describe him."

"Tall, white, muscular."

"What color shirt is he wearing?"

"Burgundy."

Devon cracked a smile. It was the same dude trying to drag Ivory onto the dance floor. "Take her to the back."

Dane lifted her to her feet and pushed her to the back.

"Wait, I told you what you wanted to know."

"We'll let you go when we're finished chatting with Cabrini," Devon said. "Behave; don't give my boy a reason to use that needle."

Dane shoved her through the door and slammed it.

"I got a fix on pimp daddy," Devon said into his headset. "Ginja, Ivory, he's on your floor. He's the guy that tried getting with Ivory. Can y'all lure him to the office?"

Ginja and Ivory tapped their earplugs twice.

"We'll be waiting." Devon watched Ivory walk up on the husky pimp and press her body into his. In less than twenty seconds, he was at the bar buying her a drink. Thirty seconds later, pimp daddy was following her to the elevator. Devon followed them on the monitors. As soon as the elevator doors closed, the white hulk was on her. He was grabbing and squeezing any part of her body he could get his hands on.

Ivory allowed him to raise her blouse and unclasp her bra. The pimp sucked and bit on her pink nipples.

Devon jumped when he heard three knocks on the door, followed by two, and then one.

Ginja walked in. "Are they on their way up?" she asked.

"Ah... yeah. They're in the elevator."

Ginja walked behind the desk and stared at the monitor. A vein zigzagged down the center of her forehead. Devon could feel the heat radiating off her body.

Rippa and Stripes knocked and walked in. "They're on their way up," Recker said. Everyone went to the back. Devon cracked the door. Ivory and the pimp came busting through the door. He was all over her.

"You sure we're going to be all right up here?" he asked, groping Ivory's butt.

"I told you, this is my brother's office, and he won't be in until later tonight."

Ginja squeezed under Devon's arm to get a peek.

"And your girlfriend is okay with this?"

"Let's find out."

Ginja shot out the door. Devon tried to grab her but she was too quick.

"Oh shit." Devon took off behind her when he saw her grab the solid brass paperweight off the desk.

The pimp heard the paperweight scrape the desk as Ginja cuffed it. The next thing he heard was GONG. Ivory stepped to the side as he fell forward. Ginja saw the red blotches on Ivory's bone white skin where the pimp had manhandled her and lost it. She brought the paperweight down on the pimp's head two more times before Devon tackled her to the ground.

Recker and the rest of the fellas hoisted the pimp to his feet and cuffed his hands behind his back. Devon couldn't believe Ginja's strength. She tossed him off of her twice. He was on his knees with his arms wrapped around her waist as she struggled to get to the dazed pimp.

Ivory hugged her. "Shhh, it's over, I'm fine."

Devon felt Ginja go limp.

"I got her," Ivory said, looking down at him.

Devon let her go and stood up. "Take her to the back," he said to Ivory. "And sit this motherfucker down," he said to Recker. Recker punched the pimp in the stomach and shoved him on the couch.

"Hey man, she told me you wouldn't be here until later tonight. I didn't mean any disrespect," the pimp said to Devon.

Devon bent down and picked up the paperweight. "We can do this the easy way or the hard way. The easy way is you tell me what I want to hear. The hard way is… my girl comes back in here and finishes bashing your head in until you tell me what I want to hear."

"I'll tell you anything you want to know."

* * *

Fifteen minutes later, Devon and Recker walked into the back. Recker snatched the woman up and escorted her out the office.

"So, what's the verdict?" Ivory asked.

"We came to an agreement of fifteen hundred dollars on Friday and Saturday nights, and seven fifty Sunday through Thursday."

"All we got to do now is find the pill man," Ivory said.

"Which is why I need you two back out there. Y'all are going on the second floor. Dane and Recker will take the first."

"Okay," Ivory said.

"You go on," Devon said to her. "I want to talk to Ginja for a second."

Ivory looked at Ginja. When Ginja nodded, Ivory left the room.

Ginja folded her arms. "I guess this is the part where you reprimand me for insubordination."

"No. I want to know what happened."

"You saw what happened. That piece of shit—"

"No. I know what happened tonight. I want to know what happened with you and Ivory. The bond that the both of you have… you would've killed that man if I didn't stop you. The way you were looking at that screen when Ivory was letting that man suck on her—"

"She didn't let him suck on anything."

"I saw the whole thing remember?"

"You saw what you wanted to see."

"Well then, help me see what I should've seen."

"You wouldn't understand."

"Make me understand."

Ginja started walking to the door. Devon ran in front of her and stood in front of it. Ginja wiped the tears from her eyes.

"Please get out of the way."

"Back in the States, I shot people… hurt people real bad… I even killed two people. After almost every incident where I had to inflict pain on someone or kill someone, I felt bad."

"Almost every incident?" Ginja tried blinking the tears back.

"I say almost, because there was this one guy. We used to work for him, Brian and I. Brian found out that this… piece of shit was abusing his own sister."

Ginja started to cry.

"I didn't' feel bad when I killed him. In fact, I felt good. I wished that I could bring him back to life to kill him again and again. Am I crazy for feeling that way?"

Ginja allowed Devon to wipe her tears. "Ivory's mother abandoned her when she was six years old. Ivory was a bookworm growing up. I couldn't understand how a girl so smart could be so naïve. She put an ad in the newspaper. She was trying to locate her mother. A woman called her and told her that she knew where her mother was. Ivory begged for me to come with her, but I didn't. So she went by herself. There was a man waiting for her. She was kind of hesitant of going with him, but he convinced her that her mother was staying just around the corner. When they walked into the apartment, there were five other men waiting. They kept her three days. They were so brutal with her the first couple days that on the third day, they didn't' have to force themselves on her. They barked commands at her and she obeyed without question."

"What happened to the men?"

Ginja chuckled. "They disappeared."

"Mysteriously."

"I guess it's not a mystery anymore."

"They got what they deserved." Devon stroked her hair.

"I made myself a promise that no man will ever hurt her again. In the elevator… the look on her face… it was the same look she had when those bastards let her go three days later. And then when I saw the marks on her…"

"I understand." Devon hugged her and kissed her on the cheek.

"I'm honored," Ginja said.

"Why is that?"

"I'm the only member of the team who got to see the soft side of the Gunslinger."

Devon straightened up. "You got someplace to be."

Ginja grabbed his hand and squeezed it. "I swear on me and Ivory's bond, nothing will happen to you that won't happen to us first." She left.

Devon walked back to the desk and sat down. He leaned back in the chair and closed his eyes. Stay focused, can't get emotional. There's no room for emotions at this level of the game.

It took the team three weeks to track down the pill pusher. All fingers pointed to a college student at the University of Amsterdam. He folded immediately when Recker brought him into the office. Devon leaned back in the chair as Recker kicked the nerd out of the office.

"So, what's next?" Recker asked.

"It's time to start going down that list and collecting."

* * *

Two weeks later, the team had their first official meeting with Dillard and Sterling since they arrived in Amsterdam. They all sat around Dillard's dining room table. Dillard's wife and daughters brought out the food and fixed everyone a plate. Devon eyed the British-bred woman. She walked with her head erect, shoulders squared. There was no doubt in his mind that she came from a family of high social standing. She kissed Dillard on the cheek and disappeared into the kitchen.

Ginja and Ivory went to work on their plates. Ginja picked up her T-bone steak with her hands and ate it like corn on a cob. Ivory picked up her tablespoon and shoveled rice into her mouth.

"Let me be the first to say that I'm very pleased with the way you all are handling things," Dillard said.

Sterling nodded in agreement.

"Did you expect anything less?" Recker asked.

"Of course not," Dillard said. "That's why I only offered you and your team the job. I must admit, though, when you told me and Sterling that we had to fire some of our personnel, we were skeptical. They worked for us for years. We would've never thought they would be stealing from us."

"But you made us believers," Sterling said.

"And, I'm digging your suave style," Dillard said.

Ginja burped. "Shit! Excuse me."

Rippa shook his head.

"Your wife can cook her ass off," Ivory said. A grain of rice flew out her mouth and onto the table. She swiped it on the floor and kept eating.

"Yes," Devon said, taking the spotlight off of Ginja and Ivory. "We know that we have to exhibit certain decorum when dealing with your clients. We want to inspire enough fear for them to pay their debts, but not too much as to scare them away."

"And it's working," Sterling said.

Devon peeped the way Sterling kept cutting his eyes at Ginja throughout the whole meal. He especially kept an eye on her when she dropped the T-bone and licked her fingers clean. Devon filed that in the memory bank. Ginja did look kinda sexy the way she was sucking on her fingers. Devon made another mental note. Ginja will be sucking on something else when he got her by herself later on tonight.

"I think I should get right to the point of why I gathered everyone here tonight," Dillard said.

Devon stopped chewing.

"Those six kilos of coke we brought from you has had our clients open for more. Your product is the purest we've come across, ever."

Devon nodded.

"It usually takes us three to four months to run through a kilo. We got rid of two in six weeks," Dillard said excitedly.

"Which brings us to this meeting," Devon said.

"Yes," Sterling said. "The quality of your coke will make all of us very rich."

"Here's the deal," Dillard said. "We would like for you to arrange a meeting for us with your connect and—"

"Not going to happen," Devon said.

"We're not trying to go around you or anything," Dillard said.

"I'm not worried about that," Devon said. "My connect is very finicky when it comes to who he deals with."

"I'm sure if you vouch for us—" Sterling began to say.

"What part of finicky don't you understand? If I go to him, talking about bringing people to him who he doesn't know, he'll probably cut me off."

"We were looking to buy a substantial amount, and we didn't think you would have the amount we were looking for," Dillard said.

"How many bricks you talking?" Devon asked.

"Twenty," Sterling said.

Dane choked on his wine, Rippa dropped his fork, and Stripes moved his lips but nothing came out.

Recker wanted to jump out of his chair and break dance. Ginja and Ivory started whispering to one another.

Devon brought his fork to his mouth and bit down on his piece of steak, his face expressionless. "How are you going to get twenty bricks from Jamaica to Amsterdam?" he asked.

"It won't be a problem for us," Dillard said.

"What about forty?"

Recker cut his eyes at him.

"What do you mean?" Dillard asked.

"I mean could you get forty bricks from Jamaica to Amsterdam?"

"If we had to, we could," Dillard said.

"Good, because I don't have twenty bricks."

Recker wanted to kick Devon in the shin.

"And the *only* way my connect will deal with you is through me, and your first buy would have to be at least forty bricks."

"Forty at fifteen thousand a piece," Sterling said, shaking his head.

"I tell you what," Devon said. "Being that we do work for you, and I know that you're going to take care of us, I'll forfeit my commission on the bricks. I'll get them for you for twelve fifty a piece."

Dillard folded his hands. "Half a mil for forty bricks."

Sterling nodded. "Sounds good."

Devon put his fork and knife down and wiped his mouth with his napkin. "We'll fly down to Jamaica this weekend and get the wheels spinning on this thing. He's going to want his money before those bricks leave Jamaica."

"That won't be a problem," Dillard said. Sterling nodded in agreement.

At that moment, Devon wanted to jump out of his chair and break dance.

* * *

"You slick talking motherfucker," Recker said as him and Devon walked into their flat. "I was about to kick you in the shin when you told them that you didn't have twenty bricks, knowing we still sitting on fifty of them things in Jamaica."

"You know I had to try them, see how serious they were." Devon smirked.

"They are definitely serious. But this poses a problem. What are we going to do when the coke is gone?" Recker creased his brow.

"We need not worry about that right now. It's going to take them close to a year to run through forty bricks. By that time, we'll be standing on our own two feet."

Recker nodded. "You really do have this whole thing figured out, don't you?"

"We wouldn't be here if I didn't."

"So, are we taking the whole team with us?"

"Yeah. I can see it in their faces, they're homesick. Everything here seems to be in order. I doubt if anything is going to jump off over the weekend," Devon said.

"That's the plan then." Recker headed to his room. "I'm going to grab some cash and meet Dane and them at the District."

"Don't trick all your money."

"Never that. What are you going to do?"

Devon pulled out his phone and dialed Ginja's number. "I'll think of something."

* * *

Back in Jamaica, the cab pulled up to Recker's house. Devon, Recker, and Ginja got out and grabbed their bags out the trunk while Ivory paid the driver.

"Yes," Recker screamed. He took off his T-shirt and let the sun hit his bare chest. "There's no place like home."

"We'll be inside, Dorothy," Devon said to Recker.

"I don't know why you wore that hot ass suit," Recker said. "And you got these airheads copying you," he said, looking at the pantsuits Ginja and Ivory were wearing.

"It's called maturation," Devon said. "We're not the same people who left Jamaica two months ago. At least that's the impression we want to give to those who knew we went to Europe to get paid."

"The only time you're going to see me in a suit is when I'm lying in a coffin."

Devon sighed and headed inside.

"It does feel good to be home," Ivory said.

"Don't get comfortable," Devon said. "We're here to go to the caves where we stashed the bricks and retrieve the forty we need." Devon pulled his jeep keys out of the kitchen drawer. "I'll drive y'all to your cribs. Tomorrow, we'll head to the caves.

* * *

The next morning, Devon pulled up to Ginja's house. Both women were on the porch with their feet kicked up.

"Hey, Gunslinger," Ginja said, checking him out in his jeans and button down short sleeve shirt.

"Good morning," Ivory said. She was wearing overalls and construction boots.

"I'm glad someone's dressed like they're ready to work," Devon said, cutting his eyes at Ginja.

"I can work in shorts and a tank top," she said. "I'm surprised Recker and them are letting you go with us all by yourself. I guess they don't mind if you disappear," Ginja said jokingly.

"They were totally against it, but Sparks called last night, he heard we were back in town, and wanted five bricks. I sent Recker and them to collect the money. Besides, you wouldn't want to make me disappear. Who's going to take care of you?"

"Umm, you right about that," Ginja said. "Maybe one day we can return the favor."

Ivory nodded, staring at his crotch.

"Let's do this," Devon said.

They walked off the porch and headed toward the ATVs. Ivory hopped on hers and started it up. "Hop on," she said to Devon. She tossed him a helmet.

He shook his head. "I'm going to ride with—"

Before he got to finish his sentence, Ginja pulled off.

"I guess you'll be riding with me, Gunslinger."

Devon watched Ginja tear around the corner. He shook his head and put the helmet on. He hopped on Ivory's ATV.

"Hold on to me, real tight, baby boy." She gunned the throttle, popping the front wheels into the air. She wheelied half a block before bringing the ATV down on all four wheels. She whipped around the corner and within seconds, she caught up to Ginja. The women didn't slowdown until they neared the trail. Devon held on to Ivory, her ATV left the ground a few times. When they entered the clearing, Devon took off his helmet.

"And I thought Ginja was reckless."

"I can ride that trail blindfolded," Ivory said.

"Let's go get dirty," Ginja said.

When they walked into the chamber, Devon moved some rocks to the side and pulled out the shovels. He handed one to Ginja and Ivory. Ginja lit the torches while Devon and Ivory began digging. When Ivory took a break, Ginja took over.

"Hold on," Devon said. He laid his shovel down and swept the dirt off of the duffel bags. He pulled them up, one by one.

"Okay, time to wash up," Ginja said. She peeled off her shorts and tank top and headed for the underground river. Devon watched her butt jiggle in her skimpy panties. When she got to the river, she came out of her bra and panties and stepped into the water.

"She's beautiful, isn't she?" Ivory said.

"Yes, she is."

"Maybe you should tell her that the next time her head's between your legs."

"Between my legs?" Devon looked at Ivory.

Ivory walked up to him and twirled one of his dreads around her finger. "I'm part bloodhound, remember? I always smell your... fluid on her breath when she comes back from one of your little episodes."

"I don't know what you're talking about," Devon said looking away.

"Umm hmm." Ivory stepped out of her overalls. She was completely naked underneath. "I'm going to go join my homegirl. Feel free to join us."

Devon stared at the sweat glistening on her naked body. Ivory didn't move until his gaze met hers.

"It's all yours whenever you want it." As she walked by him, she gently grabbed the growing bulge in his pants and massaged it. Devon watched her walk to the river, her butt bouncing. He looked at Ginja. She was wading in the water. She waved for him to join them. He shook his head and sat on a rock. His heart was pounding a million beats a minute. Any man in his shoes right now would have stripped out of their clothes and dived into the river dick first. He had to be strong though, he had to show them that he controlled his desires, and that it wasn't the other way around. He watched them for a half an hour, splashing in the water, blowing him kisses, and shooting him the most seductive looks he ever saw.

Finally they got out of the river and got dressed.

"So, what's next on our agenda?" Ginja asked.

"We head back to the house, see if Recker got that money, and then the rest of the weekend is yours."

"Well, being that we can't spend it with you," Ivory said, "We'll have to do the next best thing."

"What's that?"

Ginja and Ivory looked at each other. "Shop," they said at the same time.

Devon shook his head. "Women."

* * *

When Devon and the girls walked into the house, Recker, Dane, Rippa, and Stripes were sitting around the kitchen table, each smoking a blunt and drinking a beer.

"How we looking?" Devon asked.

"It's all here," Recker said. "75Gs."

Devon dropped the duffel bag with the five kilos at Recker's feet. "Make sure he gets what he paid for." He turned to Dane. "The forty bricks are in the jeep."

Dane stood and looked at Rippa and Stripes. "We got work to do."

"You remember the address Dillard gave us?" Devon asked.

"I got this," Dane said.

Devon held his hands up. "I'm just asking."

"I'll call you when Dillard and Sterling's man in customs has the bricks in his possession," Dane said.

"Cool," Devon said, as he headed to his room. Quana came to his mind. He stopped at his bedroom and made a sharp left into Recker's. He grabbed the phone and went into his room. He laid on his bed and dialed her number.

"Hello?"

"Quana, it's me."

"You said you were going to call me every couple days."

"I know, but I got caught up and—" Quana was crying. "Quana? What's wrong?" he asked as he sat back up.

"The jury found Brian guilty."

Devon went numb. "Wha... wha..." He knew what he wanted to say, but he couldn't get the words out.

Quana started crying hysterically. "I can't function. Everybody is looking toward me for strength, but I'm on the verge of having a nervous breakdown. The judge sentenced him to fifty years, Devon. Fifty years!"

Devon dropped the phone. He stood up and felt lightheaded. He fell into his dresser. The loud crash brought Recker, Ginja, and Ivory to the door.

"Cuz, what's up?" Recker asked.

Devon stood. His legs wobbled and he leaned against the dresser.

"Yo, Cuz. What the fuck?" Recker ran into his room to get his gun when Devon started crying.

Ginja and Ivory ran to him. "Talk to us, baby," Ivory said.

He pushed them away. "I can't breathe; I got to get out of here."

"Wait," Ginja and Ivory struggled to restrain him.

Recker was back at the door, MP-5 in hand. "Who we got to kill?"

Devon hugged Ivory tight and cried harder. Ginja saw the phone receiver on the floor. She walked to it and picked it up. She tried calming Quana down, while Ivory hugged Devon back and cried with him. Recker was pacing back and forth, getting more hyped with each step.

"Ask him who it is," Recker said to Ivory. He stopped in mid stride. The last time Devon cried like this, the General told him the story of his father. Recker hit himself in the head with the butt of his gun. "I'm about to jump in my car and kill every Villainy motherfucker I see." Recker took off. Ginja was focused on talking to Quana, Ivory was focused on comforting Devon, who was so out of it, that none of them heard what Recker said, nor did they hear when he left.

Chapter 8

Three days later, Devon was posted up on the back end of his jeep, scanning the throng of people exiting the airport. He perked up when he saw her. Quana fidgeted with the strap on her overnight bag as she peered out into the line of vehicles. She forced a smile on her face when she saw Devon waving her over. She walked into his embrace and broke down.

Devon kissed the top of her head as she cried. "C'mon, now, you know Brian wouldn't approve of this."

Quana hugged him tighter as she tried to stop crying. She finally lifted her head out of his chest and looked up at him. "I'm sorry, I'm just so sick right now. Brian is like a brother to me."

"He's like a brother to me, too."

"I soaked the front of your tank top." She looked down at his tan cargo shorts and sandals. "I guess I'm kinda over-dressed, huh?"

Devon looked at her fitted jeans and silk blouse. "You'll have plenty of time to let me see you in a bikini."

"You so stupid," she said, slapping his arm.

He grabbed her overnight bag and placed it in the back of his jeep. Then he opened the passenger side door for her to climb in.

Quana looked around the interior of the jeep as Devon headed out of the airport.

"What?" he asked, as a thin smile appeared on her face.

"Nothing. I was just checking out your ride."

"It's banging right?"

"Yeah, back in 1993."

"You got jokes, huh? So, how was your flight?"

Quana sighed and leaned back in her seat. "Long, but I needed the time to pull myself together. Ever since Brian got arrested, everybody, from his parents to Sonia, has been turning to me for strength and answers. And let's not forget I was still dealing with my own issues. That shit with Jason's trifling ass getting my cousin, Teshawna, pregnant still got me fucked up. I loved that boy... I gave him all of me. I swear to you, if I could get my hands on him or knew someone who could—"

"Don't worry about Jason. He's going to get what his hand calls for."

Quana shook her head. "I still can't believe Brian got all that time. Fifty years? I tried to do everything in my power..." She turned her head as her eyes started to water.

Devon reached over and put his hand on her knee. "I know you did everything you could. Sonia knows it and so does Brian. Listen, I invited you down here to take your mind off of what's going on in the States. You are in Jamaica, now. You hear me? When was the last time you left the States?"

She placed her hand on top of the one he had on her knee. "The States? I've never been outside the 5 boroughs."

"Well in that case, these next days are going to be ones you'll never forget." Devon pulled up to the beach house he rented for three days.

Quana stepped out of the jeep and stared at the property.

"C'mon let me show you the inside." He grabbed her by the hand and led her inside.

"Nice," Quana said as she walked through the foyer and looked around the spacious interior.

"You can pretty much see where everything is, the kitchen, dining room, living room." He led her up the spiraling staircase and down the hall to the last door on the right. He opened it and walked in with Quana on his heels.

"This is where you'll be staying. Mine is right across the hall."

Quana walked into the center of the room and looked around. "What's that?" She asked, pointing to a door adjacent from the closet.

"That's your bathroom."

She walked back to him and took her bag from him. "I don't know why I let you talk me into only bringing an overnight bag. I should've—"

Devon held his hand up. "Didn't I tell you I got you covered? Tonight, we're having dinner on the beach, under the stars. And tomorrow..." Devon started to back out of the room.

"What's happening tomorrow?" Quana said following him into the hallway.

"You had a long flight. Go back into your room, take a hot bath, and relax. I'll go downstairs and get everything ready for our dinner under the stars. I'll come get you in about... an hour."

"And when you come back, you're going to tell me what we're doing tomorrow."

"Of course." Devon said.

"Don't try and play me, Devon. You know I hate surprises."

"I promise. I'll tell you all about it over dinner."

Devon headed into his room and took a shower. Three days ago when he called Quana and she told him that the judge had given Brian two 25-life sentences running consecutive, he dropped the phone and his body went numb. When he picked the phone back up, Quana was crying, saying that she let everybody down, especially Brian. She was on the verge of a nervous breakdown when Devon decided he needed to do something. He calmed her down as best as he could and then convinced her to go and see his Uncle Clifford in Florida.

When she arrived at his uncle's, he took her to his office and handed her the phone. It was then that Devon told her that he was in Jamaica and he desperately needed to speak to her face to face. After she hung up, Clifford reached into his drawer and pulled out a first class plane ticket and a wad of money. Per Devon, Clifford gave the money to Quana and made Fredricka take her shopping just for enough things to put in an overnight bag.

Devon hopped out the shower a half hour later. He put on a pair of Bermuda shorts and a tank top and then headed downstairs. An hour later, he heard Quana coming down the stairs. "I was just about to come up and get you," he said over his shoulder.

"Well, I saved you the trip."

Devon turned around and was amazed at the transformation. He was so used to seeing Quana in jeans and boots that he had to do a double take at the teasing white sundress she was wearing.

"I know it's kind of cheesy," she said, smoothing it out, "but this was the best dress I could find in that boutique your uncle's secretary took me to."

"I like it," Devon said staring at her.

She also ditched her customary ponytail and let her Indian-straight hair cover the tops of her shoulders.

"What the hell are you staring at?"

"Nah, I was just… your hair."

"I look crazy, right?" she said, as she started to pull it back and put it in a ponytail.

"No," Devon stopped her. He grabbed her hands and pulled them down. He combed her hair with his fingers until it fell back around her shoulders. "This is the first time I've seen you with your hair down. It looks nice."

"Brian used to tease me when we were younger. He used to say I looked like a tar-black Pocahontas."

Quana was dark-skinned, but she was a devil's food cake dark, and right now, Devon's sweet tooth was acting up.

"I don't know why Brian would say such a thing. You look beautiful like that." The sparkle in her eyes told him she wasn't used to being complimented on her looks.

"So, where's the food?" she said, looking around the kitchen.

Devon pointed outside. "I got everything setup on the beach already."

"This is crazy," Quana whispered as they walked toward the blanket Devon had laid out for them.

"What's crazy? And why are you whispering?"

"The view... it's so amazing. I've never seen a sunset this beautiful. And I'm whispering because its sooo quiet. We're outside, and the only noise I can hear is us walking on the sand. I'm so used to music blasting, horns blaring, people chatting on their cell phones... I see why Jamaicans are so laid back." She cut her eyes at Devon as they got closer to the blanket. The fringes of the gigantic blanket were held down and decorated with flickering candles encased in rose-colored crystal balls. There were three stainless steel serving trays with lids on them in the center. Next to the trays was an ice bucket with a champagne bottle sticking out of it. "You really went out of your way, I see."

"But of course." Devon waved his hand for her to sit down.

She sat on the blanket with him and eyed the ice bucket. "You know I don't drink, right?"

Devon reached into it and pulled out the champagne bottle. He popped the cork and poured some into a champagne glass and handed it to her.

Quana shook her head.

"Trust me."

She took the glass from him, sniffed it, and kept her eye on him while she took a sip. "Umm, this is carrot juice."

Devon winked.

"Damn, I drink carrot juice on a regular and it never tasted this good." She finished the whole glass.

Devon filled her glass back up and then reached for one of the serving trays. "Check this out." He removed the lid.

"Jamaican beef patties?" Quana's eyes lit up.

"These aren't Jamaican patties from Queens," Devon said with his heavy Jamaican accent. "These are Jamaican patties from Jamaica."

Quana took one from the tray and bit into it. She nodded her head while she chewed. "Every taste bud on my tongue is tingling, right now."

"Good, right?"

She closed her eyes as she took another bite. "Good isn't even the word," she mumbled.

"I saved the best for last," Devon said, reaching for the other serving tray. He removed the lid and placed the tray before her. "Peas and rice with curried chicken."

"That's my favorite. How did you know?"

"I remember being in the backseat of Brian's Pathfinder on our way home and he would stop at the West Indian restaurant. When I asked him what was up, he would say 'Quana called me earlier and told me to pick her up an order of peas and rice with curried chicken.' He used to make me go in with him and he would complain the whole time. He would say, 'I ain't her man. How come she can't call Jay and have him get this. She's lucky I was planning on coming in here, anyway, because if I wasn't...' He would go on and on, knowing he had no intentions on stopping in if you didn't ask him to."

"That sounds just like his punk ass," Quana said as she started to laugh.

"That's what I've been waiting for." Devon winked.

"I can't remember the last time I laughed."

Devon took the last bit of beef patty from her and ate it. He pointed at the peas and rice for her to try.

"Ummm, you know what's going to happen right?" she said between chews. "When I get back to Queens, I'm not going to want to even step foot into the West Indian restaurant. Their food don't taste anywhere as good as this."

"I'm glad you like it."

"I love it."

Devon watched her as she wolfed down the plate.

Quana looked up at him embarrassed. "You got to forgive me, but I didn't eat anything on the flight and I haven't had a solid meal since the day Brian got sentenced."

"Don't apologize. Eat. Seeing you eat, let's me know that you're feeling a little better."

Quana held her glass out for him to refill it. "Well being that you gave me the green light, you better go inside and grab some patties for yourself, because when I'm done with this chicken, I'm coming for those three left on the tray."

Devon laughed. "Now that's the Quana I know."

After Quana knocked off the three remaining patties and carrot juice, Devon reached for the last serving tray and removed the lid.

"This will be the best carrot cake you will ever taste."

Quana shook her head. "I can't eat anymore."

Devon sliced a piece off with his fork and ate it.

Quana stared at his mouth as he slowly chewed it and swallowed. "Maybe I'll take just a little piece."

Two pieces later, Quana stood and rubbed her stomach. "I can't believe I ate so much."

Devon stood and took her by the hand. He led her toward the water. He stopped at the wet sand. A few moments later, the water came in and swirled around their ankles.

"It feels like we're on a deserted island. I haven't seen anyone around since we got here."

"That's the beauty of it. You get a chance to think, clear your head, no distractions." Devon realized that he was still holding her hand and let it go. "Let's walk."

"I appreciate you being patient with me, Devon, but I know it's killing you. I know you want to know exactly what happened."

"Yes but only when you're ready to talk about it."

"I think I'm ready. I'm at peace, my belly is full, and this is the longest I've gone without crying."

"So then, talk to me. What happened?"

"The trial seemed to be going well. The lawyer that I got for Brian was cutting the D.A.'s case to shreds. The only thing the D.A. had was Jason's confession implicating you and Brian on a robbery that went bad. Jason said you pulled out an Uzi and shot the woman and Brian shot the man."

"He said *I* shot the woman? That lying…"

"The D.A.'s case really took a turn for the worst when Jason refused to take the stand. They brought him down from up North and everything. The D.A. threatened him with everything he could but Jason didn't care. I guess he couldn't get on that stand and look Brian in the face and spout all those lies."

"So, how did Brian get found guilty?"

"That's the crazy part. The judge, D.A. and Brian's lawyer just knew that the jury was going to bring back a not guilty verdict, but they surprised us all."

Devon shook his head.

"It wasn't until the day the judge actually sentenced Brian that Sonia realized Brian was never coming home. She lost it, right there in the court room. She fainted and hit the floor with a thud. Brian tried to rush to her, but the bailiffs jumped on him and pinned him to the ground. When Sonia came to and saw them piled on top of him, she went berserk. She jumped up from off the floor and attacked the bailiffs. She was clawing and biting them and everything. Me and her father had to pull her off them and calm her down."

"How was she doing the last time you saw her?"

"Terrible. That's why I didn't want to leave her. She has no one to lean on. Her parents are trying to convince her to give the baby up for adoption after giving birth."

"That's fucked up."

"Who you telling?" Quana hugged herself as the chill of re-telling the story hit her.

"What are we going to do, Devon? We just can't let this go down like this. Talk to me. I know you have a plan. That's why you got me down here, right?"

"Yes, of course."

"What is it? What are we going to do?"

"First, I know Brian's lawyer is going to appeal the guilty verdict."

"Of course he is."

"We're going to see what happens with that."

"And if that doesn't work?"

Devon grabbed her by her shoulders and looked into her eyes. "Brian is not going to spend the rest of his life in prison, Quana. *I'm* getting him out of there, one way or another." Quana began to say something, but he cut her off. "There is no *we* in this, you understand? Devon Carter is wanted for murder and God knows what else. My life as I know it is over. You, on the other hand, have a life and you're going to live it without having to worry about the police hunting you down. I'm going to wait and see what happens with the appeal. If it doesn't work out in Brian's favor... I don't have to say any more, right?"

Quana shook her head. "If anyone can pull off what you're talking about, it's you."

"Thanks for the vote of confidence."

Quana smiled. "This might sound crazy, but I used to be scared of you."

"Scared of me?" Devon looked at her surprised.

"Hell yeah. Every time you, Brian and Jason came around, Brian and Jason did all the talking and laughing. You would just stand off to the side, looking around, watching, and waiting. And the stories Brian used to tell me about you."

"Stories?"

"Is it true that after a stick up y'all pulled off, the police had you cornered on the roof of a two-story building and you jumped off?"

"That's not true. It was a three-story building."

"How do you jump off the roof of a three-story building and not get hurt?"

Devon pulled up the left pant leg of his Bermuda shorts to show her the jagged scar on his shin. "My shin bone was sticking out, and my whole body ached for like eight months. I can't believe Brian told you about that."

"I think he had to tell someone because he couldn't believe it himself."

"Well, as you can see, I can talk, I can smile, and I'm not a bad guy once you get to know me."

"No, you're not."

"We better get back," Devon said. You need your sleep for tomorrow."

"What's happening tomorrow? You said you were going to tell me over dinner."

"Tomorrow, we're going on a boat ride."

"A boat ride?"

"Yeah, a boat ride."

* * *

Devon and Quana arrived at the harbor at 9:00 am. Devon climbed out of his jeep and slid on a pair of Ray-Ban shades. His unbuttoned Louis Vuitton silk shirt flapped in the wind as he walked around to open the passenger side door for Quana. He made sure the doors were locked before they headed toward the docks. A man dressed in a navy blue uniform stepped off of a black and white speedboat and began to walk toward them.

"Good morning, Mr. Carter," the man said with a bow.

"Good morning. Quana this is Cecil."

"Good morning, Ma'am."

"Good morning, Cecil," Quana responded.

Cecil helped them on board. "We'll be there in thirty seconds," he said as he turned to go untie the boat from the dock.

"You got me up at seven o'clock this morning to go on a thirty second boat ride?" Quana asked.

As Devon began to speak, Cecil started the engine and shot out of the harbor. Devon leaned over and put his lips to Quana's ear. "This isn't the boat ride, that is," he said, pointing in the direction of a black and white Super yacht.

Quana's heart fluttered. She looked at Devon, but he just kept looking forward. She stared at the 121 foot long, 26 foot wide, and 31 foot tall vessel.

Cecil pulled up to its backside where another crewman, named Ennis, dressed in the same navy blue uniform caught the speedboat's lines Cecil tossed to him and secured them to the yacht's boarding platform.

Ennis introduced himself to Quana as he helped them board the *Black Snapper*. Ennis led them up the steps to the main deck.

"I can take it from here," Devon said to Cecil and Ennis.

"Yes, Mr. Carter."

Devon led Quana inside to the master suite. He opened the door and let her walk in. "This is where you'll be staying for the next few days."

"Few days?"

"Yes, we're going on a boat ride."

"Are you serious?"

"For the next few days, this boat is going to be our mobile island. We got ourselves a crew of six, which includes a gourmet chef, and entertainment center, not one but two hot tubs, and my favorite, a masseuse. We're also going to jump ship and visit a couple secluded beaches."

Being that Quana was too stunned to say anything, Devon moved past her and opened the walk-in closet and turned on the light. "I had the hostess buy you a few dresses, outfits, and bathing suits for the occasion."

Quana stepped into the closet and looked around, and then looked at him.

Devon looked at his watch. "I'll give you time to get yourself together. I know you don't want to walk around wearing the same dress you wore last night. I'm going to go see about getting the chef to whip us up some kind of brunch or something."

As he turned to leave, Quana grabbed him by the arm and dragged him to the bed. She sat and pulled him down next to her. "What in the hell are you into, Devon?" she whispered.

"I'll explain everything over brunch."

"Fuck a brunch. Explain now."

"Quana—"

"Quana, nothing. I want to know everything from the night Brian came to my house with a bag of money to get Jason a lawyer up til now." Devon put his head down. She picked it back up and made him look her in the eye. "Whether you want to believe it or not, I'm in the middle of this, whatever *this* is. I took money from Brian, I took money from you, I used a fake ID and passport that your uncle gave me to come here, the FBI came to my house asking about you… I deserve to know what's going on, and I want to know now."

"I can't tell you everything—"

"Fuck you mean you can't tell me everything?" she said, punching him in the chest. She jumped up to leave.

"Quana wait."

"Get off of me, Devon. I'm getting the hell out of here. I don't know what the fuck I was thinking of even coming here in the first place."

Devon blocked the door. "Okay, Quana. All right. Just please sit back down and I'll tell you everything."

Quana wiped the tears from her eyes, but she didn't budge.

"Please, Quana. Just hear me out. And if you still want to leave… then I'll get you to the airport."

Quana walked back to the bed and plopped down.

Devon pulled up a chair and sat in front of her. "Here's the deal from beginning to end." He began from the night they robbed and killed Tequan's Lieutenant on his doorstep to the night he came to her house and left her the money for Brian. He stopped to get her reaction on what he shared with her.

"Keep going," she said, folding her arms.

He then proceeded to tell her about his arrival in Jamaica. She reached over and put her hand on top of his when he got teary-eyed talking about his father's murder.

"So you see, Quana, this vacation isn't just for you, it's for me as well. While the team was spending their share on bullshit, I was stacking mine. I decided to spend a little to charter this yacht so we can spend a few days away from the chaos in our lives."

Quana scooted to the edge of the bed and hugged him. "Thank you for trusting me."

"I guess that makes two people in this world I trust."

"My head feels like it's going to explode, right now. You really dropped some heavy shit on me. If you don't mind, I need a minute to get my thoughts together."

"Sure." Devon stood up and walked to the door.

"And Devon."

"Yes."

"See what's up with that brunch."

Devon smiled. "Sure thing."

* * *

Quana was pinning up her hair when the cabin phone rang. "Hello?"

"It's me. I'm on the sky deck. C'mon up when you're ready."

"I'm on my way."

"My God," Quana said huffing and puffing. "They need to put an elevator on this big ass boat."

Devon sat up from the recliner and flipped his shades up. Quana looked like Miss Jamaica with the strapless floral dress she had on.

"How do I look?" she asked.

"Like you're ready to enjoy your vacation." Devon walked her to the table where fruits, vegetables, fish, meats, and breads had been beautifully arranged.

"I am definitely taking advantage of that," Quana said, eyeing the large hot tub.

"No doubt."

Quana bit into a peach. "So, you got anymore surprises for me?"

Devon shrugged.

"Devon?"

He flipped his shades back down and smiled.

* * *

"I should punch you dead in your face," Recker said to Ginja, balling up his fists. "If anything happens to Devon, I swear…"

"I called you as soon as I could," she said.

"Called me? You shouldn't have called me. You should've shot that pussy boy in the head."

"In the middle of the street? In broad daylight?" Ginja asked.

"That's what I did!"

"Yeah, and you missed."

Recker slapped her.

"That's enough, Recker," Ivory said.

The day when he saw Devon crying, he jumped in his car and headed downtown. As fate would have it, not only did he spot a member of Villainy, but it was Grim, the second in charge. Without thinking, he hit his brakes. His screeching tires put Grim on point. He looked just in time to see Recker pointing his MP-5 out the window.

Recker emptied half a clip in his direction. Grim was able to dive behind a truck before the shooting started.

Recker drove onto the sidewalk and chased Grim into the street where he opened fire again. Grim must've had an angel watching over him because he escaped the hail of bullets Recker unleashed on him. Recker got out of his car, but lost him in the crowd of people running for cover.

Earlier this morning while Ginja and Ivory were downtown shopping, Grim and three members of Villainy got the drop on them. They robbed them of their jewelry and money and groped on them until Grim grew tired of playing with them.

"Tell Recker and his cousin that Irons is coming for them." The men walked off laughing. Ginja cut her eyes at her car. In five seconds, she could get her gun out the glove compartment and run up on them bastards.

Ivory must've read her mind. "Don't even think about it. We're going to call Recker," she said.

Recker grabbed his bald head and paced back and forth. "Anything yet?" he asked Dane, who was calling Devon's cell phone.

"It keeps rolling into voice mail."

"Let's go," he barked.

"Where are we going?" Dane asked.

"To that beach house he rented."

"How's that supposed to help us?" Rippa said.

"Maybe I can find the name of the yacht he chartered, if so, we can contact the yacht, somehow."

"Seems like a long shot."

"Do you have a better idea?"

"No."

"Then shut the fuck up and get into the car."

* * *

When they pulled up to the beach house, Recker tried calling Devon on his cell phone again. "Fuck." He got out of his car and waved for Dane, Rippa, and Stripes to exit Dane's truck. "Y'all stay in the car," he said to Ginja and Ivory.

"Why?" Ginja asked.

"Because I motherfucking said so."

Recker picked the lock on the backdoor and opened the front door for his boys.

"Rippa, Stripes, search the rooms upstairs," Recker said. "Look for mail or anything that may have the yacht's name on it. Dane and I will check down here."

A half hour later, they met up in the living room.

"Nobody found anything?" Recker asked.

They shook their heads.

Recker rubbed his bald head and then kicked the sofa.

"I see you still have your temper tantrums, aye Recker?" Irons walked through the front door. His smile was menacing, his appearance demonic. His six feet, broad frame was concealed under a wool poncho that hung to his kneecaps. His dreads hung loosely on either side of his shoulders and cascaded down his chest, stopping at his waist. His brillo pad beard jutted down the front of his poncho, tapering to a jagged point. He had one arm around Ginja and the other around Ivory. "You have to be more careful about where you leave your women, Recker. You never know who can come along and drag 'em off." Irons was the leader of the much feared posse in Jamaica, *Villainy*.

"Get over here," Recker said to Ginja and Ivory.

"Go to him," Irons said. "I dare you to leave from me."

Ginja and Ivory stayed rooted under his arms. Recker looked over his shoulder as he heard a chorus of combat boots marching in. The first wave of guerrilla soldiers that entered from the backdoor sealed off the way they came. Each man wore black fatigues and field jackets. They had their assault rifles trained on Recker, Dane, Rippa, and Stripes. The second wave, dressed similarly, came through the front, sealing the way they came in. Recker, Dane, Rippa, and Stripes were boxed in, literally.

"What's all this about?" Recker asked, refusing to be intimidated.

"You don't know?" Irons asked suspiciously.

"Why don't you tell me?"

"How about you tell me where this Devon has run off to?"

"I don't know."

Irons smiled. He flung Ivory into the arms of the soldier next to him, and then he wrapped his free hand around Ginja's neck and lifted her off her feet. Ivory struggled to break free of the soldier as Ginja batted and clawed at Irons's arm.

"She'll be dead in one minute, Recker." Irons snarled.

"I don't know where he is. If I did, would I be here looking for him?"

Irons felt Ginja going limp. He let her feet touch the floor. Her legs wobbled. The only thing holding her up was his choke hold.

"You're killing her!" Ivory screamed.

Irons looked at Recker. "She means nothing to you, huh?"

"When have you ever known me to give a fuck about a bitch?" Recker's eye twitched.

Irons nodded. Ginja's eyes rolled to the back of her head as she went totally limp. Irons tightened his grip and shook her like a rag doll.

"Motherfucker." Recker drew his gun and walked right up on Irons and brought the butt of his gun down on the side of Irons's head. Ginja's body hit the floor with a bone chilling thud as Irons stumbled back. Dane, Rippa, and Stripes were amazed that not one soldier broke formation; they kept their guns locked on them.

Recker switched the safety off his gun and aimed at Irons's forehead.

Irons gave him a hard stare and then busted out laughing. "You getting soft, Recker. The Recker I used to know wouldn't have given a fuck about a piece of pussy."

Recker cocked the hammer.

Irons laughed harder. "How's your mommy and daddy?"

Recker's eye twitched.

Irons walked up on him and rested his head on the front of Recker's gun. "Pull the trigger, bad bwoy. Sign your parent's death certificate."

Recker carefully thumbed the trigger down and lowered his weapon.

"Do you remember what happened the last time you thought your gun was faster then mine, Recker?"

Recker looked at his missing trigger finger.

"I remember." Irons played with the gold chain around his neck. He slowly tugged on it til Recker's skeletal trigger finger, preserved in gold, popped out and rested on his poncho.

Recker's hand shot out quickly to snatch it, but Irons reaction was stunningly quicker. He shot out a straight-armed punch. Recker staggered back, holding his mouth.

Irons tucked the chain and finger ornament back under his poncho. "And you," Irons said to Dane, Rippa, and Stripes. "You call yourselves rude bwoys and you stand by and watch one of your own get choked out and your leader punched in the mouth?"

"You're a real rude bwoy with your soldiers around to protect you," Rippa said.

Irons's head whipped in his direction, but he spoke to the soldier on his left. "Take all of their guns, except his."

The soldier left Rippa with his gun, as instructed.

"Don't do this," Recker said.

"You don't tell me what I can and can't do. Take them out back to the beach. I'll be there in a second," Irons said to Grim. "You stay," he said to Rippa.

His soldiers cleared out, dragging Recker, Dane, Stripes, and Ivory to the beach.

Irons put his left hand under his poncho and with one swipe; the poncho flew over his head and landed behind him. Rippa stared at the bullet and knife scars on Irons's chest and abs. His eyes widened as Irons rested his hands on the butts of his holstered pistols. "Now, let's see just how rude you are... bwoy."

Irons took a few steps back, widening the distance between him and Rippa to twenty feet. "Say when, rude bwoy."

Rippa shook his head.

"I'll make it fair. Pull your gun out and put it by your side."

"Irons..." Rippa's voice was shaky.

"Pull your gun out and put it by your side. I'm not going to say it again."

Rippa slowly pulled his gun out and rested it on his leg.

"Good. Now, say when."

Rippa's breathing became ragged. He clenched and unclenched his jaw.

"That's it. Get hype, rude bwoy."

"Suck out your mother!" Rippa raised his gun and...

As Rippa started to raise his gun, Irons's nickel-plated Colt 45s were already out, and bucking.

Recker flinched when he heard the gunfire. A few moments later, Irons walked out and headed toward them, grinning devilishly. Recker, Dane, Stripes, and Ivory were on their knees when Irons walked up on them. He put his poncho back on. He looked to Grim. "Shoot them in the head and make him watch," he said, referring to Recker. "And then let him go."

"Irons!" Recker screamed out.

Ginja jerked awake as she heard a popping sound.

Disoriented, she got to her hands and knees. She heard another pop and then Ivory scream. She got on her feet and ran to the back where she heard Ivory's screams. She stumbled out of the backdoor. She nearly doubled over in shock when she saw a soldier put his handgun to Ivory's head and start to pull the trigger.

"No!" Her scream got everybody's attention. Some of the soldiers started shooting at her. She dived back into the house, screaming. She crawled all the way to the front door and then stumbled through it. She ran to Recker's car and jumped in. She went to turn the key in the ignition, only the key wasn't there. She jumped out of the car and ran to Dane's truck. The keys were in the ignition. She jumped in and started the truck. As she peeled off, the first soldier out the front door opened fire, shattering the back window. She instinctively ducked. A group of soldiers jumped into their truck and took off after her.

Ginja's hands shook as she tried keeping the truck on the road. She looked up in the rearview mirror and screamed. The soldier's truck was catching up to her. She ran every stop sign and ran a car off the road. She swerved as she heard a bullet hit the back of the truck. She wiped the tears from her eyes as she smashed the gas pedal to the floor. She dug into her pocket and pulled out her cell phone. Her hand was shaking so hard that she dropped it. She swerved past a bus, missing it by inches.

"Where the fuck are you?" she screamed, referring to the police. Black smoke started rising from under the hood. "No. Don't do this to me!" She banged on the steering wheel. Her head jerked back when the soldier's truck rammed her. She fought to keep the truck on the road as it swerved. The truck pulled up beside her and rammed her. She screamed, fighting to keep from being road kill. One of the soldiers opened fire on the truck. He shot out both tires on the driver's side. Ginja lost control of the truck as it slid off the road.

It took a minute for the soldier to stop the truck and back it up to where he ran Ginja off the road. The soldiers hopped out and ran into the brush. They spotted the truck on its side. They checked inside the cab. It was empty.

"We don't go back til we find her," one of the soldiers said.

* * *

"Fore!" Quana yelled, as she blasted the golf ball off the tee. She and Devon watched the ball sail high and long into the ocean. "Yes!" She pumped her fist in the air.

"Let a pro show you how it's done," Devon said, moving her to the side. He reached into the basket and retrieved a ball and placed it on the tee. He rotated his neck and did a couple waist twists before lining his golf club up with the ball. "Fore!" He swung for the clouds.

"Mine went farther then yours," Quana said jumping up and down.

"No it didn't."

"Tell him Cecil," Quana said.

"Sorry Mr. Carter. Hers did go just a little farther."

"I told you," Quana said, pushing him.

"I think we need another pair of eyes out here," Devon said, jokingly.

"Move," Quana said, pushing him to the side. She bent down to retrieve a ball out of the basket and put it on the tee. Devon couldn't pull his eyes off of her apple-shaped booty that was stretching the shorts she was wearing to the max. As she stood back up, Devon reached into his pocket and pulled out his handkerchief. He wiped the sweat from his brow and took a swig from his glass of ice water.

Cecil winked at him, letting him know he peeped what just happened. Devon winked back.

"Fore!" Quana whacked the golf ball farther than she did last time.

"I can't understand it," Devon said, shaking his head. "Cecil just showed us both how to hit a golf ball and you're better at it than me."

"Girls learn faster than boys."

"Really?"

"Really."

"I don't think so. I'm just not feeling this golf thing."

"Don't make excuses, now, because I've been kicking your ass since yesterday."

"Since yesterday?" Devon pretended to be surprised.

"Did you forget the five games of pool?"

"Oh that."

"And the three games of ping pong?"

"It was windy."

"We were indoors. I even beat you in basketball." Quana reminded him.

"You know that court on the bottom deck isn't regulation. Plus, my jump shot was off."

"That's what that was? I thought you were building a house with all those bricks you were shooting."

"Oh, you got jokes?"

Devon looked at Cecil when he heard him snicker. "Whose side are you on?"

"Sorry Mr. Carter."

"You," Devon said, pointing at Quana. "6:30, up here, in the hot tub. We're going to watch the sunset and then I'm going to think of a game to kick your ass in."

"Where are you going?"

"I need to take a power nap."

"I'm going to go to the kitchen and see what Winston can chef up for us tonight."

"Yeah, you do that." Devon headed down to his room.

* * *

When Ginja slid off the road, she braced herself as Dane's truck mowed down shrubs and fallen branches. She stomped on the brakes. That made matters worst. The wheels locked and caused the truck to fishtail. The steering wheel whipped out of her grip and spun. When Ginja regained consciousness, she realized that the truck was on its side and wrapped around a tree. Her eyes landed on her cell phone. She picked it up and climbed out the passenger's side window. She stumbled and fell a couple times before gaining her bearings. She looked around, trying to ascertain where she was. She spun around at the sound of a dry twig snapping. She ran deeper into the woods, knowing Irons's soldiers wouldn't give up until she was dead. The first clearing she got to, she tried to get a signal on her cell phone.

No such luck.

In the distance, she saw a landscape that looked familiar. Her mouth was so dry that she felt like she was chewing on cotton. She ducked behind a tree, thinking she heard something or someone. Instinctively, she broke into a sprint. She ran until her chest burned and her legs were numb. She leaned against a tree and tried her phone again.

No signal.

She was about to smash it against the tree, but she caught herself. She screamed when the soldier grabbed her by the arm and spun her around.

* * *

"Girl, what are you doing out here?" the man asked Ginja. The man who she thought was one of the soldiers had a shotgun on his right side and his Labrador retriever on his left. "Are you high?"

"Some men are after me. I need help."

"What men?"

"They... they killed my friends." Saying the words out loud that had been repeating themselves in her head, made her buckle.

"Whoa." The man dropped his gun and grabbed her before she fell. Ginja hugged him as she cried. The man slowly bent down and picked up his gun. He looked around before he spoke. "Let's get out of here."

When Ginja saw his pickup truck, she ran toward it. She pulled on the door latch.

"It's locked," the man said, as he caught up to her.

"Hurry and unlock the doors. We have to get out of here, now!"

"You see this?" he said, holding up his shotgun. "Nobody is going to come anywhere near us." The man's dog turned in the direction they just came and started barking.

"That's them," Ginja yelled.

The man dug into his pocket and took out his keys. As he walked toward the truck, a soldier seemed to run out of the woods in slow motion. Ginja opened her mouth to scream, but it was too late for the man. The soldier already pulled the trigger. Bullets ripped through the man's back and embedded themselves into the truck; some of them shattering the driver's side windows. Ginja ducked behind the truck when the shooting started. The soldier ran around the truck and pointed his assault rifle at her. He took a step toward her as she fell to her knees.

"Who you call?"

Ginja followed his eyes to her cell phone she had in her death grip.

"Who you call?" he asked again, nudging her head with the tip of his rifle.

"No one." She put her hands in the air. "I didn't call anyone. I couldn't get a signal, see?"

The soldier snatched the phone from her. His first mistake was lowering his weapon, and his second was taking his eyes off her to look at the screen. From her knees, she delivered a wicked uppercut to the soldier's balls. He dropped his gun, the cell phone, and grabbed his nuts. He fell on top of Ginja, trying to pin her down with his body weight. She squirmed from under him. He wrapped his legs around her waist as she rolled on top of him. He reached up and wrapped his hands around her neck. She tried to pry his fingers loose, but they were locked like a pit bull's jaws. She felt herself blacking out. As her eyes closed, she saw it. Strapped across his chest was a hunting knife. She stopped struggling with his fingers and groped for the knife. By the time the soldier realized what she was reaching for, Ginja had the knife out of its sheath. She stabbed wildly at the soldier's face and arms. When she felt his grip loosening, a surge of energy gave her the strength to plunge the knife into the soldier's chest. She yanked his hands off of her neck and wiggled out from between his legs. The soldier looked down at the knife in his chest and then tried to get to his knees. Ginja scuttled backward until her back hit a tree. The soldier started coughing up blood and then collapsed. His dead eyes stared at her. Ginja turned away from him and threw up.

* * *

Devon jumped up when the cabin phone rang. He leaned over and picked it up. "Yo."

"Yo? I know you're not still in bed," Quana said.

"What time is it?"

"Six o'clock."

"Shit." Devon jumped up. "I'll be up in ten minutes." He hung up and headed for the bathroom to shower and brush his teeth. Twenty minutes later, he arrived on the sky deck in a pair of swim trunks and a towel draped over his shoulder. Quana was lying on a lounge chair. "What's up with the robe? You naked under there?" Devon asked, as he sat next to her.

"You wish. I'm black enough. I don't need to have the sun blazing on my skin."

"So what's for dinner?"

"Stuffed red snapper."

"Sounds delicious."

"It is."

Devon looked at her.

"What? Winston let me taste some while he was preparing it."

"Look." Devon pointed to the redness in the sky.

"This is our third sunset together," Quana said.

"What does that mean?"

"I don't know what it means to you, but I will never look at a sunset the same, ever again."

"Aw, that's so sweet."

"Shut up."

After thirty seconds of silence, Devon stood up and walked to the hot tub. He stuck his big toe in. "Yep, I can see myself falling asleep in this thing."

"You just woke up."

"And this hot tub is going to put me right back to sleep." He stepped in and sat down.

"Is it all that?" Quana asked.

"Why don't you come and find out for yourself? I don't bite."

Quana stood up and removed her robe.

Holy shit! Devon sat up.

"Fuck is you looking at? You act like you ain't ever seen a woman in a bathing suit." Quana walked toward him like a runway model. She stopped at the rim of the tub and struck a pose. Then she slowly twirled around. Devon's eyes dropped to her butt and then to the backs of her thighs and then to her calves. When she turned back around, Devon was red in the face.

"You got drool right there," Quana said, pointing to the corner of his mouth.

Devon wiped his mouth before realizing Quana was joking. She started laughing.

"Just get in, and make sure you stay on your side of the tub," Devon said.

"Which side is that?"

"The side that I'm not on."

When Quana got into the water, it made matters worse for Devon. Now, that her bathing suit was wet, it clung to her body. She dipped her head underwater and slicked her hair back. Devon quickly looked away from her when he felt himself hardening.

"Oh, wait a minute." Quana got out of the tub and walked to the table, her butt jiggling, her hips rotating. Devon's meat was now harder than concrete. She returned with a platter of strawberries.

"I almost forgot my fruit," she said, as she stepped back into the hot tub.

"How can you eat more than me and still have a body like that?"

"Genetics, I guess." She bit into a strawberry and closed her eyes.

Devon zoned in on her lips.

"You've got to try one of these," Quana said, grabbing a strawberry off the platter and walking to his side of the hot tub. Her body was inches from his. She put the strawberry to his lips. Devon bit into it and nodded. "Sweet, right?"

"Yeah," Devon said.

She put it to his lips again. Devon opened wide and let her put the rest of it into his mouth. Juice ran down the side of his chin. Quana swooped in and licked it off. Her bold move paralyzed him. She followed the lick with a gentle kiss on his bottom lip. His arms automatically wrapped around her waist as she pushed her body into his. Her tongue was sweeter than the strawberry. Quana slid her arms around his neck.

"Wait." Devon broke the lip lock.

"What's wrong?" Quana asked.

"This. You and me…" He couldn't think.

"Quana—"

"I thought this is what you wanted."

He ran his hands around the curvature of her butt and then cupped it. "I got to go." He backed away from her and began getting out of the hot tub.

"Devon, wait."

"I'll be in my room." He grabbed his towel off the lounge chair and took off.

* * *

After Ginja threw up, she stood up and limped to the truck. She looked down at the dead man, realizing the keys were in his hand when the soldier started shooting. His hand was empty. She searched the ground around him, but couldn't find them.

"Jundi!"

Ginja froze. A soldier was calling out to the dead one. She picked up the dead soldier's assault rifle, her cell phone, and took off running. She noticed the terrain started to incline slightly. Forty minutes later, she dropped to the ground out of breath. She opened her phone, praying for a signal.

"Thank you, God," she whispered. She started to call the police and stopped. By the time they sent someone out to find her, she would be dead. She scrolled down to Devon's number and hit dial. "Devon don't do this to me. Pick up. Pick the fuck up." She hung up and hit redial. She hung up and texted him a message. She dropped the phone and held the assault rifle with both hands. The soldiers weren't trying to be quiet in their search. They were catching up to her. She picked up her phone and took off.

* * *

What the fuck was I thinking? Devon thought as he plopped down on his bed. How could I not see this coming? I fucked up. She's so vulnerable, right now. And what do I do? I fly her down here, intoxicate her with the beauty of Jamaica, then get her on a yacht, in a fucking hot tub, in the middle of the ocean, and watch the sunset while she's feeding me strawberries. Brian will kill me if I take advantage of her. He could still feel the softness of her lips on his. He shuttered when he imagined bending Quana over in the hot tub and digging into her from behind. Fuck it. She's going back to New York tomorrow. I'm tearing that ass up tonight. As soon as he pulled the handle on his cabin door, his phone rang. He walked to the dresser and looked at the number. It was Ginja.

He was about to answer it, but he wasn't ready to deal with the team yet. He let it ring. A moment later, Ginja started to text him. "Give me a break," he said as he began reading the text. The blood started to drain from his face as he read the first couple words. *The whole team is dead. They're trying to kill me...* He called her cell phone immediately.

* * *

Ginja stopped running when her cell phone rang. "Devon!" she screamed into it.

"You knew I wasn't going to answer my phone, so you texted me some bullshit so I can call you?"

"They're dead, Devon, all of them."

"What do you mean dead? What are you talking about? Put Recker on the phone."

"God dammit, Devon. Aren't you listening to me? Everyone is dead. They're after me, right now. I can't keep running, Devon. I'm so tired."

"Where are you?" Devon ran out of the cabin and ran to the entertainment room. "I have no idea where that is Ginja. Wait, hold on."

"Hold on?"

"Cecil!" Devon grabbed him by the collar.

"Mr. Carter. What did I do?"

"Just shut up and listen. Ginja, I'm putting somebody on the phone. Tell him exactly where you are."

Devon handed Cecil the phone.

"Hello?" Cecil listened. "Yes, I know where that is."

Devon grabbed the phone from him. "How far are we from there?"

Cecil shrugged. "Maybe, forty five minutes."

"Forty five minutes? Damn, Cecil. I need to get to her now."

"Well, if we took the speedboat, we could be there in fifteen minutes give or take."

"Tell her where to meet us," Devon said, handing him back the phone.

"Mr. Carter. I can't just take the speedboat. The captain needs to give permission."

"Fuck the captain. We'll be back before he misses us."

"Mr. Carter—"

"Two thousand dollars when we get back."

"Sir?"

"I will give you two thousand American dollars when we dock tomorrow."

Cecil reluctantly grabbed the phone from him and told Ginja that they would be there in fifteen minutes and where she should wait for them.

"Let's go!" Devon said, leading the way.

* * *

"There!" One of the soldiers said, pointing at Ginja leaning on a tree. They opened fire.

Ginja screamed as bullets hit the tree. She dived to the ground. When the firing stopped, she crawled away from the tree and started running.

* * *

When Cecil got a safe distance away from the yacht, he hit full throttle. The speedboat hit 75 M.P.H. in under twenty seconds. As far as Devon could see, there was no land in sight. We're not going to make it there in fifteen minutes, he thought. His eyes started to tear. Could his cousin really be dead?

* * *

Ginja stopped in her tracks. She realized that the only way to get to where the man on the phone told her to be was to go back the way she came, the way that was now filled with

Irons's men. She fell to her knees and cried. She was going to die on this mountain. She thought of Dane and Stripes lying on the beach, their brains splattered on the sand. She thought of the soldier putting the gun to Ivory's head and Ivory crying. "Motherfuckers! If I'm going to die, I'm taking some of you with me! You hear me?" She got to her feet and fired a round in the air. She ran off to find herself the perfect spot to take her last stand.

* * *

"How much longer before we get there?" Devon asked.

"Five minutes, tops."

"Shit, we told her fifteen minutes. That was twenty minutes ago."

"Look!" Cecil pointed. "She should be right over there."

The little bit of light that was left in the sky was quickly fading. Devon strained to look on the shore. "I don't see her, anywhere."

"This is where I told her to be."

"We're too late."

* * *

Ginja was tired of running; she ducked behind a grouping of boulders and caught her breath. This was it, no more running. She crouched down and peeked around the boulders, ready to pop the first head coming out the bush. She swatted at the fly buzzing around her ear a few times before realizing the buzzing sound was the sound of a speedboat's engine. "Oh shit, Devon!" Ginja jumped up and ran to the edge of the cliff. There, in the distance, she saw the speedboat. She waved her hands in the air, but they weren't looking for her up there. She looked at the rifle, aimed for the sky and let off a burst of shots.

* * *

"Yo, you heard that?" Devon asked Cecil.

"It sounded like gunfire."

"There, right there!" Devon pointed to the flash shooting out of the muzzle as Ginja fired a hail of bullets into the sky again. "Head that way. That's her." Devon ordered.

"But, how is she going to get to us from up there?"

"Just go!"

* * *

Ginja threw the gun down and jumped for joy when she saw the speedboat heading in her direction. She peered over the edge and saw darkness. It was her only way to get to Devon. She had no choice. She got on her stomach and dangled her legs over the edge. She found a toehold and placed some of her weight on it. When she was sure her foot wouldn't slip, she put her whole weight on it. She worked her way down, slowly. She froze against the cliff when pebbles fell on her head. The soldiers were at the edge of the cliff.

"What do you see?" one of the soldiers asked another.

"Nothing," he said as he peered over the edge.

"Are you sure?"

"She's not down there."

"Look over there, a speedboat. It's heading this way."

* * *

"She's crazy," Cecil said.

"Devon watched Ginja scaling down the side of the cliff. He thought she was going to make it. Then he saw men peering over the edge. His hands curled into fists. I feel so helpless without my guns, he thought.

"What are they doing?" Cecil asked.

"I don't know," Devon said. "Wait! No!" The soldiers started firing over the edge of the cliff.

* * *

Ginja's muscles were burning as she tried to stay absolutely still. The soldiers were about to turn and leave when her hand slipped.

"She's down there," one of the soldiers said. They couldn't see her so they fired indiscriminately. Their bullets were getting closer, her muscles were cramping. A bullet ricocheted inches from her face. She lost her footing, lost her grip. She fell into the darkness.

* * *

"Oh my God, she fell!" Cecil said.

Devon was speechless.

"What do we do, Mr. Carter?"

"Get closer."

"But... she couldn't survive that. No one could survive a fall from that height."

"She landed in the water."

"Yes, but the height—"

"Just get me closer, Cecil, please."

"Mr. Carter—"

"There! I see her," Devon pointed.

Cecil saw her. Ginja was afloat, but wasn't moving. Devon dived off the speedboat and started swimming toward her. When he got to her, he got under her and kept her head above water as he swam back to the boat. "Ginja, can you hear me? I'm here. I got you. You're safe." Devon kept swimming back to the boat. "Grab her," he said to Cecil.

Cecil held her afloat until Devon got back on the boat and then they lifted her onboard.

"Get us back to the yacht," Devon said.

* * *

When Cecil pulled up to the yacht, Devon lifted Ginja up and carried her to his cabin and laid her on the bed. He was shivering in his clothes. He quickly undressed and put on some dry ones. He jumped when he heard the knock on his door.

"Devon, we need to talk."

Shit. Devon cracked the door, slid out of it, and closed it behind him. "Now is not a good time, Quana."

"I just wanted to say I'm sorry for what I did in the hot tub. I had no business—"

"No, Quana. Don't apologize. Tonight, in the hot tub, felt so right."

"But the way you left."

"I can explain that."

Quana waited for the explanation.

"I just can't explain it right now."

"Why not?"

"Something's come up that I really have to deal with."

"Something like what?"

They both jumped when they heard Ginja screaming. Devon opened the door and ran in. Ginja had a lamp in her hand about to launch it at him.

"Ginja, it's me."

She stopped screaming and stared at him. "Devon?"

"Yes, it's me."

She dropped the lamp and ran into his arms. She was shaking like a leaf. Devon peeked up at the door. Quana stood there not knowing how to react.

"Quana let me explain."

"You don't have to explain yourself to me." She stormed off.

Devon sighed. He tried to pull away from Ginja, but she wouldn't let him go. She kept crying. "Ginja, tell me what happened."

She shook her head and hugged him tighter.

He tried to pull her hands from around his waist and she screamed. "Okay, okay, we'll just stand here for a minute."

A half hour later, Devon couldn't take it anymore. "Ginja, you're safe. Whoever was chasing you can't get to you. You're going to have to let me go and tell me what happened."

She shook her head.

"Listen to me. We're walking over to the bed. You and I are going to sit down, okay?" Devon dragged her with him to the bed and had to force her to sit. He exhaled when she released her death grip from around his waist. He grunted when she straddled him and then wrapped her arms around his neck and her legs around his waist.

"Ginja!"

Cecil walked into the room with blankets and towels.

"Cecil. Help me get her off of me."

Cecil placed the towels on the bed and stood behind her. As soon as he grabbed her shoulders and attempted to pull her off Devon, she started to scream. Cecil backed up and nearly tripped over the couch.

"Okay, Ginja," Devon said, rubbing her back.

She calmed down, but she was still shaking.

"Mr. Carter. I think she's in shock."

"What am I supposed to do?"

Cecil held his finger up. "I'll be right back." A few moments later, he returned with a box the size of an eyeglass case. He opened it and showed Devon the needle and glass bottle. "It's a sedative."

Devon nodded. He rubbed Ginja's back as Cecil prepared the injection. Rubbing her back seemed to be the only way to keep her calm.

Cecil rested his arm on her shoulder, she didn't move. He injected her with the needle. She still didn't move. Devon sighed as he felt her grip loosening. As he stood up, her legs fell from around his waist. He laid her on the bed. "Thank you, Cecil. How long is that shot going to last?"

"Until morning."

"Tomorrow, I'm going to need you to give her another one so that I'll be able to get her off the yacht without attracting attention."

"Sure, Mr. Carter." Cecil backed out of the room and closed the door.

Devon was about to cover her with a blanket, then realized the reason why Ginja was shivering. Her clothes were soaked. He draped a sheet over her and then removed her shoes, pants and shirt. Then he grabbed a sweat suit out of his closet and put it on her. He then covered her with the blankets. For the first time, he noticed the bruises on her neck. He bent down and kissed her on the cheek. As he backed out of the room, he turned out the lights and locked the door. He dashed to Quana's room and knocked on her door. "Quana it's me."

She opened the door. "What's up?"

Devon immediately noticed she was wearing the jeans and shirt she had on when he picked her up at the airport.

"What's up with this?" he asked, pointing at her outfit.

"These are my clothes."

"Why are you wearing them?"

"What do you want, Devon?"

"Can I come in?"

She backed away from the door. "You can do anything you want. This is your yacht until tomorrow."

"Quana, what you saw, it's not what you think."

"You want to know what I think, I think I made a fucking fool of myself."

"Quana, I'm sorry."

"Don't be. This isn't even about you. I'm mad at my own damn self. It never fails with me. A guy shows me a little affection and I'm ready to open my legs for him."

"Quana, if you'd just give me a chance—"

"What a chance to make a fool of me again? I don't think so. I just want this trip to be over so I can go home."

Devon walked toward her, but she put her hands up.

"Just go, Devon, please. I want to spend these last few hours by myself."

Devon wanted to tell her about his cousin and the team, but he didn't want to add anymore stress to her already stressful life. "Look in your overnight bag; you'll see that I put something there for you. Just so you know, the only woman I ever gave anything to was my grandmother." He looked at her one last time and then walked out.

Quana waited a few minutes before digging into her bag. She spotted the blue velvet box and pulled it out. She opened it and stared at the platinum chain with a platinum and diamond cross. She put it around her neck and looked at it in the mirror. She remembered seeing this same chain around Devon's neck; and she remembered Brian telling her why he wore it. For Devon, it was a reminder to trust *no one*. She understood that by him giving it to her, he trusted her. Quana kissed the cross and lay down. She curled up into a ball and held the cross in her hands and cried.

Chapter 9

Cecil helped Devon put Ginja into the backseat of his jeep while Quana looked on in silence. With nowhere else to go, Devon rented a room at the same motel they first sold Dillard and Sterling six bricks of coke.

Devon sat on a wooden chair, loading shells into the Block Buster. Physically, he was preparing for battle, mentally, he thought about the car ride to the airport. Quana was silent the whole time. She hugged him with no emotion at the boarding gate. Devon didn't want to let her go. He kissed her on the cheek and backed away. His eyes dropped to his chain around her neck.

"I'll take good care of it," Quana whispered.

He touched it and then removed a strand of hair from her neck. "I don't care about the chain. I care about the person wearing it."

Quana placed her hand on top of his and squeezed it. "Take care of yourself."

"That's what I do best."

He slid the last shell into the shotgun. He cradled it in his arms and leaned back in the chair. He sat back up when Ginja stirred in her sleep. He leaned the shotgun against the wall and walked toward the bed. Ginja opened and closed her eyes, trying to focus.

"You're up, finally."

She tried to talk, but her throat was dry. Devon grabbed a glass of water off the table and held it to her lips. She took a couple sips and then tried to sit up.

"Lie there for a moment."

"Where are we?" Ginja croaked.

"How are you feeling?"

"Sore all over."

"You ready to tell me what happened?"

"Can I sit up?"

"If you can."

She groaned as she slowly sat up against the headboard. She looked down at the black sweat suit she was wearing.

"I had to get you out of those wet clothes."

Ginja looked around the tiny bedroom, "I don't even remember how we got here."

"I had you heavily sedated."

"Sedated?"

"You were in shock. Do you remember anything?"

"I remember falling. I remember a boat."

"And before that?"

"Ivory… and the rest of the team…" She started to cry.

"I know this is hard for you, but you're going to have to tell me what happened, and you can't leave anything out."

"I can't—"

"You can, and you will. Recker and the rest of the team are dead. I need for you to tell me who I got to kill."

"You can't kill him."

"Irons did this?"

Ginja nodded.

Devon punched the wall. He started pacing like a caged animal. He grabbed his duffel bag of guns and slung it over his shoulder, then grabbed the Block Buster. "This ends tonight."

"You'll never find Irons. He's constantly moving."

"I don't have to find him. He's looking for me, remember? Now if you don't mind, get your ass up and let's go."

"Where are we going?"

"We're going to see the General."

* * *

Grim cut his headlights off when he got to Ginja's block and coasted down the street.

"Is he still in the house?" Irons asked from the passenger seat.

"According to our men, he's been in front of the TV. the whole time."

"Is he by himself?"

"Yes."

Irons stroked his coarse beard. "This is too easy. It's like he's waiting for us."

"Maybe he thinks he can work something out with us."

"Work something out? Send someone to the front door. Let's see how he answers it."

Irons watched as one of his soldiers walked up to the front door and knocked. Devon didn't move from in front of the TV. The soldier knocked again.

Irons shook his head. "Something's not right."

That's when it happened.

The house exploded, killing the soldier at the front door instantly. The windows in Grim's Hummer shattered. Irons blinked, trying to stop from seeing double. As his eyesight started to clear, he saw his soldiers falling. Someone had opened fire on them. Irons tumbled out of the Hummer, holding his head. There, he saw fire spitting out of a machine gun from across the road. He pulled his guns and started firing at the gunman. His soldiers followed suit. The gunman stopped firing. Soldiers charged the nook where he was firing from.

"There!" Irons shouted pointing to the figure running down the block. Grim slammed the Hummer into drive as Irons jumped back in and took off.

Devon was running like a track star. All one could see was elbows and knee caps. Ginja was at the corner revving her ATV. With a hop, Devon was airborne. As soon as he landed on the back of the ATV, Ginja popped the clutch and they shot down the avenue.

Grim's Hummer careened around the corner. Irons's soldiers were right behind them in their truck.

"Faster," Irons said, hitting the dashboard. Grim smashed the pedal to the floor.

Devon let go of Ginja and turned around. He leaned against Ginja's back as he fired the two Uzis strapped to his shoulders.

Grim swerved as the bullets pelted the front of the Hummer. Irons stuck his hand out the window and fired back.

"I'm out of range. Can't this thing go any faster?" Irons hit the dashboard.

"No," Grim said.

Ginja tapped Devon on the thigh, letting him know that their turn was coming up. He turned back around and wrapped his arms around her waist. She veered to the left.

"Stop!" Irons said, smashing his feet on the Hummer's floor board. Grim hit the brakes. They skidded past the turnoff. As Grim backed up, Irons's men caught up with them.

"They turned into there!" Irons said. Grim turned onto the dirt road.

The first time Ginja rode this trail with Devon, she was going 20-30 miles per hour. Now, she kept the ATV between 40 and 45.

Four minutes into the trail, Grim's Hummer slowed down to 15 miles per hour.

"C'mon, mon," Irons said. "A big truck like this and you can't ride it faster than this on a simple path?"

"If I go any faster, we'll flip over."

Irons hit the dashboard.

Ginja throttled through the clearing. Devon jumped off the bike and reached for his flashlight. He turned it on and waved it toward the mountain where the General built himself a nest.

A moment later, the General flashed his light at Devon.

"Okay, we're good," Devon said to Ginja.

She was shaking.

"You did good," he said, hugging her. "We got to go. C'mon." They headed to the mouth of the cave.

Ten minutes later, Grim's Hummer busted through the clearing with Irons's men right behind him. Irons looked around. "What is this place?"

"Look!" Grim said, pointing at the figure at the mouth of the cave.

"Devon," Irons called out. "If you make me come after you, I promise you, you'll be sorry."

"He went into the cave," Grim said. "Let me send the men in to flush him out."

"No. I'm in control. He will come to me. Go get our insurance."

Grim went to the back of the soldier's truck.

"Devon," Irons called out. "I have something you may want."

Grim came back dragging Recker and Ivory.

"Look at who I brought with me?" Irons yoked Recker up.

"He's coming back out," Grim said.

"Yes, Devon. Who's in control now?"

"I am."

Everyone turned around too late. Devon never went to the mouth of the cave with Ginja. He doubled back and came up behind Irons and his men. Armed with two MP5s on rapid fire, he opened fire. The six soldiers in line of the MP5s were dead before they crumpled to the ground.

The ones who had enough time to raise their guns got sniped by the General. Irons and Grim were too busy running for cover to realize that Ivory and Recker were sprinting to the mouth of the cave.

Devon pulled the string on the belt of hand grenades he had rigged and threw it toward the Hummer. In the wake of the explosion and with the General covering him with sniper fire, he ran to the mouth of the cave.

As Ivory and Recker reached the cave, Ginja hugged Ivory and covered her face with kisses. "I thought you were dead."

"I thought you were dead," Ivory responded.

Ginja saw Devon running. She remembered what she had to do. She pushed Ivory and Recker into the cave and raised the Uzi Devon gave her and started shooting in the direction of Irons and his men.

Irons peeked over the boulder he was hiding behind and saw Devon hightailing it to the cave. He drew his pistol and started firing.

Devon zigzagged as bullets ricocheted off of the ground around him. Only yards from the cave, Ginja moved to the side and let him dive in.

He rolled and came to a full stop at Recker's feet. Recker held his hand out to him. He grabbed it. Recker hoisted him up and hugged him.

"I love you, too, Cuz," Devon said. He winced.

"You all right, Cuz?"

Devon removed his hoodie and then took off the Kevlar vest. He had two welts on his back. "Did the bullets go through?"

"Nah, Cuz, you good."

They ducked when they heard gunfire. Devon peeked out. The soldiers who were still alive were shooting toward the General's direction, giving Irons, Grim, and a handful of men time to run toward the cave. "They're coming, we got to go," Devon shouted.

"Give me one of the MPs," Recker said.

"You know how to use one of these?" Devon joked.

"We're about to get our asses shot off and you still got jokes."

Devon reloaded the MP5 and tossed it to him. Then he tossed Ivory a 9mm. He winced as he put the vest and hoodie back on.

"Where are we going?" Ivory asked.

"We're splitting up," Devon said. "Ginja and I are going to take the sharp right that leads to the old slave hideout. Y'all head straight toward the caverns. You do know these caves, right Ivory?"

"Like the back of my hand."

"Good. Irons only has a handful of men, so if they split up, we will have even more of an advantage." Devon gave Recker 5 clips for the MP5 and gave Ivory 5 for the 9mm. "Let's do this."

* * *

A few of Irons's men concentrated their fire on the General while Irons, Grim, and six soldiers headed toward the cave.

"Anyone peeks their head out of that cave, shoot it off," Irons said.

When they reached the mouth of the cave, Grim was the first one to go in. "It's clear."

Irons walked in and looked around. "So, he wants to play hide and seek. You," he said to one of his men, "stay here in case they try to double back. Shoot to kill."

"We should head back," Grim said. "This boy wanted us to follow him in here. We don't know these caves."

"Neither does he," Irons replied.

"What about the girl?"

"What girl is going to know about these caves? Stop being scared and let's finish this. We have plenty of ammunition and men."

"But—"

Irons shoved him. "But what?"

"Nothing."

"Then, let's go."

Irons stopped walking. "See that opening?" he asked Grim.

"Yeah."

"Take three of the men with you. I'll take the other two and go straight."

Grim and the three men squeezed through the opening. Grim stood on the sixty foot high cliff and stared down at the chamber below. They started to work their way around the columns with assault rifles leading the way.

* * *

"They did split up," Devon whispered to Ginja. They were lying on their stomachs looking down at them.

"That's Grim," Ginja whispered. "Irons's right hand man."

Devon started to climb down from their perch.

"Wait. Where are you going? This isn't part of the plan."

"There's been a change. Don't let them out of your sights."

"What are you going to do?"

"When I start shooting, I want you to take out the soldiers. Can you do that?"

Ginja swallowed hard and then nodded. She watched him slither down the cliff and run behind one of the columns. "Devon, I hope you know what you're doing!"

* * *

Irons had both pistols out as he and his men crept down the cave's interior.

The man in the front stopped and stooped down to examine the boot prints in the mud. "There are only two sets of prints," he said.

Irons holstered one of his guns and examined the prints. "Let's go back," he said. "That boot print belongs to Recker, and the other one is female." They turned around and headed back to catch up with Grim.

* * *

Devon was fifty yards away. He grabbed the Block Buster strapped across his back. He then pulled out one of his P89s. He crept up on them, closing the distance to forty yards. Grim and the three men were now in the chamber.

Devon's hand tightened around the pistol grip of the Block Buster as he aimed at the chamber's ceiling. He knew that the echo from the shotgun blast would shock them long enough for Ginja to take care of the three men.

* * *

Grim looked down the path leading out of the chamber and saw nothing but darkness. "Fuck this. We're heading back."

Grim nor the other men knew where the ear splitting sound came from, but after witnessing Ginja's house exploding, they ducked for cover. One of the men wasn't quick enough. Ginja lit him up. Eight of the twenty bullets spitting from the MP5 hit him. The two remaining soldiers shot up at Ginja.

Grim emptied his gun in Ginja's direction. As he ejected the clip and reached for another one, an arm wrapped around his neck, cutting off his air supply.

* * *

After Devon shot the Block Buster in the air, he slung the shotgun across his back and ran toward Grim. Ginja was only able to take out one soldier, but her gunfire distracted the rest of them. With the P89 in one hand, he ran up on Grim and yoked him from behind. He shot one of the soldiers twice in the back. The last one spun around. He got two bullets in the chest from Devon and five in the back from Ginja. Grim dropped his gun and was trying to wretch Devon's arm from around his neck.

Devon holstered his gun and used both arms to tighten the choke hold. Grim yelped.

"I don't want to kill you, so stop fighting me."

Grim struggled for a few more seconds and then stopped.

"Good boy." Devon loosened the lock just enough for Grim to suck in a few breaths. "You don't have to talk, just listen. The way I see it, I'm doing you a favor. When I kill Irons, you'll be the new leader of Villainy."

Grim became absolutely still.

"Yeah, I figured that would get your attention."

"Devon!" Irons stood on the cliff looking down at him. He had Ginja hanging off the edge with his gun to her head. "She won't survive this fall, trust me."

Devon let Grim go.

Irons and the two men with him worked their way down the steep cliff. Grim loaded his gun and pointed it at Devon.

"No!" Irons called out. "He's mine. Leave him." Irons pulled off his wool poncho when they reached the chamber. He kicked Ginja in the back of her legs, dropping her to her knees. He drew one of his Colt .45s and put it to her head and cocked the hammer. "This is what I should've done the first time."

"Wait!" Devon held his gun in the air. "I challenge you."

"Challenge me?"

"Me and you, your pistols against mine."

Irons's eyes widened, and then he busted out laughing. "I don't think so." He began to pull the trigger.

"Scared? You only shoot it out with people you know you can outdraw, people like Curry?"

Irons removed his gun from Ginja's head. "What do you know about Curry?"

"He was my father. Can't you see the family resemblance?"

"Your father? Curry?"

"So are we going to do this?"

"I hope you're faster than your father."

Devon held the P89 at his side.

Irons holstered his gun and let his hands hover over them. "Say when."

Devon's hand flew from his side. Irons drew and fired from the hip. His first bullet skinned Devon's right forearm, causing him to fire off a wild shot. Irons's second and third bullets hit him in the chest. The impact from the Colt .45s hurled Devon into the dark tunnel leading to the other caverns.

"He was faster than his father, but not fast enough." Irons holstered his pistols. His eyes widened when the head of the man standing next to him exploded, then he heard the sound of the shot. Another shot rang out, hitting the remaining soldier in the neck. Irons and Grim fired into the darkness where Devon had disappeared.

Devon stumbled out of the darkness and fell to one knee.

"What kind of madness is this?" Irons roared.

Devon unzipped his hoodie and began taking off the Kevlar vest.

Irons began to finish him off.

"Wait!" Devon held his hand up. The pain from the impact of the bullets coupled with his adrenaline made him throw up.

"Enough of this," Irons raised his gun.

Devon reached behind his back and drew the other P89 from its holster. Irons fired, but Devon was already rolling and firing. Devon hit Irons four times in the stomach. Devon leaned against the wall exhausted. Ginja crawled to him. She took the gun from him and pointed it at Grim who had his pointed at them. Ginja's hands shook as she tried to hold the gun steady.

Grim heard a click in the darkness. Recker and Ivory emerged with their guns trained on him.

"I'm going to make you suffer," Recker said.

"No," Devon called out. "Let him go."

"Hell no!" Recker's finger tensed on the trigger.

"Let him go," Devon said again.

"You're not thinking straight, Cuz. He'll round up the rest of Villainy and hunt us down."

"No, he won't. Isn't that right, Grim?"

Grim nodded slowly.

Ginja helped Devon to his feet. "Drop your gun and walk out of here."

Grim lowered his gun, but he didn't drop it.

Devon hopped to him. He grabbed the gun from him. "Spanish Town."

Grim looked at him surprised.

"Yeah, I know where your kids live and what schools they attend. You come after me, my family or any of my team... now, go."

Grim backed up. He turned around and climbed out of the chamber. Devon fell to the floor and grabbed his ankle.

"Devon!" Ginja ran to him.

"I twisted it when I dove behind that boulder when Irons and Grim started shooting at me."

Recker walked up to Irons's dead body and snatched the chain off his neck with his finger on it, and then he emptied half a clip into his corpse.

"Did that make you feel any better?" Devon asked.

"Hell yeah."

Ivory walked up to Irons and shot him twice with the 9mm. "Yeah that felt reeeal good."

"Why'd you let Grim live?" Recker asked.

"Someone has to tell the story of the legendary Gunslinger."

"You so stupid," Ginja said. "Can you wiggle your foot?"

Devon winced. "Barely."

"I don't think it's broken. Let's get out of here so we can let the General take a look at it," Ginja said.

"The General?" Recker said. "What the hell does the General know about broken bones?"

"He said he was a medic in the armed forces before he was recruited by Special Forces to be a sniper," Devon said.

"A sniper? And you believe that bullshit?"

Devon and Ginja looked at each other and started laughing.

"What the fuck is so funny?" Recker said, confused.

Chapter 10

Devon, Recker, Ginja, and Ivory returned to Amsterdam after attending their fallen comrades' funerals. Before leaving Jamaica, Devon had convinced what was left of the team that, more than ever, they had to go hard. Dillard and Sterling would be keeping a close eye on them.

The team, although still in mourning, did turn it up. Everybody who owed paid; everybody except one. Devon stood across the street from the corporate building. He looked at his watch and back at the parking garage. It was three thirty one. He's a minute late, he said to himself. Being a minute late to most people is a small thing, but not to David Hagen. He was a stickler for sticking to schedules.

At three thirty one and forty five seconds, David Hagen exited the building. Hagen crossed the street and then looked at his watch. Fucking cocksucker. He thought of how his supervisor waited til the end of the day to want to brief him about the Gaskin's case. He walked into the parking garage and groped in his coat pocket for his keys. He stopped in his tracks when he saw Devon leaning on his car.

"How's it going, David?"

"Boy, I'm glad to see you. You've saved me the trouble of trying to contact you."

"It's not hard to contact me, David. Just pick up the phone and dial my number."

"Yeah, I've been meaning to call you."

"I thought something happened to you."

"To me?" David looked puzzled.

"Yeah, I know how you corporate execs get when you start losing money or get into debt. Y'all tend to jump out of windows."

"I would never jump out of a window."

"That's the thing. I don't think the others jumped. I think they were… pushed."

"Hold on a minute—" David turned to his right when he saw a figure step from behind one of the pillars. Ivory had on a pair of shades, a knit hat, and was wearing a trench coat identical to Devon's.

"That's another thing," Devon said. "We've been holding on for some time, now. Or should I say holding back?"

"I got the money."

"All of it?"

"A little over half, but—"

"There's nothing else to talk about, David." Devon stuck his hand out. "Give me the Rolex and the wedding band."

"Wait, wait, wait, I got something for you. Something worth twenty times what I owe."

"Not interested."

"Please." David held his hand up. "There's an American investor by the name of Harvey Gaskin. He was convicted of tax evasion and embezzlement. He didn't show up for his sentencing again today. He's disappeared. In two weeks, his corporation is planning on selling off eight properties. No one knows about this except me and my supervisor."

"I don't need property, David, I need money, the money that you owe."

"I can get you these properties for next to nothing," David said talking faster. "A couple storefronts, a couple boutiques, and brownstones in choice locations all over London. The land that they're on is worth hundreds of thousands alone."

Devon walked up to him and put his arm around his shoulders. He walked him to his car. "And how are you going to get me these properties?"

David looked around, and then spoke. "I can set you up a corporation. Then I'll contact James Roth, he's the lawyer in charge of auctioning off each piece of property. I tell him I have a buyer and a fat commission for him and that's that."

"And it's that easy?"

"Yes."

Devon wasn't paying him any mind. When he asked the question, he was looking at Ivory for the answer. She subtly nodded. He took David's car keys out of his hand and tossed them to Ivory. She unlocked the doors and hopped into the driver's seat. Devon opened the back door.

"Hop in, David."

"Where are we going?"

"I'm getting you to a computer so you can build me a corporation."

* * *

"That's it," David said, looking up from the computer screen.

Devon in turn looked at Ivory who was on another computer tracking his every move.

"We're in business," she said.

Devon patted David on the shoulder. "I don't have to tell you what will happen to you and everyone you love if you screw me on this, right?"

"This deal is legit, I swear on my daughter's eyes."

"You have David's parting gift?" Devon asked Ginja.

She held an eight ball of coke in her left hand and his car keys in her right.

"Good," Devon said. "Walk him to the door."

As soon as Recker heard David's car pull off, he lit up a blunt. "I don't like this, one bit."

"What don't you like about it?" Devon asked.

"The whole computer aspect, people can do all kinds of things with computers these days."

"Ivory was following his every move."

"That don't mean shit. What's to stop him from going home and tapping into that bank account he just set up for us in the Cayman Islands?"

"Fear," Devon said.

"He transferred a little over half a mil to that account. Greed supersedes fear in my book."

"And I thought I was the paranoid one. Don't worry about David Hagen. He has more to lose than gain if he crosses us."

"Even if he doesn't cross us, I still don't trust them computers. One glitch and five hundred thousand becomes five hundred dollars," Recker said.

"The days of stuffing our money into the mattress are long gone."

Ginja came back into the room. "Dillard just called. He wants to know what we're going to do about the new kids on the block. Yesterday, they ransacked one of their stores and threatened the manager. They want their dues by the end of the week or else."

"Young punks," Devon spat. "Nothing better to do but try and extort the local businesses."

"We'll take care of them," Recker said.

"We need more manpower," Ginja said.

"I said, we will fucking handle it."

"There's only four of us," Ginja said.

"And there's about to be three if you don't shut the fuck up."

"Enough," Devon said. "Recker, I know this is a touchy subject for you, but Ginja's right. We can't be rocking suits and ties, making power moves by day, and then be suited down in Timbs and hoodies putting in that body and fender work by night."

"Why not?"

"Because we can't."

"We were doing it when Dane, Rippa, and Stripes were here," Recker countered.

"They're not here, now, and we're expanding. The majority of our cash flow is coming from the shit we're doing behind Dillard and Sterling's back. We've been lucky so far."

"Lucky?"

"Yes. Lucky that we haven't ran into anyone who's willing to go toe-to-toe with us," Devon said. "We can't afford to get our hands dirty."

"And who do you think can take Dane, Rippa, and Stripes's place?"

"No one can take their place. You know that."

"You damn right."

"But that doesn't negate the fact that we need to beef up the team."

Recker took a deep pull of the blunt and held it out to Ivory. She declined. "Fuck you then!" Then he held it out to Ginja. She declined, as well. "What the fuck? Y'all don't smoke anymore?"

Ginja fanned the smoke with her hand. "We haven't smoked since we got back."

"What, y'all trying to emulate this motherfucker?" he said, pointing to Devon.

"It ain't even like that," Ivory said. "We just got to be on top of our game."

"I think you just trying to get on top of his dick."

"Fuck you, Recker!" Ginja shouted.

"Fuck me? Fuck you, you skank bitch! You're the fucking reason why my boys are dead. You and that white trash were outside, sitting in the car. How the fuck you let Irons and them sneak up on us? Maybe you didn't, maybe that was part of the plan." Recker was getting angrier by the minute.

"You sick bastard," Ivory said. "I can't believe you just said that."

"Yeah, I said it. And what?"

"Go for a walk, Recker," Devon said.

"Walk for what?"

"Just go. Get some fresh air, now."

Recker popped off the couch and stormed past him. He slammed the door on his way out.

Ginja sat on the couch and wiped the tears from her eyes.

"You know he didn't mean that," Devon said. "They were like brothers."

"We had love for them, too," Ivory said, walking to the couch and sitting next to Ginja.

"I know y'all did. Recker knows that you did. He's just hurting right now."

"What are we going to do, Devon?" Ginja asked. "You were right when you said we've been lucky."

"We got to do some recruiting," Devon said.

"Recruiting from where? Here in Amsterdam? We can't trust anyone here."

"Trust? You know how I feel about trust."

"So, who are we going to turn to?" Ginja asked.

"There's only one person to turn to. Let's just hope Recker doesn't pop a blood vessel."

* * *

"Are you out of your mind?" Recker shouted. "Yo, Cuz, you know there've been some decisions that you've made that I was against, but I rolled with you none the less, but this one? I am now convinced that you've lost your fucking mind. I'm not putting my life in their hands," Recker said pointing at the gentlemen sitting on the couch.

"Can't put ya' life in our hands? Me been saving ya' narrow ass since you were a snot-nosed punk," the General said, standing up. The two men on his right and left stood as well. "You must've forgotten all de' times me intervened on ya' behalf when de' rude bwoys were ready to shoot you like a stray dawg. You must've 'ave also forgotten who was on dat' mountain sniping all of Irons's men so you and 'dat pretty white gal' over 'dere could get away. And speaking of Irons, it was out of respect for me 'dat de only thing 'em cut off was ya' finger."

Recker got in his face. "I got a lot of respect for you, old man, but that don't give you the right to fly all the way here to Amsterdam and disrespect me in my own fucking crib."

"And me didn't fly all de' way to Amsterdam just to be disrespected in ya' own fucking crib." The General walked to the other side of the living room.

"Chill out, Recker," Devon said. "The General doesn't have to be here. He came out of respect for what happened to the team. He's the only one in the world that we trust, right now. And these two gentlemen are the only two in the world that he trusts."

Recker eyed the two men. They were still standing. Both let their hands fall below their navels, right hand cuffed over left. He remembered seeing them on the beaches back home hustling trinkets to tourists. Both men were in their late fifties. They had taken off their suit jackets and had rolled their sleeves up to their elbows. Their forearms were all sinew and muscle like the rest of their bodies. They were in better shape than men half their age. Neither man said a word, other than hello when they first walked in. Now, they stood, watching, waiting.

"And what's their story?" Recker asked. "What's their motivation for coming?"

"I'm dere motivation," the General said. "We've long retired from de' Brigade, but de' war for us isn't over."

"Oh, God," Recker sighed. "Just what we need. A couple of shell shocked beach bums. They probably don't even remember how to fire a gun." Recker stuck his hand into his jacket and began drawing his gun. Both men sprung at him.

"Ahh, get the fuck off of me," Recker yelled.

Knots, the shorter of the two men, had swept Recker's feet from under him. While he was falling to the floor, Porter, the other older gentleman had wrenched Recker's arms behind his back. Recker hit the floor, chest first.

"General!" Recker yelled.

"Enough!" the General barked. Both men jumped off of Recker just as fast as they jumped on him.

Ginja and Ivory looked on in shock.

Devon noticed that Knots had Recker's gun tucked in his waistband. He busted out laughing. "I'll make a deal with you, Recker. Either you agree to put them on the team or I'm telling everybody back home that two old, shell shocked, beach bums, who probably don't remember how to shoot took your gun from you and had you screaming like a little bitch."

"Nobody will believe you."

"I got witnesses."

Ginja and Ivory waved at him.

"Y'all are some trifling bitches." Recker snatched his gun out of Knots's waistband. He acted like he was putting it back in his shoulder holster, but then leveled it at Knots's head. "I could do you a big favor and put you out of your misery right now, old man."

Knots smiled. He opened his left hand. In the palm of his hand the clip to Recker's gun was staring him in the face.

"Old fool," Recker spat. "You forgot about the one in the chamber."

Knots's smile grew wider as he opened his right hand.

"How the fuck...?" Recker stared at the bullet that Knots had ejected out of the chamber.

Devon busted out laughing again.

Recker looked Knots in the eyes and couldn't help but smile. "The only reason why y'all got the drop on me is because I ain't smoke no weed yet."

Knots and Porter nodded and smiled.

"Y'all don't talk much, huh?" Recker asked.

"The General does the talking, we do the rest," Porter said.

Recker nodded. "All right. Fuck it, I like their style. They're down with the team."

"Good," Devon said, clasping his hands together. "Ginja, Ivory, I want you to bring the General, Knots, and Porter up to speed. Tomorrow, I'll introduce them to Dillard and Sterling."

"No problem," Ginja said.

Devon and Recker were the only ones left in the room.

"So what do you think?" Devon asked.

"I can honestly say that they scare the shit out of me."

* * *

The General and his men didn't waste any time stomping out the new kids on the block. The General's solution was simple. Eliminate the head, eliminate the threat. When the crew saw their leader strung up on a light pole, butt naked, with his head nearly decapitated, they didn't know how to respond. And when their second in command went missing, the crew hightailed it out of Amsterdam. For the first time in weeks, Devon kicked back and relaxed. He sighed and looked at his phone. He thought of Quana and how they parted. He picked up his phone and dialed her number.

"Hello?" she answered on the fourth ring.

"Hi," Devon said.

"Hi, stranger."

"I know it's been a while. Things have been kind of hectic, but things are starting to calm down a bit."

"That's good to hear."

"What's up with my boy?"

"He hasn't been upstate a full two years yet, and already he's hustling."

"Hustling?"

"He got Andrea smuggling drugs into the facility."

"What the hell is he doing that for? He got plenty of money."

"It's not even about the money for him. It's just playing the game."

"You need to talk to him, Quana. He needs to be easy until that appeal comes through."

"I know, I already tried and he's not listening to me."

"How's Sonia?"

"She had a baby girl, she named her Briana."

"My boy's a father; I can't believe it. How are you holding up?"

"I'm taking it one day at a time. I filled out some college applications."

"That's good."

"Yeah, I stopped procrastinating. I got to do something to get my mind off of Brian and his situation, you know?"

"Yes, and you're doing the right thing."

"How about you, are you doing the right thing?"

"As right as I can do it."

"Just be careful, Devon."

"Of course. Seen any beautiful sunsets, lately?"

"None like in Jamaica."

Devon closed his eyes. "Our vacation was cut short. I swear, I'm going to make it up to you."

"You don't have to make anything up to me."

"Sure I do. And I will."

"That girl that I saw on the yacht, was that Ginja?"

"Yeah, how did you know?"

"I remembered talking to her on the phone that day you called me and I told you that Brian was found guilty. She was trying to calm me down. Actually, she did. She seems like a beautiful person."

"She is, but she's just a friend. She will always be just a friend."

"I'm taking good care of your chain."

"You better be. That's my heart you're wearing on your neck."

"Your heart is safe with me."

"I know." Devon sighed. "I have to go. Please try to keep Brian out of trouble. Talk some sense into that hard head of his."

"I do every chance I get."

"Take care, Quana."

"Be careful."

"Always." Devon hung up and stared out his window. A minute later, his cell phone rang. "Talk to me."

"It's done," David whispered.

"All eight properties?"

"Yes, all eight."

"You're a good man. I'll see you at the lounge tonight. Drinks and… everything is on me."

"Thank you for giving me the chance to do this for you."

"See you tonight."

* * *

Six months later, Devon called the team together for a meeting in London. It had been the first time the whole team had been there since Devon had the storefronts and boutiques renovated, and the brownstones converted into Bed and Breakfast hotels.

One of Devon's secretaries escorted them to the top floor of one of the brownstones. The top floor was Devon's operations center when he was in London. Recker, Ginja, Ivory, the General, Knots, and Porter all sat around the conference table waiting for Devon to show up.

"Where's this dude at?" Recker said. Devon had been in London for the past three weeks taking care of business while the rest of the team held down the fort in Amsterdam.

They all turned their heads toward the solid oak door when it opened and Devon stepped in.

"What... the fuck..." Recker's jaw dropped.

"Oh my God," Ginja said. She got up and ran to Devon. "What did you do?" she said rubbing his bald head.

"I had to recreate myself."

Ivory peeped the Armani suit and platinum bracelet on his wrist. "Damn, you look sexy as hell."

"Don't he?" Ginja said, gazing into his eyes.

"Yes, Sir," the General said. "Back in my day, before joining de' Brigade, I used to dress like that dere'. Did I ever tell you about de' time when—"

"Yeah," Recker said. "A thousand times already."

Everyone started laughing.

Devon walked to the table with Ginja. He took his seat. "I got some good news and some great news."

"That's the type of news I like to hear," Recker said.

"The good news is, we are now officially caking in London."

"Let's celebrate," Recker said, pulling a blunt from his shirt pocket.

Devon shot him a look.

"What the fuck? We can't celebrate?"

"You know the rules, Recker"

"Who the fuck came up with that no-smoking-weed-at-meetings rule anyway?"

"We did."

"No, we didn't."

"Everyone agreed, but you. We out voted you," Devon said.

Recker tucked the blunt back in his shirt pocket. "Y'all are killing me with all these new rules and recreating yourselves bullshit."

Devon pointed to Recker's suit. "I see you're wearing that suit I sent you."

"That's only because his girlfriend said he look like Lil Wayne in that *Lollipop* video," Ivory said.

"Suck my dick." Recker grabbed his dick for emphasis.

"Grow one, little dick bastard," Ivory shot back.

"See," Recker said to Devon. "You need to tell that trifling skank to recreate herself and learn how to talk to people."

"Alright," Devon said. "Now for the great news, Mr. David Hagen has been able to acquire two more properties for us in France. Khufu Incorporated is now the proud owner of a boutique in Paris, and a warehouse in Lyon."

Everyone clapped.

"I don't have to tell you what the warehouse is going to be, right?" Devon said.

"You think Dillard and Sterling will be upset that we bit their idea?" Recker asked.

"Dillard and Sterling can go fly a kite for all I care," Devon said. "We don't work for them anymore. Starting today, we work for Khufu Incorporated." Devon picked up the phone in front of him and pressed a button. "Yes, Mary, come in."

A few moments later, Mary, the secretary walked in.

"Everybody, this is Mary. She's in charge of daily operations here at the brownstone. This brownstone is going to be our command center. Everything will be ran out of this building. Mary, please show my colleagues to their rooms."

"Yes, sir, Mr. Carter."

Everyone stood. Devon removed his suit jacket. "Ginja, Ivory," he called out. "You two stay." Everyone else followed Mary out of the office.

"What's up?" Ivory asked.

"Mary is efficient and trustworthy, but you know I got trust issues. I already told her that you will be her supervisor. At the end of everyday, I want a status report on our finances and any unusual occurrences at any of our businesses."

"No problem."

"You can go."

Ginja opened the door for her. She shut the door behind Ivory and turned to face Devon.

"So, you like me with or without dreads?"

She walked up to him and leaned on the desk. "With dreads, you had that rugged, Gunslinger look. With the baldie, not only do you look fine as hell, but you got that strictly business persona emanating from you."

"That's good to hear, because you know I'm strictly business."

"Of course you are."

"You did what I asked you to do?"

Ginja got off the desk and turned her back to him. She slowly hiked her miniskirt up, exposing her bare behind. "No panties, just like you ordered." She bent over the desk, giving him a full view of her freshly shaven peach.

Devon stood up and walked up behind her. He slapped her butt and watched it jiggle. He pulled his pants and boxers down in one motion. He rubbed his semi hard head up and down her moist slit. When he became brick hard, he penetrated her to the hilt.

She let out a low cry as he entered her. His phone on the desk started to ring.

"Fuck," he said as he tried to ignore it, but it wouldn't stop. He sunk his shaft deep inside her and paused. He reached over and answered his phone. "What?" As he listened, Ginja continued to grind and wind. Devon tried to focus on the conversation as he felt her muscles tighten around him. He knew she was about to cum.

"You're where?" he said pulling out of her.

"No," she pouted and reached behind and tried to put him back in. He swatted her hand away. "Don't worry about a thing. Just keep your mouth shut. I'm sending my lawyer over there, right now." He hung up and sat back in the chair.

"What's wrong?" she asked.

Devon stood back up and bent her back over. After they both climaxed, he collapsed back into the chair. "I really needed that," he said panting.

Ginja pulled the silk handkerchief out of his top pocket and sat on the edge of the desk with her legs cocked open. She wiped as much of their juices out of her as she could before pulling down her skirt.

"Talk to me, what was the phone call about?"

It never ceased to amaze Devon how Ginja could fuck him for hours at a time and as soon as the act was over, she could talk to him as if nothing happened.

"I just fucked you."

"Yes, you did."

"How does that make you feel?"

"How am I supposed to feel?"

"You don't feel anything?"

"I feel your cum dripping down the insides of my thighs." Devon sighed.

"You're not catching feelings for me, are you, Gunslinger?"

"Never that."

"So, why are you worried about what I'm feeling?"

"That was nerdy-ass Warren the pill man on the phone," Devon said, changing the subject.

"What happened?"

"He's in jail."

"Jail?"

"Someone at the University snitched him out."

"I wonder how that's going to effect his scholarship?"

"Who cares? I'm sending our lawyer, Yantz, to bail him out. That's the least I can do for all the money he's thrown our way."

Ginja twirled a lock of her hair and stared off into space.

"What Ginja? I know that look."

"We can use him."

"Use him?"

"He's a fucking genius. Who do you think taught Ivory all that shit she knows about computers? He's a wiz when it comes to hacking into databases."

"How does that help us?"

"Hacking into databases? He can hack into, let's say, American Express and get you a dozen platinum cards under various names. He can hack into any DMV and get you a driver's license. He could hack into the hall of records and get you a birth certificate and social security card under any name you want. He can hack into security cameras, GPS navigational systems—"

"All right. I see your point. I'll run it by the rest of the team in the morning. For now, get your hot behind out of here before Recker and them suspect something."

Ginja got up to leave.

"Ginja."

"What?"

He pointed to the office's private bathroom. "Go in there and wash up, thoroughly. I don't need Ivory smelling me on or in you."

Ginja cracked a smile and headed to the bathroom.

Chapter 11

In a little under two years, Khufu Incorporated became a reputable conglomerate of businesses investors were standing in line to invest in. As the corporation grew in size and publicity, Devon knew he had to play the shadows. Being wanted in the United States for murder and numerous other charges would cripple their newfound enterprises. So, in trying to keep things in the family, and honoring their fallen friends, he flew Dane's uncle to London and made him the CEO, and the Face of Khufu Incorporated.

David Hagen had earned his way onto Devon's payroll by using his inside connects to secure prime real estate for Khufu Inc. With legit money coming in from multiple sources, Devon was able to focus on what mattered to him the most: Getting his boy out of prison.

He spoke to Quana a few weeks back, and she told him that Brian's appeal was denied. Then she followed up the bad news by telling him the Bloods had a hit out on Brian over the jail house drug empire Brian was trying to build. Then she capped it off with a revelation that blew Devon away. Sonia admitted that Briana wasn't Brian's daughter. She purposely had a one night stand on Brian to make him jealous; a one night stand where she wasn't smart enough to use protection.

The only man that Devon had love for was going through hell, while he was living the life of luxury. He was traveling to a different country every month. And from every country he vacationed in, he made sure to send Brian a postcard. A few times he contemplated going back to the States to visit him, because the identities that Warren produced for him were so authentic that the only way a person would know his true identity was through his fingerprints. But the last thing he needed was to get fingerprinted for some bullshit in New York. But he couldn't just sit idle knowing that his boy had beef with the Bloods.

He did the unimaginable. He reached out to a person who he knew had people in the New York State Department of Corrections. He contacted Grim. He offered to pay him five hundred thousand if his men could meet with the Bloods and call off the hit.

Three weeks later, Grim called him back. The Bloods agreed to the truce as long as Brian didn't violate it. That business deal opened the lines of communication between Devon and Grim. Devon of course took full advantage of it. He told Grim that he was pulling his team out of Dillard and Sterling's employment. He told him that he would suggest to Dillard that he and his team take over. This offer sounded good to Grim. It also sounded good to Dillard and Sterling who knew Villainy's "don't play" reputation.

It especially sounded good to Devon, because he knew Villainy's "don't play" attitude would be Dillard and Sterling's downfall. Villainy thrived off of violence and treachery. It will only be a matter of time before Dillard and Sterling became victims of it.

Devon sat in his penthouse suite reading the London Times when his phone rang. "Yes."

"It's me."

"What have you got, David?"

"I know you're specific when it comes to geographical locations, but I had to run this deal by you before it gets out."

"What is it?"

"A chain of dollar stores are going to be put on the market in two weeks."

"Where?"

"North Carolina, but—"

"What did I say, David?"

"I know, you're only interested in properties on this side of the hemisphere, but this deal was just too sweet not to run by you."

"What's so sweet about it?"

"These dollar stores are the hottest thing out. They're popping up all over the United States. The owner of this particular chain became a millionaire overnight."

"So, why is he selling them?"

"He was diagnosed with terminal cancer a few months ago. He's spent hundreds of thousands on medications and treatments. He has finally faced reality. His doctor gave him six months to live."

"Damn, that's fucked up."

"What's fucked up is he has no family to leave the business to. So, he's decided to cash out and spend the next six months living like a king."

"Sounds good, David, but I don't have anyone in the United States to close the deal nor run something like that."

"I know some people and—"

"That's the problem. They're your people, not mine."

"I understand, Mr. Carter."

"Call me when you have something on this side of the world."

"Yes, I will."

Devon hung up and shook his head. He picked up his newspaper and opened it. He was reading, but he wasn't focused. That was the third time David had called him with a sweet deal that he couldn't touch, because he didn't have anyone he could trust in the United States. He thought of his uncle, but that's all it was, a thought.

"Fuck." He balled up the paper and threw it. He picked up his phone and called the General.

"Yes, Devon," he answered.

"Can you hold the fort down without Knots?"

"Yeah, what'a gwon?" The Genral Asked.

"I'm going to need him for a few days."

* * *

Quana sat cross-legged on her twin-bed with her back against the wall. Her textbook was still opened to the last page she was reading before she fell out. She jumped when Cindy, her roommate, walked in and slammed the door. She was screaming at somebody on her cell phone. She stopped to look at Quana and hung up on whoever was on the other end of the phone. "Nah, ah," she said. "That economics exam is not that serious for you to be cooped up in here studying like that."

"I got to ace this test and the midterm in order to get a B," Quana said, rubbing her eyes.

"What you got to do is get your face out of that book and start getting ready for the club tonight."

"Nooo," Quana whined. "I told you I wasn't going. I have to work tonight."

"Study and work, study and work, that's all Quana does. When are you going to unwind and enjoy your freedom?"

"My freedom?"

"Freedom, girl. You're out from under your parents's roof, you're in the 'Dirty South' where anything goes, and you're a Spellman girl."

"A Spellman girl who's about to lose her scholarship if my grades drop any lower."

"That's your problem. You worry too much. Call in sick tonight, come to the club, enjoy yourself, find yourself a man and you know…"

"I don't have time for a man, right now."

Cindy sat down on the edge of Quana's bed. "Right now? You've been here for two years, and I've never seen you with a man." Cindy's mouth dropped open. "Don't you sit there and tell me you ain't been with a man in two years."

"Like I said, I don't have the time."

"A woman has got to make time to get her coochie scratched."

"I'll have plenty of time when I graduate."

"So, you're talking about going another two years without a man? That's totally unacceptable."

"Okay, maybe I was exaggerating about going two more years, but I'm just not ready for a relationship, right now."

"A relationship? You don't have to be in a relationship to get some TLC."

"I'm just not ready."

"What are you waiting for?"

"I don't know."

Cindy opened her cell phone and called Quana's job. "Yes, hi, my name is Cindy Mayers. Yes, I'm LaQuana's roommate. I'm just calling to let you know that she's come down with a virus. Yes, she's throwing up and she has diarrhea."

Quana swatted her on the arm.

"Yes, I'll tell her, bye-bye."

"I can't believe you did that."

"Your boss says she hopes you get better soon and call her tomorrow to let her know how you're feeling. Well, being that you don't have to work, tonight, it's time for you to get up and get ready for the club."

* * *

Quana couldn't remember the last time she went to a club. She sat in a booth with Cindy and three of her friends. Quana sipped on a club soda while Cindy and her friends slurped down pineapple cosmos.

Quana kept adjusting the front of her dress. She couldn't believe she let Cindy talk her into wearing one of her too short dresses with a plunging neckline.

"Girl, stop fidgeting," Cindy said.

"I feel like everyone is staring at my breasts."

"You've got beautiful breasts. You need to show them off more often."

"You know how many women would kill to have a set of melons like those?" Saphari, one of Cindy's friends said.

"You're definitely snagging a man with those tonight." Cindy said, giving her girls high-fives.

"Y'all are crazy." Quana looked around the club and noticed a brown skinned brother making his way to the table. She turned back around and sipped on her soda.

"Ladies." The fine brown skinned brother greeted them.

"How you doing, Mel?" Cindy asked.

"Not too good. All these women in here and I can't find one to dance with."

Quana sneaked a look at him. He was fine as hell, clean shaven and well-dressed.

"How you doing, Quana?" he asked, focusing his attention on her.

"How do you know my name?"

"I see you around on campus. You work at the diner over on Peachtree right?"

"Yeah."

Mel nodded. "Can I get you something a little stronger?" he asked, eyeing her soda.

"I don't drink."

"Do you dance?"

"I—"

"Yes, she does," Cindy said, cutting in.

Quana looked at her.

"Go on, we'll be all right."

Quana looked up at Mel. He held his hand out. Quana allowed him to lead her to the dance floor. Mel was smooth. He kept his steps simple. He gave Quana her space. She expected him to try and press his body up on hers, but he didn't. When the DJ slowed it down, he put his arms around her waist, but he didn't crowd her. He's nice, she said to herself.

It didn't take long for her to loosen up. They danced, they laughed. It was the most fun she had in years.

Mel leaned in and whispered in her ear. "You want to go get something to eat?"

Quana looked back at the booth Cindy and her friends were sitting at. They were gone. She looked around and saw them on the dance floor. "Uh, I don't want to leave Cindy."

"She can come with us."

"A third wheel? I don't think so," Quana said, jokingly. "I'll be right back." She made her way to Cindy and told her she was going to go get something to eat with Mel.

"Ready?" Mel asked her as she walked back.

"Yes."

At the diner he pulled Quana's seat out for her to sit.

"Ah, that's so sweet," Quana said.

"My momma taught me to respect women."

Quana eyed him as he sat down. He had a nice build, and his cornrows were freshly braided.

The waitress brought them menus.

"What are you having?" Mel asked.

"Why don't you order for us?"

"Okay. You eat seafood?"

"Yes."

Mel ordered two seafood platters and two tall glasses of iced tea.

"So what's your major?" he asked.

"Business administration. What about you?"

"Micro biology."

"You serious?"

"Nah, I'm just kidding. I'm majoring in communications. I had to pick something, so—"

Quana had a confused look on her face.

"I'm here on a football scholarship. I'm going to the NFL after college."

"I didn't know you play football."

Mel leaned back in his chair. "Girl, stop playing, you know I play football."

"No, I didn't."

"I'm Jamel Jackson, the star running back."

Quana shrugged. "I'm sorry. I don't keep up with sports."

"Wow, you are probably the only person on campus who doesn't know who I am."

"Well, look on the bright side; at least you know I'm not having dinner with you because of who you are."

Mel nodded. "That's definitely one way of looking at it."

After dinner Mel told Quana he was going to take the scenic route back to the campus just so he could enjoy her company just a little while longer. He was the perfect gentleman all the way up to the point when he walked her to her dorm. He gave her his number and ended the night with a kiss on the cheek and a hug. Quana sighed when he embraced her. He definitely had a football player's physique.

She thought about sneaking in, so she wouldn't wake Cindy, but she knew she was most likely sitting on her bed waiting for the details. As soon as she opened the door, Cindy jumped off her bed and shut off the TV.

"Well?"

"Well what?"

"Girl, don't play with me. Give me the rundown."

"Why didn't you tell me he was a football player?"

"Everybody knows Mel is on the football team."

"Not everybody."

"Everybody but you. So, talk to me."

"We had a nice time."

"And?"

"And he brought me home."

"Y'all plan on hooking up again or what?"

"Yeah, on Tuesday, my day off."

"Girl, look at you. Going out with a football player and everything."

"We're just enjoying each other's company."

"Umm, humm, just make sure you get your *enjoyment* off first."

"It's not going to be that type of enjoyment."

"Umm, humm."

* * *

Mel called Quana the whole weekend. And the times they weren't talking on the phone, he was at her dorm. Quana was enjoying herself so much that she didn't pick up her economics textbook since Friday. She kept telling herself that the test was on Wednesday, so she had plenty of time to study.

"Are you ready to order, sir?" Quana asked the man sitting at one of her tables."

"Yes, I'll have the scramble eggs, sausage links, and a black coffee."

"It'll be here, shortly."

"Thank you," he said, checking her out in her uniform.

When Quana turned her back, she rolled her eyes. When she complained to Brian about her bum job, he told her on more than one occasion to use some of the money she was holding for him. She couldn't bring herself to use any. She had to prepare for the reality. What if he had to do all that time? Or what if he wanted to do another appeal? She wasn't going to touch the money, even if it meant having to put up with the ogling and an over-demanding boss.

She worked the breakfast shift, went to classes, and then returned to work the night shift. As usual, her boss picked her to stay back and help her close up.

"Good night, Miss. John," she said after she shut off the lights and held the door open for her. "I'll see you Wednesday."

"Wednesday? You mean tomorrow, don't you?"

"I thought I was off tomorrow."

"You were, but you called in sick last Friday. That was your day off."

"Are you serious?"

"I'll see you tomorrow night." Miss John headed to her car.

I can't believe this, Quana said to herself as she walked back to her dorm. Her cell phone rang. She dug in her bag and answered it.

"Hey, you," Mel said.

"You must've felt me thinking of you," Quana said. She was going to tell him she couldn't go out tomorrow night because she had to work, but he cut her off.

"I've been thinking about you like crazy, too. I'm just calling to say that I'm going to have to cancel our dinner plans. I totally forgot that we have practice that afternoon. By the time I get back, take a shower—"

"It's okay," Quana said.

"I know that you're off tomorrow night and all."

"Yeah, but—"

"Just don't be too mad at me, okay?"

"I'm not mad at you."

"I got to go. I'll give you a ring tomorrow."

"Okay, bye." She tucked her phone back in her bag and picked up her pace. She had been looking forward to going out with Mel again. It must not be meant to be, she thought. I got to work and he cancelled.

* * *

Quana punched in the next night. Her boss had the nerve to be shooting her a dirty look. She was only five minutes late. Quana shook her head as she changed into her uniform.

Between six and eight was when the diner became the most hectic. Her feet were killing her and for the fifth time that night, a customer grabbed her by the hand and tried to get her number. She politely pulled her hand out of his and told him she had a man. For some, it worked, for others, it made them try harder. Thankfully, this particular customer believed the line. She headed to the pickup counter and grabbed one of her orders the cook just finished preparing.

She nearly dropped the order when she saw Mel walk in. Pam, who used to tutor her in Chemistry, had her arms wrapped around his waist. Quana felt the blood rushing to her face as she watched Mel pull the seat out for her to sit.

Pam said something and Quana read Mel's lips. "My momma taught me to respect women." Quana took a deep breath and continued carrying the order to her customer. Out the corner of her eye, she saw when Mel spotted her. She could tell he wanted to leave, but she purposely turned toward him and locked stares with him.

He smiled, she smiled back.

"How was practice?" she asked, as she walked up on them.

"What? Oh yeah, practice was good. I didn't know you were working tonight."

"Shit happens, you know?"

"Hi, Quana," Pam interjected.

"What's up?"

Pam could hear the tenseness in her voice.

"What can I get you?" Quana asked.

"You can get us some menus," Pam said.

Quana cut her a wicked look. "Yeah, right, I'll be back."

Quana walked to the break room and sat on the bench. God, I can't believe this. Men ain't shit. That's why I've been by myself, just because of men like him.

"Laquana," Miss John yelled.

"Yes, I'll be out in a minute."

"We're getting backed up out here; you don't have time to be in that bathroom."

Quana clenched and unclenched her hands. Fuck him, she thought. He wasn't my man, anyway. He can see whoever he wants. She got herself together and headed back out.

"Can I take your order?" she asked the elderly couple.

"Excuse me," Pam said. "We're still waiting on those menus."

"I'm sorry; I'll be with you in a minute."

Pam sucked her teeth.

"Is there a problem?" Quana asked, as she stuck her pad and pen in her apron pocket.

Pam peeped the move and pushed her chair back a couple inches from the table. "You need to ask yourself that question."

Mel stood. "Quana can I talk to you for a second?"

"We have nothing to talk about."

"Please." She allowed him to lead her to the back. "I didn't mean any disrespect. If I would've known you were working tonight, I would've never brought Pam here."

"You're not disrespecting me, you're disrespecting yourself. You called me and canceled out because you said you had practice. You didn't have to lie to me. I'm not your girl."

"This thing with me and Pam has run its course. After tonight, I'm not messing with her anymore."

"And why are you telling me this?"

"We got something, Quana."

"We don't have anything, Mel."

He chuckled. "So, what are you saying?"

"I'm saying backup off me, and put your girl in check before I do." She tried to walk past him.

He shoved her against the wall and balled up his fists. "This is how you gonna treat me? I tried being nice to your ass, and you gonna just brush me off like some chump." Quana started to move. Mel put his finger in her face. "I'm fucking Jamel Jackson, bitch. You better recognize."

"Quana!" Miss John yelled. "I'm not telling you anymore."

"Can I please go, now?" Quana said.

Mel moved to the side and let her pass.

Quana tried not to look shaken up when she took the elderly couple's order.

"We're ready to order," Pam called out.

Quana stood in front of their table with her pad and pen in hand.

"Just get us two seafood platters and two tall glasses of iced tea," Mel said.

Quana wrote it down and walked off without a word. She could feel the tears of humiliation forming in her eyes, but she refused to let them fall. As she walked by a customer's table he grabbed her hand. That was her breaking point. She turned around and opened her mouth to take all of her frustration out on him.

"Seen any beautiful sunsets lately?"

Her heart stopped. Her tears fell, but they weren't tears of frustration. They were tears of joy. "Oh my God… oh my God…"

"Is that all you can say?" Devon asked.

"Oh my God. What are you doing here? And what happened to your dreads?"

"How long did you think I could be away from my heart?"

Quana touched the chain around her neck. "You risked everything to come here for your chain?"

Devon stood up. "No, I risked everything to come here for this." He leaned down and kissed her gently on the lips. Quana melted into his arms. When he pulled back, he wiped the tears from her face.

Quana felt the daggers hitting her in the back of her neck. She turned around and saw Miss John glaring at her. She looked toward Mel and Pam. They were clocking her as well.

"A diner, Quana?" Devon asked.

"A scholarship doesn't pay for everything."

"Take that apron off."

"I just can't leave. I don't get off for another three hours."

"You're done, now. My woman works for no one."

"Devon," Quana whispered. "I can't quit my job."

"Laquana," Miss John yelled out.

Quana closed her eyes and bit her tongue.

"You work for me, now," Devon said.

"Laquana," Miss John yelled out again.

Quana's eyes popped open. She untied her apron and walked toward Miss John. Devon couldn't hear everything Quana said, but he heard old and cunt. He smiled when Quana threw the apron at her and stormed back toward him.

"You ready?" he asked.

"In a minute." She grabbed a glass of water off the old couple's table and threw it in Mel's face. He jumped up. Devon looked him dead in the eyes and subtly shook his head. Mel could see fire and brimstone behind Devon's eyes. He tensed as Devon walked toward them.

When Pam realized Mel was going to let Quana get away with splashing him, she jumped up. Mel quickly grabbed her as Devon approached. Mel had no doubt in his mind that Pam could get it too.

Devon put his arm around Quana and dragged her away from Pam. Quana didn't stop calling Pam every curse word in the book until they got outside.

"When I see that bitch tomorrow—"

"Shh," Devon pulled her to him. "Damn, you look sexy when you get angry."

She pushed him away, but she couldn't stop the smile appearing on her face. "Now, I'm sexy? I wasn't sexy enough in a bathing suit feeding you strawberries?"

"That was three years ago, Quana. Things were different then."

"And what's so different now?"

They both turned toward the Lincoln Town Car when Knots whistled. Devon turned to see what Knots was looking at. Mel got a little heart when he realized three members of the football team were in the diner. They saw what had taken place and amped Mel up. They headed toward Devon. Quana squeezed his hand. "Let's go."

Devon looked at her. "In a minute."

"Yo, Homie, can I talk to you for a second?" Mel yelled out as they approached.

"Sure... Homie."

Quana jumped when she felt a calloused hand grab her by the elbow. Knots pulled her behind him and stood next to Devon.

Devon listened to Mel's boys getting him hyped as they walked toward him. Devon smiled.

Mel screwed his face up. "What's so funny?"

Devon stopped smiling. Mel stopped walking. He stood a little out of arm's reach.

"Check this out," Devon said. "Before this turns into something it doesn't have to, why don't you and your boys go back inside and finish your meal?"

"Why don't you suck my dick?" Mel said.

His boys got ready to laugh, but froze when Knots whipped out the biggest handgun anyone of them ever saw. He took aim at Mel and cocked the hammer. Mel's eyes nearly popped out of his head as he stared down the barrel.

Devon walked up to him. "Suck your dick? Now, I would be wrong if I made you get on your knees and suck my dick in front of your boys and little girlfriend back there, right?"

Mel turned around and saw Pam and a few other people standing in front of the diner. "I was just talking shit, Homie," Mel said.

"Devon," Quana called out from behind Knots.

"You not fucking my woman, are you?" Devon asked.

"No, hell no. We just met a few days ago. She didn't tell me she had a man."

"Yeah, once people know who I am and that she's my shorty, they tend to treat her differently. She wanted to be just like any other student here at Spellman, you know?"

"Yeah."

"From this night forward, my woman will be respected, and you're going to make sure of that, right?"

"Nobody's going to disrespect her, you got my word."

Devon shook Mel's hand and gave him a hug. Then whispered in his ear. "When people ask what happened, just let them know it was one big misunderstanding." Mel nodded. "Good, I'll be seeing you around, champ."

Mel did an about-face and headed back to the diner with his boys close behind. Knots put his gun away.

"You should be ashamed of yourself," Devon said to Knots. "You could've whipped them boys with your bare hands."

Knots nodded. "True, but I wasn't trying to whip 'em."

Quana looked on in shock.

Devon took her by the hand. "Let's get out of here." He led her to the backseat of the town car. Knots climbed in the front and pulled off.

"Where are we going?" Quana asked.

"To the crib," Devon replied.

"To the crib?"

"To the crib."

* * *

Knots pulled up to the iron gates of the 26,000 square foot mansion. He pushed a button on the visor and the gates started to open. Quana looked at Devon.

"A lot of things have happened since we last saw each other," he said.

"I can see that." She eyed his two-piece suit and shiny bald head. "I still can't believe you're here. And what's all this?" She asked pointing to the mansion.

"I'm just stunting, right now. This place and the car belong to an investor friend of mine. He's letting me use the place for a few days."

"A few days?"

"You know I can't stay long."

Knots pulled up to the front door, and let Devon and Quana out. Devon unlocked the front door and allowed Quana to go in first.

"Whoa, this is really nice."

"This is nothing compared to where I live in London."

Quana spun around. "London?"

"Follow me." He led her to the den and sat down with her on the plush sofa. He laced his fingers in between hers and looked her in the eyes. "Before you even ask, I want to tell you everything. I don't ever want to keep anything from you again." He told her about Dane, Rippa, and Stripes's executions, the story of Ginja escaping certain death, and the showdown with Irons.

"My God," was all Quana could say.

He then went into the Dillard and Sterling arrangement and then from there, how he started Khufu Incorporated.

"Khufu? Wasn't he a king of Egypt and a pyramid builder?"

Devon nodded. "I'm impressed."

"Don't be. I only remembered that, because I helped my roommate put together a paper on ancient Egypt and the pyramids."

"That stops tonight," Devon said squeezing her hands.

"What stops?"

"You selling yourself short. You believing that you're not as pretty as the next girl, or that you have to jump on any man who shows you a little attention."

She dropped her head. "Back at the diner you said my woman works for no one."

"Look at me." Quana picked her head up. "You are the only woman, outside of my grandmother I *ever* trusted." He looked at his chain around her neck. "I gave you my chain for a reason."

"It's your heart."

"Not anymore. You're my heart, now." He kissed her. Their tongues danced, timid at first, but then they connected like two magnets.

Quana gently pulled away. "I'm going to take your advice."

"What's that?"

"I'm not going to jump on you just because you're showing me a little attention," she said jokingly.

"Woman, don't play with me," he said laying her back on the couch and climbing on top of her. "I flew half way across the globe; put my freedom on the line just to finish what we started in the hot tub three years ago."

"We're not in a hot tub."

Devon got off of her and pulled her up from the sofa. "I can fix that," he said, leading her to the hot tub in the master bathroom.

* * *

The next morning, Quana stirred as she felt Devon covering her face with feather soft kisses. She smiled as she opened her eyes.

"Good morning," he whispered.

"Good morning," she whispered back.

"How you feeling?"

"Satisfied."

"Hungry?" Devon asked.

"A little."

"Knots cooked us some breakfast."

"What kind of name is Knots?"

"One that you don't' want to know the reason for."

"Is he your bodyguard?"

"Something like that."

Quana caressed his face and stared into his eyes. She didn't have to say anything. Devon could read the affection in her eyes.

"We have a busy day ahead of us. So, you need to get up, take a shower, and come on downstairs to eat."

"A busy day? What are we doing?"

Devon got off the bed and started walking to the door.

"Devon, you know I don't like surprises."

"We're going shopping."

* * *

By midday, the trunk of the town car was filled with shopping bags and shoe boxes. Quana allowed Devon to only buy her two pieces of jewelry after seeing the nine thousand dollar receipt for the diamond necklace and earring set.

"Where is Knots taking us to, now?" she asked, as she laid her head on his shoulder in the backseat of the car.

"We're here," Devon said, as Knots pulled into the car dealership.

"Oh, no" Quana said, shaking her head.

"My woman doesn't walk or take public transportation, any more."

"You're doing too much for me."

"This is just the beginning."

They exited the car and walked into the showroom.

"Can I help you?" one of the salesmen asked as he approached them.

Knots stepped up. "I'm Mr. Byrd, from Khufu Inc."

"Ah, yes, Mr. Byrd, we've been expecting you. If you'll just follow me, we can start the paperwork."

"You already have one picked out for me?" Quana asked.

"I can't do all the work, now. I just called ahead so we could expedite the paperwork. You got to pick out your own car."

Quana hugged him and then walked down the aisle of Audis. She stopped at a black and silver Cabriolet convertible. She opened the door and got in.

"You like it?" Devon asked.

"I love it!" Quana exclaimed.

Devon got Knot's attention and pointed at the car. Knots nodded. It was a done deal.

Chapter 12

After a two hour sex marathon, Devon stroked Quana's hair as she rested her head on his chest. She moaned and snuggled closer to him.

"You're spoiling me," she said. "What am I going to do when you fly back to London?"

"You're going to keep doing what you're doing."

"Nah, I'm flying back with you."

"I wish it was that easy."

"It is."

"Nah, you're going to stay here and get your education. Then you're going to work for a real estate agency in New York."

Quana lifted her head. "What are you talking about?"

"I'm talking about your future. I have the wealth and the connections to make sure you'll never need for anything, ever. My future, on the other hand, is limited. I'm constantly looking over my shoulder, expecting for some task force to arrest me and bring me back to New York."

"You got wealth and you got connections, you can buy a team of lawyers that will give you a fighting chance."

"I'd rather take my chances lying low, or as Knots says, 'hiding in plain sight'."

"But what about us?" Quana wanted to know.

"Right now, it's about you. Anything can happen to me at anytime. If so, I want to go out knowing that you're straight. If you're situated, Brian and my grandmother will be taken care of."

"I don't like the way you're talking, Devon"

"I'm talking reality. And you know that."

"I still don't like it."

"You only got two more years to do. Switch your major to Business. Don't worry about that scholarship or money for that matter, I'm paying for everything. Once, you graduate, the real estate company in New York is going to take you on and school you. Once you're confident enough to take the next step, we'll take it together."

"What's the next step?"

"You're going to be the American Representative for Khu-fu Inc."

"Meaning?"

"Meaning, you will purchase and oversee all businesses and properties we buy here in the U.S."

"Your company is making power moves like that?"

"Like that."

"And you need me for this to happen?"

"You know I do. I wouldn't trust anyone else to do this."

Quana climbed on top of him and eased his semi-hard erection into her. "Being that you *need* me, it seems like I can lay down some demands."

"Is that right?"

"That's right."

"What do you demand of me?"

"First," she said, beginning to ride him. "I want, no, I demand to see you at least once a month."

"Not a problem," Devon moaned as he became fully erect.

"And it has to be in the country of my choosing." She dangled her breasts in his face.

"Not a problem." He began sucking on her nipples.

"And last but not lease, *this*," she said, taking his whole shaft inside her. "Is for my pleasure only."

"That definitely won't be a problem."

* * *

Cindy lay in her bed with the blankets pulled over her and watched Quana while she packed her last suitcase.

Quana zipped it up and plopped down on her bed with a sigh. "What?" Cindy was still staring at her.

"I'm hating on you right now," she pouted.

"You need to stop."

"Month before last, you spent the weekend in Canada, last month you spent the weekend in Puerto Rico, and this month you're spending the three day weekend in Africa. Africa, Quana. How many times have you heard me talk about going to Africa one day to see the pyramids, the Nile River, and the Sphinx?"

"Too many times."

"I would kill to have a man like yours. All this time we were roommates and you never talked about him."

"Our relationship wasn't that serious."

"Wasn't that serious? He came to town and brought you clothes, jewelry, shoes, and a car. All in the same day. And you no longer have to work at the diner because he takes care of your every need. And let's not forget that night at the diner when he pulled a gun out on Mel, and put his ass in check."

"He didn't pull a gun out on Mel. His bodyguard did."

"And that's another thing. A bodyguard? Only real important people have bodyguards."

"He's not that important."

"Let you tell it."

Quana's phone rang. "Hi, baby."

Cindy pulled the covers over her head.

"You all packed?" Devon asked.

"Yes, I'm all ready to go. Where are you?"

"I'm still in London. I should be in the air within the hour."

"Sweetheart, baby."

"What's up?"

"I was wondering. Would it be too much trouble if I wanted to bring Cindy along?"

Cindy whipped the covers off of her head and sat up.

"Umm, no, all I would have to do is send word to the pilot that he will have two passengers instead of one, but why would I do that?"

"Because she's my best friend and she's been dying to go to Egypt her whole life."

"Umm, no."

"Because you love me?"

"Umm, no."

Quana turned away from Cindy and whispered into the phone. "Because I'll wear the outfit."

"What outfit."

Quana continued to whisper. "Stop playing, you know which one."

Devon had been trying to get her to wear the red thigh-high boots and thong bikini he brought for her when they were in Puerto Rico. Even though he only wanted her to wear it around the house, she was still too shy to put something like that on.

"I'll have my secretary make that call."

"I love you, baby," Quana said. She gave Cindy the thumbs up.

Devon had to pull the phone away from his ear. Cindy grabbed it from Quana and was screaming how grateful she was for the last minute invitation.

"It's my pleasure," Devon was able to finally say. "Can you put Quana back on?"

"Yes, sure, I have to go pack. Bye."

Devon met Cindy twice, both times, she peaked his interest with her extraordinary ability to retain facts and figures in that pretty head of hers. Quana joked about her being a walking encyclopedia. He could use a mind like that in the States.

* * *

The trip to Africa was well worth Devon's time. He got to spend quality time with Quana, and he got a chance to get inside of Cindy's mind. Devon came to find out that not only was she a walking encyclopedia, but she was also a charismatic speaker. Devon watched the chemistry between her and Quana. They were a perfect match. The most entertaining part of the weekend for Devon was when Cindy corrected their tour guide a few times about his historical facts. She got on his nerves so much that he asked her if she wanted to take over. Not being one to back down, she stepped up and humbled him. There was definitely going to be a spot for her on his team after she graduated.

On their last night, Devon and Quana decided to spend it outside on the screened-in porch. They sat on the swinging bench and held each other as they stared at the star-studded sky.

"I'm not going to see you for a whole month," Quana said as she laid her head on his shoulder.

"I know, but look on the bright side. Next month you got a whole week off from school, so we can spend a week together instead of just a weekend. Have you decided where you want to go?"

"Yes. I want to come to London. I want to see how the big boss player runs his corporation."

"London, interesting. I think we can do that." He made a mental note to have a looong talk with Ginja.

"I have some good news for you," Quana said.

"You waited until now to tell me?"

"It's about, Brian. I know how you get depressed when we talk about him. I didn't want to ruin our three day weekend."

"What's up with him?"

"He's in Green Haven Correctional Facility and he's chilling. No more fights, no more going back and forth to the box, and he finally hit Sonia with the divorce papers."

"That is good news.

"Remember a girl named Arlene?"

Devon nodded. "The girl in the park."

"She was visiting a friend at Green Haven—"

"Get the fuck out of here. Don't tell me her and Brian hooked up."

"How about they're getting married?"

"Now, that's what I call true love. She knows that he ain't got nothing but time, yet she's willing to stick by his side."

"When I went to see him, he was telling me about this old guy who took a liking to him. He said the old guy got him on the boxing team and is keeping him in check."

"Boxing?" Devon started to laugh.

Quana squeezed his hand. "He asked about you again."

"What did you tell him?"

"I told him what you told me to tell him. That I haven't seen or heard anything from you. God, I hate lying to him, Devon. And you know I'm not a good liar. I think he knows I'm hiding something, but he doesn't push it."

"I'm sorry for putting you in that predicament, but he can't know about me, about us."

"Why not?"

"I want to be the one to tell him."

"And how are you going to do that?"

"When I get him out of there."

Quana stiffened.

"The less he knows about me and what I'm doing, the easier it will be for me to do what I have to do to get him out."

"Okay, let's talk about something else, you're stressing me out."

"Let's talk about how you had me harder than steel when you put on that bikini and thigh-high boots."

"I can't believe you made me wear that."

"I knew you were going to look sexy in it. It made you feel sexy, didn't it?"

Quana blushed.

"Tell the truth."

She nodded.

"I can't wait to see you in that bikini when we hit the white sands of Jamaica this summer."

Quana pinched his arm. "You playing yourself, now. You know that's never going to happen." She sighed and kissed him on the neck. "So, did my friend pass the test?"

"Huh?"

"Don't 'huh' me. I got you down to a science. Everything you do, you do with a purpose. You were picking her brain the whole weekend."

Devon smiled.

"I knew you were up to something."

"Relax," Devon said, putting her head back on his shoulder. "We leave in the morning. So, let's enjoy our last night here gazing at the stars, or…"

"Or?"

"Or I can gaze at you in that bikini."

"Shut up and look at the stars."

* * *

Devon sat in his office, leafing through the monthly report Ivory put together. The monthly profits spiked a whopping sixty percent. David called with a deal on a boutique in France. Devon was elated. This was going to be their third boutique and it was on one of the busiest streets in Marseilles. He closed the portfolio and called Ginja. "I need to see you," he said when she answered her phone.

Ten minutes later, she knocked on his door.

"Come in."

"What's up?"

"You hungry?"

"If you're paying."

Devon stood up and put his suit jacket on. "Let's go get something to eat."

As they entered the posh café, the Maitre d' got the attention of one of the waiters and sent him scurrying off to prepare Devon's regular table.

"Mr. Cartier, it's a pleasure to see you," he said to Devon. "And it is a pleasure to see you as well, Miss. Smith."

Devon and Ginja both nodded, as they headed to their table. Ginja arched her eyebrow when Devon pulled her chair out. She jumped when he kissed her on the side of her neck.

"What's wrong with you?" she asked.

"I can't kiss you on the neck?"

"You know the rule."

"That's your rule."

"Whatever, just don't do it again."

"Let me get this straight, I can fuck you whenever I want, but I can't kiss you?"

"Correct."

"So, how are you doing?" Devon changed the subject.

"How was your trip to Africa?"

"It was beautiful, but let's not change the subject. How are you?"

"I'm good."

"Are you ready to order?" the waiter asked.

"Yes, I'll have the chicken salad," Ginja said.

"And I'll have a roast beef sandwich without onions," Devon said. The waiter bowed and left. "Quana wants to come to London next month." Devon watched Ginja's reaction. There was none.

"Okay, what do you need me to do?"

"I need you to stop acting like a fucking robot and tell me how you feel about it."

"I don't feel anyway about it."

"How do you feel about me and Quana as a couple?"

"I don't see how my feelings have anything to do with you and Quana's relationship."

"Your feelings have a lot to do with *our* relationship," Devon said, pointing back and forth between them.

"We don't have a relationship."

"We've been intimate for years, Ginja, what do you call that?"

"An arrangement."

"Arrangement?" Devon leaned back and folded his hands. "I want you to look me in the eye and tell me you don't have feelings for me."

"I have feelings for you, Devon. I mean, if you were to die tomorrow, I would be sad."

"You are unbelievable."

"What do you want me to say? I'm trying to be honest with you. That's what you want, right? That's what this whole conversation is about. You don't want Quana coming here and sensing that something is going on between us. I'm surprised you didn't think of sending me away when she comes."

"You know, this is going to sound funny, but David called me today and told me that he has a boutique for me in Nice. And I was going to send you and Ivory to go close the deal."

"And when is this supposed to take place?"

"Sometime next month."

"Whatever, Devon."

The waiter brought their food. They ate in silence.

Ginja finished her chicken salad and dabbed the corners of her mouth with her napkin. "So, if I was to die tomorrow, would you be sad?"

"Keep fucking with me and you'll die today."

Ginja cracked a smile. "You really feeling me, huh?"

"Nope," Devon said, taking a sip of his drink.

"You must've forgot, I know you better than you know yourself. You're not worried about Quana sensing that I have feelings for you. You're worried about her sensing that you have feelings for me."

"You are absolutely, one hundred percent, wrong. And you sound crazy for even saying some stupid shit like that."

Ginja reached across the table and placed her hands on top of his. "Feelings are only good for one thing. Remember telling me that?" Devon didn't answer. "Feelings are only good for one thing, getting you killed."

"I was wrong."

"No, you weren't. The Devon I used to know trusted no one, especially a female. The Devon I knew would've never gone back to the States, especially for a female. Can't you see what your feelings are doing to you? You're risking everything—"

"For a female."

"No, for love. Believe me there's no such thing."

"And what makes you an expert on feelings and love?"

Ginja pulled her hands back. "You're right. What do I know?"

There! In that tenth of a second, he saw it. A clinck in her armor. The way her body sagged and her eyes looked down and to the right. An image from her past came to mind. Before Devon could blink, she caught herself and straightened up.

"Okay, Mister Softie, I'm ready to go."

Devon pulled out his Black card and signed the bill. He held them both up for the waiter to come and get them.

"Did you sign Cartier or Carter?" Ginja asked.

"Oh shit." Devon pulled his pen back out and squeezed an i in between the t and the e. "It's hard getting used to the new last name."

"What would you do without me?" Ginja said.

* * *

Devon swore it was a coincidence, but while Ginja and Ivory were on their way to the airport, Quana was on her way from the airport. They spent the first two days inside the brownstone. The last five, Devon took Quana for a scenic tour around London. What would leave a lasting impression on her though was Recker and the General. They both kept her laughing. Recker with his "weed is the answer to everything" philosophy, and the General with his thousand and one stories. Any topic they talked about reminded him of a war story. And he started everyone off with, "Me know y'all never heard this one." Of course Recker and Devon heard them all. The General told them to be quiet, because he knew Quana never heard it before.

He was a great story teller, Quana gave him that. And if he did half of the things he said he did, then he was a very dangerous man.

Every month like clockwork, Devon hooked up with Quana and they spent their weekends strengthening their bond. Before either of them knew it, she and Cindy were graduating, with honors.

Quana and Cindy moved to New York and started working for the real estate firm that Devon had ties with. A year later, Quana was the representative for Khufu Inc. and Cindy was her CEO. As Devon sat back and watched everything fall into place, the famous words from one of his favorite TV show characters came to mind. "I love it when a plan comes together."

Chapter 13

Quana met Devon at JFK airport. She hugged him stiffly and started heading to the car.

Devon grabbed her by the arm. "Hey, slow down. That's all I get after not seeing me all month?"

"I don't like this at all. Let's just get to the car and get out of here."

"Everything's going to be fine," Devon said, as he got into the car. "It's been seven and a half years since I've been back here."

"There's no statute of limitations for murder."

"Stop stressing, woman, please."

"I can't, and I won't until you're back on that plane. For the first time I can honestly say I can't wait for our weekend together to be over."

"It's good to see you, too."

Quana sighed. "You know I don't mean it like that."

"Yeah, whatever."

"I just... we've come so far, I can't afford to lose you."

"And you're not." He leaned over and kissed her on the cheek. "I can't wait to see your flat."

"Excuse, me, Mr. London. We're in America. We don't call our residences flats. We call them apartments or in my case penthouses."

"Well, I can't wait to see your penthouse, and it better be fly."

"Cindy's penthouse is fly. Mine, is sick."

Quana pulled into the building's underground garage. Devon eyed the cars and SUV's, none of them cost under fifty thousand. Quana pulled into her parking spot, which was next to the elevator.

"How'd you manage to get this spot?"

"I negotiated. That's what I do remember?"

When they got on the elevator, she stuck her key into the penthouse keyhole on the panel and turned it to the right. The top floor light lit up. Devon nodded.

The elevator opened up into a carpeted hallway. As soon as Quana stepped off, she took her shoes off and then her jacket. Devon followed her into the living room.

"You like?" she asked.

He took in the hardwood floors, the plush furniture, and the paintings on the walls. "You did good."

She took him through the state-of-the-art kitchen and up a spiral staircase. She led him into the master bedroom and stepped to the side.

"This is nice," he said.

She showed him the rest of the rooms and then she took him out onto the terrace and showed him its panoramic view. "This place isn't too small, is it?"

"Are you kidding? This place is huge."

"Good, because you're not leaving it."

Devon walked around her and hugged her from behind. "You're not going to take me to your office?"

"My office is the room across from the study."

"You can show me all your records from there?"

"I didn't know this was an audit, Mr. Carter, I mean, Mr. Cartier."

"So, what you're telling me is I'm under house arrest?"

"Call it what you want."

"You're serious, aren't you?"

She turned to face him and put her hands on her hips. "I'm dead serious."

"You better lose that attitude."

"I'm gonna have this attitude until you understand that you're not leaving this penthouse."

"I think you better lose it now."

"And why's that?"

"It's turning me on. As a matter of fact, just seeing you in that pantsuit and glasses with your hair in a bun is turning me on."

Quana softened.

"I know your male employees are always trying to holler at you, don't they?"

Quana put her head down.

Devon palmed her butt and pulled her close. "I bet they fantasize of doing what I'm doing right now." He kissed her on the neck and squeezed her butt. "You ain't letting one of them dude's tap mines right?" He slid his hand into the front of her pants. Quana moaned as he touched her most sensitive spot.

"And why would I do that?" she whispered.

"Maybe I'm not hitting it right." He sucked on her neck.

"Umm, you are hitting it just fine."

"I'm the man, right?"

"Yes, you are the man."

"I call the shots, right?"

Quana pulled his hand out of her pants. "You may be the shot caller with everyone else, but as long as you're in New York, I'm calling the shots. And I say you're not leaving this penthouse. Am I making myself clear?"

"Okay, okay. You're fucking up the mood."

"You fucked up the mood, trying to run that weak-ass game on me just now."

"There you go again with that attitude. You know it's turning me on. Come here." He grabbed her by the waist. "I promise you, I will not leave this penthouse."

Quana stared at him.

"I promise. Now you got to do something for me."

"What?"

Devon pulled his pants down and sat on a hardwood chair. "I want you to keep on the top half of your suit and your glasses, and come over here and sit on this chair."

"There's not enough room on it for me."

"I think I can find a spot on it for you to sit on," he said, pulling his rock hard beef out of his boxers.

Quana looked like a crackhead staring at a crack pipe. She ran her tongue over her lips and then pulled her pants down. She was going to ride that wagon until the wheels fell off.

* * *

Devon and Quana christened every room in the penthouse with their insatiable love making. After showering, Devon headed to the kitchen and began cooking dinner. Quana sat in the study in her robe, checking her e-mails. She finally shut her computer down and headed to the kitchen. She stood at the threshold of the kitchen watching Devon pull the steak out of the oven and check it. "Isn't it a violation of some health code for the cook to be cooking in just a pair of boxers?"

He grabbed the apron off the hook and put it on. "Better?"

"You're crazy."

The kitchen phone rang.

Devon looked at Quana. "Can I answer it?"

"Go ahead, I have nothing to hide."

"You better not." He picked up. "Hello?"

"This is MCI; you have a collect call from... Brian Moore an inmate at..." Devon's mouth fell open.

"What's wrong?" Quana asked. "Devon!"

He jumped and passed her the phone. She grabbed it.

"… If you wish to accept the call, press three now." Quana pressed three.

"Thank you for using MCI."

"Quana, what's up?"

"Hey, I was beginning to worry about you. I haven't heard from you in a couple weeks."

"Who was that nigga that just answered the phone?"

Quana looked at Devon. "That was my man." Devon stopped breathing.

"Put him on the phone."

"No, I'm not putting him on the phone. You called to talk to me, right?"

"Yeah, shit's been kinda hectic here. Remember the Shaykh I was telling you about?"

"The old man?"

"Yeah, he died."

"Oh my God!"

"What?" Devon whispered.

"He had a heart attack," Brian said.

"I'm sorry to hear that. I know how close you two were."

"Yeah, he kept it official, no doubt. I also called to tell you that he and the Muslim leader here named Ali put together a brief for me and this shit is high-powered. I'm definitely coming back down on appeal with this, word."

"That's good news."

"Yeah, when the judge reads this, he's going to have no choice but to vacate the sentence."

"Do you need me to get you a lawyer?"

"Nah, no more lawyers. I got this."

"Are you sure?"

"I work in the law library, remember? I got my paralegal certificate."

"I'm coming to see you this Saturday."

"Yeah. You didn't ask me about my family reunion visit."

"Oh, yeah, Arlene did come up last week didn't she? So how was it?"

"It was beautiful. I fell in love with her all over again."

"I'm so happy for you."

"I think this is it, Quana. I'm coming home, I can feel it."

"I hope you're right."

Brian got quiet.

"What's wrong?" Quana asked.

"Nah, I was thinking. The *only* thing that would stop the judge from throwing the case out is if the DA can get Jason to testify."

Quana gripped the phone and closed her eyes.

"What?" Devon whispered.

"He didn't testify before, let's just pray he doesn't this time," Quana said.

"That fucking rat motherfucker. I swear, if I didn't promise my wife…"

"Don't worry about him, Brian; focus on how you're going to represent yourself."

"Yeah, you right. Devon still didn't contact you yet?"

Quana put her head down. "No."

"Damn, I figured he would've got at you by now."

"He still sends you postcards, right?"

"Yeah, but I just thought… fuck it. I know once I get out there, he'll know and he'll find me."

"I know he will."

"I got to go, I got to call wifey."

"Okay, don't forget, I'll be there Saturday."

"I love you, Quana."

"I love you, too."

"Yeah, and let that nigga know he better treat you right, cause I'm coming home."

"Bye, Brian." Quana hung up. Devon had broken out in a cold sweat. "You okay?"

"No, I'm not okay. That was my boy. Everything I am today I owe to him. I wanted to snatch the phone from you so bad."

"Why didn't you? Why can't you talk to him?"

"Those phone calls are being recorded. I can't risk the staff knowing or suspecting. How is he?"

"He said the old man who took him under his wing died of a heart attack."

"Umm, I'm sorry to hear that."

"He also said he's coming home."

"Stop playing."

Quana couldn't stop smiling. "That's what he said. He said the old man put a brief together that's going to force the judge to dismiss the case."

Devon hugged her. "Get on the phone and get him the best lawyer in—"

"He said he didn't want a lawyer."

"What? No, he needs a lawyer."

"He said he didn't want one."

"I don't care what he said. Get him one anyway."

"It's obvious you forgot who we're talking about here. If Brian walks into the courtroom and sees a lawyer, what do you think he's going to do?"

Devon rubbed his bald head. "There has to be something I can do to make sure he beats this."

"There is."

"What?"

"He said the only way he wouldn't be able to beat this is if the DA gets Jason to take the stand."

Devon balled up his fists. "Say no more."

* * *

Monday morning, Devon was up bright and early as usual. Quana turned over and looked at him. He was staring out the window at the sunrise.

"Where are you, right now?" she asked.

"Jamaica. Me, you, Brian, and the girl from the park."

"You mean his wife, Arlene."

He smiled. "Yeah, Arlene. There's no doubt in my mind that they're made for each other."

"Why do you say that?"

"She's from Albany, he's from Queens, she's a good girl, and Brian is a bad boy."

"Was a bad boy," Quana said.

"On the surface, they're the total opposite. Then she just happens to stumble upon him while visiting a friend in Green Haven? That's crazy."

"How's this for crazy, I'm a good girl, you're a rude boy, you trust no one, I trusted everyone. On the surface, we're the total opposite."

Devon walked to the bed and kneeled down. He pulled back the strands of hair that hung in front of her face. "So we're like them in every way, except…"

"Except?"

"Except we're not married."

Quana sat up and looked him in the eyes. "What are you trying to say, Devon?"

"When my boy comes home, he's going to be my best man at our wedding."

Quana threw her arms around him. "I love you."

"I love you, too." Devon's mind flashed back to the conversation him and Ginja had in the café. What did she know about love, anyway?

* * *

Recker was at the airport waiting for Devon. Recker saw him and waved him over. As Devon got to the car, Recker jumped in and started it up.

"Damn, Cuz, no welcome back hug?" Devon asked.

"We don't have time for that."

"What's up?"

"I think I fucked up."

"Fucked up? You lounge around all day and smoke weed. How can you fuck up?"

"I killed Dillard and Sterling."

"You wha… stop the car. Stop the fucking car."

Recker skidded to a halt. Devon got out and walked around in circles holding his head.

"They came to the brownstone and—"

"You killed them in the brownstone?"

"Shit got crazy—"

Devon pointed at him. "Don't you say another mother-fucking word." He sat on the curb. A few minutes later, he looked up at Recker. "Where was Grim?"

"He wasn't there?"

"They go nowhere without him."

"He was the reason why they came to the brownstone in the first place."

Devon stood up. "Let's get the hell out of here."

On their way home, Devon contacted everyone on the team and told them to be in his office in fifteen minutes. When he and Recker arrived, he walked straight to his office and sat down. He looked at everyone and shook his head. "I was gone for two days. Just two days."

"And you left me in charge," Recker said. "I made a judgment call."

"A judgment call? You killed two people in our place of business. What the hell happened?"

Recker began. "As soon as you left for the States, they were calling all the lines off the hook demanding to speak to you or be put through to you. They got tired of Mary putting them off so they took the next flight here."

"What was so important?"

"They said every month Grim kept demanding more and more money for his crew's service. Finally, when they grew some balls and told him they weren't giving him another penny, Grim flipped on them. He started robbing the spots they were paid to protect."

"How did that conversation cause you to kill them?"

"I'm telling you the story in a calm manner. They were screaming and shouting. They demanded that you do something about Grim, being that it was you who recommended him. You know I was calm throughout the whole ordeal because I just finished smoking a big ass spliff."

"Fast forward to how the gun got in your hand."

"I told them that you were out of town and you would deal with it when you got back. They said that wasn't good enough. Then Sterling said, I better get you on the phone right now or else."

"Or else what?"

"They knew about your situation in the States."

"Impossible!"

"Once they said that, it blew my high. That's when I got pissed off. They couldn't live after that."

"No," Devon said standing up. "There's no way they could know. No one outside of this room knew."

"You mean outside of us and Unc."

"Clifford? Why would he tell them?"

"It seems that we had more in common with Dillard and Sterling than we knew. They used him to smuggle the forty bricks of coke into Amsterdam."

"I can't believe he gave me up."

"He didn't. After I put two in Sterling's melon, I gave Dillard my word that I would let him live if he told me how they came across that information. He said Sterling was boning one of Clifford's secretaries."

"Fredricka," Devon said.

Recker nodded. "He said she didn't know exactly what you did, but you had to get out of the States in a hurry."

"She needs to be dealt with," Ginja said.

"I agree," Ivory responded.

"General, you think you can scare her into keeping her mouth shut?" Devon asked.

"Me don't know. She may keep quiet or she might run to de' police."

"There's only one way to deal with her," Ginja said.

Devon put his head down.

"Devon—"

"I heard you!"

"Ivory and I can take care of it."

"No," Devon said picking up his phone. "Put him on the phone," Devon said into the receiver.

"And what do I owe this pleasure?" Grim asked.

"Dillard and Sterling."

"I know them two bitches didn't come crying to you."

"You know they did."

"So, this is what this call is about? They want you to talk to me?"

"I want to talk to you, but it's not on their behalf. What was theirs is now yours."

Grim was quiet for a moment. "I know they're not trying to hear that."

"Dead men don't hear."

Grim got quiet again.

"I'm flying out to see you tomorrow. You cool with that?" Devon asked.

"You know where to find me."

Devon hung up. "We're flying out tomorrow. General, call our people in Amsterdam, tell them to pull out the big guns."

The General nodded.

"Everybody out except you Recker."

"What about Fredricka?" Ginja asked.

"She'll be taken care of."

When everybody left, Recker closed the door.

Devon walked toward him. "You know if it was anybody else, they would be dead, right now. We were planning on taking their spots over, now I have to give them to Grim."

"You don't have to give him shit."

"If I don't, how do you propose we get Villainy out of Amsterdam?"

"You should've killed that motherfucker in the caves."

"By letting him live, Villainy became our unofficial muscle in Jamaica, Amsterdam, and in New York. What did you accomplish by killing Dillard and Sterling?"

"I wasn't thinking."

"And that's the type of shit that we can't afford. You always have to be thinking."

"So, what is giving Grim their businesses going to accomplish?"

"It's going to keep things between us stable. We will still acquire Dillard and Sterling's properties; it's just going to take us a little longer. Grim doesn't know the first thing about business. It will only be a matter of time before he runs them into the ground." Devon grabbed him by the back of his head. "Think Cuz. I know that weed hasn't fried all your brain cells."

"That was my bad, Cuz. You know how my temper is."

"Yeah, that's why I should've left Ginja in charge."

* * *

The bouncer removed the rope and let Devon and Knots into the club. Devon looked around. The club hadn't changed a bit. A dread made a beeline toward them. He led them to the elevator.

When the elevator doors closed, he spoke. "Y'all packing?"

"We're not, but my army on the top floor is."

The dread chuckled. "The top floor, huh?" When the doors opened, the smile fell off his face. The General, Porter, and Ginja were standing in the corridor, automatic weapons held at their sides.

Devon smiled at the dread.

"How did they get up here without triggering the alarms, and not being seen by the cameras?" the baffled dread asked.

Knots grabbed the dread by his collar and pulled him out of the elevator.

"How many in the office?" Devon asked the General.

"He confirmed four. Two men in de' back room, Grim and a woman on the couch." The *he*, he was referring to was Warren. He was the one who disabled the alarm system and he was the one who was using the cameras to pinpoint where Grim's men were posted. There were hidden cameras in the office Devon had installed so he could spy on Dillard and Sterling. Now, Warren was using them to identify who was in the office and where.

Devon looked at Ginja and Porter. "Let's go." The General and Knots posted up in the corridor, and made the dread sit on his hands against the wall.

Devon knocked.

"Come in," Grim said. He jumped off the couch and started buttoning up his shirt when Devon walked in. The female didn't bother buttoning up hers. She just crossed her legs and stared at Devon. "How the hell did you get up here—"

"We used to run this spot, remember?" Devon winked.

Grim watched Ginja and Porter as they walked in. The female's eyes widened when she saw the guns at their sides.

"Is that necessary?" Grim asked.

"I don't know, is it?"

"I thought you came to talk."

"Anybody in the back room?"

"No."

Devon shook his head. "And I was just beginning to trust you. Tell the two goons to come out here so we can get this over with."

Grim looked toward the room and then back to Devon. "How did you—"

"We're wasting time."

"Aye, yo, come to the front."

The two men walked out with their guns in hand.

Grim waved at them. "Put those away." The men obeyed. Devon looked at Ginja and Porter. They put their guns away.

"So, talk," Grim said.

"Not with them in the room."

Grim looked at his men and the woman. "I trust them."

"I don't. They can go out in the hallway and keep their man out there company."

Grim scratched his head. "Wait outside." The men and female walked out.

"Okay," Grim said.

"Dillard and Sterling are out of the picture."

"So, is this the part where I'm supposed to thank you?"

Devon smiled. "Leave," he said to Ginja and Porter. Ginja stared at him, but she turned with Porter and left. When they closed the door, Devon spoke. It's just me and you now, Grim."

"And?"

"And you can drop the tough guy act."

Grim snorted.

"I made you the leader of Villainy, I put you on to this gig, and now I'm handing it over to you."

"And I'm still wondering why."

"The why is simple. One hand washes the other."

"You washed up Irons, Dillard, and Sterling for me, so, who I got to wash up for you?"

Devon dug in his pocket and handed Grim a piece of paper with Fredricka's name and information. "Just scare her into not talking about business that doesn't concern her."

Grim nodded.

Devon handed him another piece of paper with Jason's name and the facility he was in. "He needs to be washed up."

Grim looked at Devon for a second and then nodded.

Devon turned to leave. "Call me when it's done."

Devon and the team exited the club with no resistance. Ivory pulled up in the all black SUV.

"How did you make out?" Devon asked her.

"It's all in the glove compartment," she said.

Devon opened the glove compartment and stacks of cash were neatly stacked inside. "What's this?" Devon asked, pulling out the gold chains and diamond rings.

"Pimp daddy hasn't sent us a penny like he agreed to. So, he had to come up off of everything."

Devon looked closer into the glove compartment and saw the platinum and diamond grill.

"Damn, Ivory. You even took his fronts?"

"Like I said, he had to come up off everything. His leather jacket and a mink his girl was wearing are in the back."

Devon shook his head. "Remind me to never owe you."

* * *

Three weeks later, at nine thirty in the morning, Devon's phone rang. He rubbed his eyes and answered it. "Hello." Quana was crying. He cleared his throat. "Quana what's wrong?"

"I'm outside the courthouse."

Devon sat up. "What happened?"

"The judge is dismissing the case," she shouted.

"Don't play with me, Quana."

"I'm serious. I spoke with the court appointed lawyer and he said when the judge comes back from recess, he's dismissing the case due to procedural errors and a lack of evidence."

"What happened to the DA's star witness?"

"He was stabbed to death in the prison yard," Quana said with no remorse.

"My boy is coming home? He needs a ride and some money and some clothes and—"

"Slow down, speedy. I'm way ahead of you."

"Damn, I can't believe it."

"What I can't believe is where you're at. What the hell are you doing in Iceland?"

"Business, what else?"

"Are there any black people there?"

"Of course there is. We're everywhere."

"Hmm, maybe our next rendezvous should be in Iceland."

"That's a thought."

"I got to go," Quana said. "I want to be in the courtroom before the judge gets back. I love you."

"I love you, too." When Devon lay back down, Ginja put her head back on his chest.

"I'm finally going to get to meet the legendary Brian Moore, huh?"

"It sure looks like it." Devon couldn't stop smiling. He jumped up.

"Where are you going? Come back to bed."

"I got to go pick up a postcard."

"You can get that at the airport on our way back home."

"Nah, I'm going to get it now. Start packing our things. We're flying back today. I got things to do before my boy comes home."

* * *

"It's taken care of," Quana said to Devon over the phone.

"What color is it?"

"The Escalade is black with gold trimming."

"Did you get the postcard?"

"Yes, Devon."

"And the bank account?"

"Seventy five thousand in the account like you said."

"How about——"

"Devon! Stop it! I got this. You don't ride me this hard when I'm closing on a million dollar deal."

"I'm sorry. I just want everything to be perfect."

"And I will make sure it is."

Ginja walked into the office.

"Okay, I got to go. I'll call you later on tonight." He hung up. "What's up?"

"Grim's here."

"Really?"

"Says he needs to speak with you face-to-face."

"Bring him in."

Ginja left and returned a few minutes later. Grim walked in behind her, staring at her butt and licking his lips.

"What's up?" Devon asked.

"Good news travels fast. I heard your partner is being released next week."

"Yeah."

"My people inside say he's a beast."

"Why are you here?" Devon asked.

Grim looked at Ginja before speaking. "I'm here to thank you in person."

"For what?"

"For all that you've done for me. I know you didn't do it exclusively for me, but I did benefit from the moves that you've made. And being that your man is home, I know that you're going to take your enterprise to the next level. I just hope that I can lend my services when that time comes."

"I appreciate the offer, Grim. I really do. You hungry?"

"Yeah."

"I know this place where the jerk chicken tastes almost like back home."

"No place makes jerk chicken like back home."

"That's why I said almost like back home."

"I'll give them a try."

"Good. Let me finish off this paperwork and we'll go grab a bite."

Grim left. Ginja closed the door behind him.

"You didn't go for that bullshit did you?" she asked.

"Of course not. What's our people in Amsterdam saying?"

"Since Grim took over, the club, bakery, and showroom have been raided by the police, they're clients are going elsewhere, the coke they're pushing has been stepped on more than a welcome mat, and there's grumbling in the ranks on how Grim's running things."

"So he comes here—"

"Offering his services, but what he really wants is your services. He needs you to bail him out. Are you?"

"What do you think?"

"I think you knew this was going to happen."

"Would I be where I am if I didn't?"

"So, what part is Brian going to play in the organization?"

"None."

"None? I thought—"

"He's married. He's expressed to Quana that all he wants to do is come home, take care of his family, and start a little home repair business."

"That doesn't sound like the Brian you've been telling me about."

"I guess spending nearly eight years in prison gave him time to see the things that matter the most."

"So, when are you and Quana getting married?"

Devon walked up on her. "Why? You want to come to the wedding?"

"Sure, why not?"

"And you wouldn't be jealous?"

"Please."

"You know if we get married, you and I won't be together anymore."

"We're not together, now."

"Oh, I forgot. We have an arrangement." He tried to kiss her on the lips, she turned her head.

"The next time you try to kiss me, I'm going to bite your d—"

"Hey, hey, I'm just trying to show you some love."

"Save your love for Quana."

Devon got serious. "After I have lunch with Grim, I'm sending him back to Amsterdam. Tell our people there to standby. I think Grim's time has expired. And with the grumbling going on, I doubt anyone in Villainy will be sad that he's gone."

"I'm on it."

Chapter 14

Down in Mexico, Devon walked out of his five bedroom villa in a pair of swimming trunks. Three Mexican women in string bikinis were swimming in the heated pool. When the women saw him, they swam to the edge of the pool and beckoned him in Spanish to join them. As soon as he stepped in, they attacked him like barracudas. The dark skinned one wrapped her arms around his neck and began sucking on his tongue. The light skinned mommy with the ocean blue eyes slid her hand into his trunks and caressed his manhood. The third one sucked on his shoulders. The one kissing him said something in Spanish.

"I have no idea what you just said," Devon said.

She smiled and guided his hand into the front of her bikini bottom.

"Oh, that's what you said."

She nodded.

The one who caressed him to full erection said the same thing in Spanish. Devon slid his hand down the front of her bikini bottom. Both women moaned and spoke rapidly in Spanish as they grinded on his finger.

Ginja walked out of the villa in a robe, phone in hand. She walked to the edge of the pool and bent down. "Devon. Phone."

He tried to look at her, but the dark skinned mommy turned his head back around and stuck her tongue back in his mouth.

"It's Quana."

Devon pulled away from the women and gave Ginja the evil eye.

"It sounds important."

He snatched the phone from her. "Yeah, baby... wait slow down, what happened?"

"That psycho bitch tied him and his family up in their home, Devon. One of her men put a gun to Arlene's head and pulled the trigger."

"Jennifer?" Devon said in shock. His shock quickly turned to rage. "Where's Brian now?"

"Him, Arlene, and the kids are on their way to JFK airport. I'm flying them to the ranch in Montana."

"I'm going to kill that bitch. I'll be in Montana tomorrow afternoon. Y'all just sit tight until I get there." Devon hung up and headed inside. He called his personal secretary, Mary. "Mary, charter me a private jet. I don't care how you do it, but it has to be ready to take off in two hours." He hung up and started getting dressed. He turned when he saw Ginja standing in the doorway. "Send the women away."

"I already did."

"Get dressed, we're out of here."

"Where are we going?"

"Just fucking get dressed!"

Ginja sucked her teeth and went to get dressed.

Devon's hands shook as he tried to button up his shirt. She put a gun to Arlene's head and pulled the trigger? She tied up the kids? How could I have not seen this coming? "Ginja!" He grabbed the car keys off the table. "I'm pulling off in five minutes with or without you."

"I'm ready." She ran out of the bedroom down the hall. She had to run to keep up with Devon's long strides.

Devon pulled into the airport a half hour later. A half hour after that, the charter jet was in the air.

Devon rocked back and forth in his seat. Ginja stared at him. She looked out the window for a moment and then looked back at him. "Devon can I talk to you?"

"Not now."

She got out of her seat and sat across from him. "This is crazy. We need to think this through."

Devon stopped rocking and looked at her. "We need to think this through? Who's we?"

"Us, the team."

"I didn't think it through when you called me with Irons's men hot on your ass. I just came didn't I?"

"This is different. He's not in immediate danger. He's on his way to Montana."

"You need to go sit your ass back over there, because I'm two seconds away from throwing you out of this plane."

Ginja sighed and went back to her original seat. The cabin's phone rang. She answered it.

"It's Recker."

"Hang it up."

"He's not listening to me," Ginja said to Recker.

"I said hang it up!"

Ginja hung up the phone and folded her arms.

* * *

When they landed, Audrey, one of the ranch's maids, was at the airport waiting for them. "Good afternoon Mr. Cartier."

"How you doing Audrey?"

"I'm doing well, sir. I tried my best to tidy up on such short notice."

"That's okay, Audrey. Did my guests arrive yet?"

"No, sir."

When they pulled up to the ranch, Devon made a beeline for the media room. He pulled down on a book on the shelf. The bookshelf slid open, exposing a staircase. Ginja followed him down.

He flipped on the light switch. Guns lined the shelves along with their respective ammunition.

"Devon," Ginja cried out as she stepped in front of him. "Please, just listen to me."

"I don't have time for this." He began to shove her out of the way. She smacked him.

"You selfish son of a bitch!" She kept hitting him until he was able to pin her arms to her sides.

"You done lost your fucking mind?"

"You bastard," she cried. "All these years, I've done everything you wanted. I gave myself to you and after all that…"

Devon let her go. "Are you crying?"

"No," Ginja said, wiping the tears from her eyes.

Devon sat her down on the couch and knelt in front of her. "I wish you could understand."

She grabbed his hands. "Make me understand."

"Jennifer and her twin sister used to work for this guy named Manny. He used to use them to set dudes up. They set this dude named Supreme up. They killed him. Then they cut his dick off and stuffed it in his mouth. Chuka, the dude that Supreme worked for swore to kill the ones responsible for killing his second in command. I had the twins hemmed up in an apartment. I called Chuka. I gave him the address to the apartment. All I wanted was for the twins to tell him that Manny was the one responsible for killing Supreme. They told him, but then this motherfucker pulls out and shoots Paula in the head. Then he points the gun at Jennifer. I was able to tackle him as he squeezed the trigger. Instead of shooting her in the head, he shot her in the chest. We tussled. I was finally able to subdue him."

Ginja shook her head.

"He tried to convince me it wasn't personal. They had to die because they partook in his man's murder. When he left, I checked on the twins. Paula was dead. But Jennifer still had a pulse. I called the police and an ambulance, and then I broke out."

"So, she wants to kill you?"

"Basically."

"You can get Knots and Porter to take care of this."

"No, this happened before I came to Jamaica. I can't ask them to do this."

"I'll do it. Ivory and I will fly to New York and—"

"No Ginja. I got to do this."

"No, you don't."

"Yes... I do." Devon stood up.

Ginja stood with him and kissed him. It was the first time Devon ever tasted her tongue.

He slowly pulled back from her and opened his eyes. "What happened to your rule?"

"It conflicted with my other rule."

"And what rule is that?"

"Always show your man how much you love him."

"I'm your man?"

"You know you are."

"I'm Quana's man."

"You were mine first, and you will always be mine."

"I know you're not catching feelings for me, Miss there's-no-such-thing-as love."

"I only caught feelings for you, because you caught feelings for me first, Gunslinger."

Ginja kissed him again. "Please let me take care of this. If anything was to happen to you—"

"Shh, nothing is going to happen to me."

"Then I'm coming with you."

"Ginja—"

"No, Devon! I don't care what you say. I'm coming, and that's that."

"Okay, you can come. But for now, I need you to do me a favor."

"Anything."

"Quana and them should be here shortly."

"You want me to disappear?"

"Just to the guest house."

Ginja narrowed her eyes at him. "I swear, if you try and go to New York without me, I will describe your dick in detail to Quana, all the way down to the freckles on your balls."

"You wouldn't do that."

"Try to pull a fast one on me and see what happens."

"Get out of here. I got things to do." He spanked her on the butt as she headed up the steps. He looked at his arsenal one more time before heading upstairs to take a bath and get dressed.

* * *

Devon perked up when he saw Audrey turning onto the property. He watched as Brian, Arlene, and the kids jumped out of the minivan.

As Devon walked down the stairs he heard Quana talking to them in the living room.

"There's plenty to do in the house, but if you want to venture outside, there's a horse barn and an indoor riding facility, and there's always the ski slopes."

"I don't think we'll be venturing out," Brian said. "Since we arrived here at Grasshopper Valley, I haven't seen any black people."

Devon laughed to himself as he watched them. Brian was different. His voice was deeper, his shoulders broader.

"You can stay for as long as you need to," he heard Quana telling him.

"Nah, we got a life, Quana. As beautiful as this place is, I want to go back to Albany and finish what I started."

Arlene hugged him from behind.

Damn, they look so beautiful together, Devon thought.

"And how do you plan on doing that?" Quana asked Brian.

"I don't know, yet, but first things first. I need to speak to Dev."

"Brian—"

"No, Quana, don't give me that I don't know where he is crap or I don't know how to contact him. There has to be a way."

"There is."

"How's that?"

"Turn around."

Devon held his breath.

Arlene and Brian both spun around. Devon was leaning on the stone fireplace, with his arms folded, and with the same emotionless expression Brian remembered as a teen. Only he was staring at a twenty-six year old version in an Armani suit.

"What's up?" Brian said.

"I'm cool," Devon said, standing up straight.

Devon could see the apprehension on Arlene's face when Brian took a step toward him. He peeped Brian when he squeezed her hand to let her know everything was all right. He walked toward Devon, all the while, looking at his bald head. I forgot he never saw me without dreads, Devon said to himself. When Brian got in arm's distance, he nodded. Devon nodded back, and for the first time that Brian could remember he saw Devon smile.

They embraced like they were long lost brothers.

"I see you hooked up with the girl from the park," Devon said, looking over Brian's shoulder at Arlene.

"That's probably the best decision I made in my entire life." Brian pulled back from him. "I thought you were over-seas."

"I was 'til I got the call from Quana last night, and she told me what went down."

Brian looked at Quana. "You had his number, and didn't give it to me?"

"I told her not to," Devon said. "She told me you were doing the right thing. You know my story. I didn't want to get you trapped off in my drama."

Brian stared at her. He knew she meant well, but he couldn't get over the fact that she had Devon's number and didn't give it to him.

Sherodd and Tamicka came into the living room out of breath. "Mommy, this place is like a castle," Sherodd said.

Damn, Devon said to himself. He remembered shorty when he was like five years old. Now he had to be twelve or thirteen.

"I was looking out the window," Tamicka said. "And I saw horses. Can I go outside and look at the horses, mommy?"

Oh shit, Devon said to himself. Brian had a baby girl by Arlene already?

Tamicka turned to Brian. "Can we go look at the horses, daddy?"

"In a little while sweetheart."

Tamicka looked Devon up and down. "You look scary," she said.

"Tamicka!" Brian said embarrassed. He turned to Arlene. "Sweetheart, why don't you take the kids outside to see the horses, so that Dev and I can talk?"

"I have a better idea," Quana said. "Me, Arlene, and the kids can go shopping. It gets kind of chilly up in these mountains."

"That sounds like a good idea," Arlene said, holding her hand out for Brian to give her his bank card.

Brian pulled out his wallet, but Devon stopped him. "That's not necessary. Quana's got everything under control."

Brian looked at him and then to Quana, and then put his wallet back. "You heard the man," he said to Arlene.

Arlene, Quana and the kids climbed into the minivan and headed into town.

"What the fuck happened?" Devon asked, unable to keep his cool any longer.

Brian related the events as they unfolded last night, including giving Jennifer his cousin's phone number. Devon didn't interrupt 'til he was finished.

"I would've done the same thing if I was in your shoes. You didn't have a choice. Don't worry about my cousin, Sheldon; I made sure he got out of that apartment. He's in Queens hiding out 'til this blows over."

"Damn," Brian said shaking his head. "I would've never in a billion years thought that I would see you in a suit."

"Well, I have a little over three-billion reasons why I need to wear one."

"All those years, while I was in prison getting those postcards from you, from all over the world, one question always popped into my mind: How in the hell did you do it?"

"It's a long, long, too long story. When my grandmother told me that the police had come to the house wanting to ask me some questions, I grabbed the money and the kilos of coke, and headed to Quana's. I left her the money to take care of you and drove to Florida, where my uncle has an export and import business. I was straight up with him. I told him I needed to get to Jamaica, to hook up with the rest of the family, and I needed him to have the coke waiting there for me when I arrived. He charged me an arm and a leg, but I said fuck it, because I knew that once I got to Jamaica and hooked up with my cousin, it would be worth it. And... as you can see, the rest is history."

"Un... fucking... believable. So, this place is yours?"

"Yeah, this is my honey comb hideout."

"Who would have ever thought? Me, you, and Jason started out as snotty-nosed, stick up kids. And our paths took turns that none of us expected, and now here we are. You're the black Bill Gates, I'm married, and Jason is probably going to spend the rest of his life in prison."

"Nah, he's not in prison, anymore."

"What? He got out?"

"Yeah."

"When?"

"He got out about two weeks before you came home."

"How the fuck did that happen?"

"In a pine box."

Brian's jaw dropped.

"It seems he had some beef with the Jamaicans in Comstock Correctional. They got at him in the yard, hit him up eight times. A stab wound for every year you did in prison. What a coincidence."

"Yeah," Brian said, reading in between the lines.

"So, what do you want to do with this bitch?" Devon asked.

"I just want her out of my life."

"Well, there's only one way that's gonna happen."

Brian closed his eyes. "There has to be another way."

"There is. You're gonna give her what she wants."

Brian gave him a mixed look.

"She wants the Dread? We're gonna give her the Dread."

* * *

"That punk, bitch, motherfucker." Jennifer cursed Brian out as she watched Stone and Jonel ransack his house. "A whole family can't just disappear into thin air," she said to Stone. "There has to be something here that can tell us where they went."

Jennifer ignored the cell phone in her pocket as it rang. "Oh shit!" she said as she fumbled to retrieve it. It dawned on her that the ring tone wasn't hers, it was Brian's. "Speak."

"I heard you were looking for me?" Devon spoke into the phone.

Jennifer closed her eyes as she felt her belly jump. For the first time in months, she desperately needed a valium. "So, the bastard did know where you were, huh?"

"He knows, now, but I didn't call to talk about him. Let's talk about us."

"What about us?" Jennifer asked, while signaling to Stone that the Dread was on the line.

"What do we have to do in order for you to leave my man and his family alone?"

"Meet with me."

"Humph. That's it? You just want to arrange a meeting?"

"Yes, I got some things I need to say to you."

"You can say them over the phone."

"I need to say these things face-to-face."

"Face-to-face?"

"Yeah, face-to-face. I need some closure."

"You're so full of shit, bitch."

"Now, that's no way to talk to a lady," Jennifer said coyly. "So watch your fucking mouth, nigga!"

"Okay, meet me at—"

"Fuck you Ras clot. You ain't calling the shots. We'll meet at the first place we saw one another."

Devon thought for a moment. "That Dyke's apartment in Brooklyn?"

"Her name is Ericka, and yes, the apartment where you helped murder my sister."

"I'll be there in two days."

"I'll see you, there." Jennifer hung up.

"So, what happened?" Brian asked.

"She wants to meet with me at the apartment where Chuka killed her sister."

"You mean she wants to kill you at the apartment her sister was killed in."

"There's gonna be some killing," Dev said, as he walked toward the entertainment room with Brian following him. Devon pulled down the book, exposing the staircase. Brian followed him down to what appeared to be a wine cellar, only the shelves weren't lined with wine.

"You think you got enough firepower?" Brian asked as he surveyed the droves of guns and ammunition.

"Got to stay prepared. Never know when you're going to have a psycho bitch trying to kill you."

Brian stood off to the side and watched as Devon grabbed a duffel bag off the shelf and started filling it with guns and ammunition.

"There's a bag over there," Devon said over his shoulder. When Brian didn't move, he turned around. "This bitch came into your house, cuffed your kids to a chair, put a gun to your wife's head and pulled the trigger. The Brian I used to know would pick up the fo'fif right there and fit as many clips in his pockets as he could."

"That's not me anymore."

"It is you, and it will always be you." Devon picked up the .45 and held it out to Brian. His first instincts were to reach for it, but he stopped himself.

"You can't go to a gunfight without a gun, Bee."

Brian looked him in the eyes. "I'm not going."

"Come again?" Devon said, screwing his face up.

"I said, I'm not going. It's not just about me anymore. I'm not that buck wild dude who felt like he had nothing to lose."

Devon stared at him for a moment. "I can't tell you how to live your life, Bee, but I know you better than you think I do. You live for this shit."

"Not anymore."

Devon zipped up the duffel bag. "I'll give you a call when it's all over."

Devon left Brian in the cellar with his thoughts.

Chapter 15

Ginja sat across from Devon on the charter jet typing on her laptop. She looked up when she felt him staring at her. "What?"

"Nothing," Devon said.

"It is something."

"I know I don't say it much, but I do appreciate all that you've done for me," Devon said sincerely.

"Much? You don't say it at all." She finished typing. "Car rental's all done. I put it under one of the false names Warren gave me, just in case we have to ditch it."

"Or blow it up."

"Let's hope it doesn't have to come to that." She started typing again. "All I got to do is the hotel arrangements and we'll be straight."

"You want some coffee?"

"Sure," Ginja said, without looking up from the screen.

Devon got up and walked to the coffee pot. He poured himself a cup and then Ginja. He looked over his shoulder and then pulled out the crushed sleeping pills he smashed up earlier. He poured the whole packet into Ginja's cup and then added creamer and sugar.

She downed the coffee and finished making their reservations. "We're staying at the Marriot."

"And where's Knots and Porter staying?"

"Knots and Porter? What are you talking about?"

"You know exactly what I'm talking about. Recker called me and told me everything. Even after I told you not to call them, you went behind my back and did it anyway."

"It's not what you think."

"I know it's not what I think, it's what Recker told me."

"What did he say?"

"You were going to convince me to go to the hotel first, and then, you were going to drug me. And while I was in la-la land, you, Knots, and Porter were going to take care of Jennifer. I trusted you."

"And I love you. What did you expect me to do? You're too valuable to us, to me. I wouldn't have been able to live with myself if something happened to you."

Devon nodded. "Okay."

"Okay what?"

"I'll stay at the hotel while you, Knots, and Porter take care of this."

"What's the catch?" She stared at him suspiciously.

"The catch is you never go behind my back again."

"I swear, I'll never go behind your back again. I swear." She yawned.

Devon yawned and reclined the seat. "I'm going to sleep. Wake me when we're about to land."

* * *

When the jet touched down, Ginja was still knocked out. Devon reached into the overhead compartment and grabbed a pillow. He put it under her head and reclined her seat. He headed to the cockpit.

"Thank you very much, Walter," Devon said grabbing the duffel bag of guns that the pilot was able to bring on board without being searched.

"Not a problem, sir."

"My friend is knocked out in the back. I don't want to wake her, so I'm going to let her sleep. When she wakes, tell her I'll meet her at the hotel."

"Sure thing."

Devon exited the jet, duffel bag in hand, headed toward Hertz. He signed the rental agreement and he was on his way to Brooklyn. As he neared Ericka's apartment, he made a pit stop behind the warehouses. He pulled out the C4 and taped it under the car's gas tank. He took a couple deep breaths and threw a couple jabs. "Okay, let's do this."

* * *

Devon pulled up to Ericka's apartment building just before sunset. He got out of the car and walked to the playground. He looked up at Ericka's window, knowing that Jennifer was probably looking down at him. He pulled out his cell phone.

Jennifer squinted at the man who stood in the playground wearing a North Face coat, making a phone call. No sooner than he put the phone to his ear, Brian's cell phone went off. She answered it on the second ring.

"Where are you?" she hissed.

"You know where I am," Devon said, waving at the window.

"Come on up."

"Nah, you come on down."

Jennifer squeezed the phone as if she was ringing his neck. She ended the call and threw the phone against the wall. She grabbed the bottle of valiums off the table and swallowed two of them. "The bastard's in the playground across the street," she said to Jonel. "I didn't expect him to come up here anyway. I would've been disappointed if he would've made it that easy. Let's go." She grabbed her 9mm off the table and headed out the door.

Stone had the appearance of the perfect father. He was pushing Ericka's daughter on the swing. He laughed with her as he pushed her higher and higher. When he saw Jennifer and Jonel storm out of the lobby toward the park, he put two and two together. The man who he suspected was the Dread was in fact him, only he no longer had dreads.

Devon stuck his hand into his duffel bag the moment Jennifer and Jonel stepped foot on the playground. He watched Jennifer as she continued to walk toward him, unaffected by his gesture. He held up his left hand for her to stop. When she kept coming, he exposed the butt of the submachine gun. Jennifer and Jonel stopped in their tracks. The only thing between Devon and Jennifer was ten feet of air.

"So what do you have to tell me that you couldn't tell me over the phone?" Devon asked, shoving the butt of the gun back into the duffel bag.

"Not only did I want my voice to be the last thing you heard, but I also wanted my face to be the last thing you saw."

Devon's words got caught in his throat when he felt the cold steel on the back of his neck. Jennifer and Jonel had been the diversion Stone needed to get the drop on Devon.

"You got me," Devon said, as he subtly took his hand off the gun and grabbed another trigger.

"Easy partner," Stone said, as he nudged Devon in the back of his neck with his gun.

A smile danced across Jennifer's face as she walked up to Devon and spat in his face.

Devon didn't even so much as blink. "What? You're gonna kill me out here in front of all these witnesses?"

"Oh, no," Jennifer said digging into her trench, and pulling out the straight razor. "Killing you comes later, much, much later. Take him to the van!"

When Devon saw that the van she was referring to was the one he just happened to park in front of, he smiled.

"Something funny?" Jonel said, puffing up his chest.

"Nigga, is you sporting a jeri curl?" Devon said, starting to laugh.

Jonel clinched his fists.

"Damn, you know who you look like? You look like one of them niggas from Full-Force from back in the days."

Jonel's nose flared.

"And I can't believe you're wearing those tight-ass pants," Devon said, continuing to taunt him.

"That's enough," Jennifer hissed.

"A cock diesel nigga like you wearing tight-ass pants. You gay?"

Jonel snapped and switched to Terminator mode. Devon braced himself. At the last second, he slightly shifted to the left, allowing Jonel's punch to only graze his cheek. As he fell to the ground, out of Stone's line of fire, he squeezed the trigger he had his finger on. The trigger sent a signal to the pouch of C4. The sudden blast disoriented everyone except Devon. He used the five second confusion to scramble to his feet and take off.

Stone was the first one to recover and take off after him. Jennifer came to her senses ran toward the van, not realizing that it went up in the explosion. She shook her head, trying to think straight. Jonel ran up behind her and shouted something but her ears were still ringing from the blast. She watched him as he ran to the Lincoln Navigator. She followed him.

When Devon hit the boulevard, he ran up to the first motorist he saw and pulled him out of his car. He peeled off just as one of Stone's slugs took out the tail light. When Devon saw the Navigator skid around the corner, he slowed down some, giving them a chance to pick Stone up and pursue him. He turned off the boulevard. He took the back streets all the way to the warehouses where the Sanitation trucks park for the night.

The Navigator was steady gaining, while a navy blue Chevy Cavalier kept its distance behind the Navigator. Stone opened fire. He shot out Devon's back windshield. Bits of glass bit into his neck, causing him to lose control of the car. He skidded into a sanitation truck. On instinct, he rolled out and dived behind a dumpster. He reached into his duffel bag and pulled out the machine gun. He heard the Navigator skid to a stop and the doors fly open. He leaned out on his side and emptied the whole clip into the truck. Out of the corner of his eye, he saw Jennifer and her goons taking cover behind one of the sanitation trucks.

Devon ejected the used clip and fished a fresh one out of his bag. "I got plenty of ammo," he yelled. "And the cops should be here any minute. So let's just squash this and go our separate ways."

Four bullets from Jennifer's 9mm pounded into the dumpster.

"You got to do better than that," he yelled. Oh shit. His eyes bulged as the hand grenade that Stone tossed bounced off the wall and landed on his lap. He swatted at it, and took off. As soon as he shot out from behind the dumpster, Stone had him in the sights of his 9mm Parabellum.

Devon stumbled as one of the slugs grazed his ear. He slid across the sidewalk when a slug hit him high in the thigh. He frantically looked around for the submachine gun. He slid farther than he thought. By the time he reached into his duffel for a hand gun, Stone was ten feet away with his gun trained at his head.

"Pull it out, I dare you," Stone said, grinning.

Devon took his hand out of the bag, empty handed. He struggled to get to his feet, so he could die with dignity, but the grinding pain from the slug in him, changed his mind.

Jennifer half-walked, half-jogged up to him and kicked him in the stomach. "Punk bitch," she said as she kicked and stomped him. When she stopped out of exhaustion, Devon laughed.

"Your hand grenade was a dud," he said spitting up blood.

"No," Stone said. "You fell for the okey-doke."

Devon nodded. "You got me."

"No, I got you," Jennifer said breathing hard. She looked at Jonel. "Drag his sorry ass to the truck."

Jonel took a step. When his foot came down, it looked and sounded like he stepped on a land mine. His left leg, from the knee down, was squirting blood. As he fell to the ground, the second slug from Brian's fo'fif blew half of Jonel's neck off.

Stone raised his gun and started firing before he even had Brian in his sights. Brian barked the fo'fif two more times before ducking behind a sanitation truck.

"I knew your punk ass wouldn't be too far behind," Jennifer yelled, as she stood her ground, hovering over Devon. "Let's make this real easy," she shouted to Brian as she pulled out the straight razor. "Come from behind that truck and drop your gun."

"Nah, fuck that."

"I thought you were going to do us all a favor and make this easy, but I guess not." She grabbed Devon's arm and ripped him from his forearm to his shoulder. Brian came from behind the truck and fired two more shots.

"Drop it," Jennifer yelled.

When Brian didn't comply, she slashed Devon across the face.

"Okay," Brian said, dropping the gun.

"Go get him," Jennifer said to Stone.

Stone jammed a fresh clip into his gun and walked toward Brian.

* * *

Perched on a warehouse rooftop half a block away, was the driver of the Chevy Cavalier. She watched all of the events unfold through her scope. Her breathing was deep and even as she became one with her rifle. In this mode, whatever spot she focused on, no matter how tiny, the tip of her bullet was going to hit it dead center.

Before anyone heard a sound, Molina's first bullet hit
Stone high in the shoulder. Before he could process what hit
him, her second bullet hit him high in his other shoulder. Her
third bullet hit him in the right butt cheek, her fourth in his
left. When her fifth one hit him in his right calf, he mouthed
her name. When her sixth bullet hit him in his left calf, he
screamed it.

Four more to go, poppy, she said to herself as she focused
on the next spot.

The seventh and eighth shots blew away both his knee
caps.

"Timber," Molina whispered as Stone finally fell face first.

Her ninth shot pierced his back and ripped through his
heart, and her icing on the cake was the tenth bullet that
entered the back of his head and blew his face off.

Brian, Devon, and Jennifer all froze, staring at Stone's
picked apart corpse. Devon scrambled away from Jennifer who
was too scared to move. The sniper's signature rooted her to
the ground. She knew if she as much as flinched, Molina
would turn her into Swiss cheese.

Brian picked up his gun and walked up to her. "Your
people are lying dead in the street like dogs. I should just put
two in you, and end all this." He got up in her face. "If you
ever come anywhere near me or my family again, I swear by
God, I will kill you slow." He cemented his promise with a
grin, a grin so sadistic that Jennifer dropped the razor and
stopped breathing.

Brian mushed her to the ground and walked toward Devon. He didn't have to see that look on Devon's face to know
that he fucked up. He spun, but there was no way he could get
a shot off at Jennifer who had already had her gun aimed at his
head. Brian closed his eyes and prayed.

His answer came from above, but it didn't come from the
heavens. It came from a warehouse rooftop. When Brian
opened his eyes, he saw Jennifer on the ground, clutching her
right wrist. He followed the spray of blood to his feet where

her right hand landed. It was still clutching the gun. Without hesitating, he raised the .45 and squeezed the trigger. It was then that he realized it was empty. He threw the gun down and wrenched the 9mm out of Jennifer's severed hand and shot her twice in the head. He took a step closer and shot her two more times in the chest.

The police siren snapped him back to reality. He threw the gun down and ran to Devon. He started to take off the leather gloves, but Devon's stare stopped him. "I'm rusty kid."

"That's hood 101, Bee. Never take your gloves off 'til it's over, and it's not over. Not by a long shot."

"We got to get the fuck out of here," he said to Devon, as he helped him to the car Devon crashed.

"It's totaled," Devon said.

Brian frantically hobbled with him to the navigator. When he saw the bullet holes Devon had put into it, he knew it was totaled as well.

"Where's your ride?" Devon asked.

"Shit," Brian screamed. "This way," he said to Devon as they hobbled together away from the scene.

A half block up, Brian leaned on the Cavalier.

"MOVE!" Molina commanded as she walked out of the shadows with her rifle slung across her back and a Glock leveled at them.

"We need a ride out of here," Brian pleaded.

"Not my problem. That wasn't part of the deal."

"But—"

"I said move!" She took a step toward them. "I'm not going to tell you again."

"I'll give you another million," Brian pleaded.

"I don't need another million."

"Three million," Devon said weakly.

"You think you can just throw numbers in the air and I'm just going to jump?"

"Four million in any account you choose by tomorrow morning." Devon said with authority.

Molina pressed the button on her key pad, unlocking the doors. "Don't just stand there," she said to Brian. "Help the man in."

Chapter 16

"How's he looking?" Molina asked, as she turned onto the boulevard?

"He's losing a lot of blood." Brian was keeping pressure on the deep cut Jennifer made on Devon's arm, while Devon held Brian's shirt to his face to stop the blood from gushing from the cut on his face.

Molina turned onto the Belt Parkway. "We have a twenty minute drive."

"Where are we going?" Brian asked.

"Away from the police." Twenty minutes later, Molina got off at the Hill Side Avenue exit. She turned onto a block of private houses. She stopped at a yellow and white one. "This is it." She got out and helped Brian pull Devon out of the backseat. They carried him through the front door and laid him on the living room couch.

Molina disappeared in the back and came back with a black portfolio suitcase. Brian looked on in shock when she unzipped and unfolded it. Surgical tools lined one side, disinfectants and medication lined the other.

"I can't afford to go to hospitals," she said. She went into the kitchen and came back with a tub of hot water and towels.

"Move out the way," she said to Brian. He moved aside and watched as she pulled out a pair of surgical scissors and cut Devon's shirt off. The cut on his arm started from the middle of his forearm and went all the way to his shoulder. She shook her head. "I can't waste time stitching this up." She reached for what looked like latex cast. She wrapped it around his arm, closing the gash as best she could. Then she removed the thin film of tape from the adhesive side and sealed the cast tight.

"What's wrong with him?" Brian asked, as Devon's eyes began to roll to the back of his head.

"Hold his legs up. He may be going into shock." She pulled out a needle and inserted it into the side of Devon's face.

"What's that?" Devon asked.

"So you won't feel this." She pulled out the needle and thread.

Brian shuddered as Molina started stitching the gash shut. Devon winced as he felt the needle piercing his cheek. Brian couldn't take it anymore.

"Is this your place?" he asked.

"No."

"Good." He turned his head and threw up.

Molina smiled as she continued to work. "Don't worry, poppy, I threw up my first time, too."

Brian nodded and then threw up again.

"I didn't throw up twice, though." Molina stopped what she was doing when Devon's cell phone rang. She looked over at Brian, he was still throwing up. She reached into Devon's pocket and answered it. "Hola."

"If you hurt him in anyway, I swear—"

"Whoa, slow down, Mommy."

"Who is this?" Ginja asked.

"I'm the one who just saved his ass."

Devon reached for the phone. Molina pulled back from him. "How you gonna talk with a needle in your mouth,

Poppy?" She hit Brian in the back of the head with the phone. "Toma, here, talk to this crazy lady."

Brian wiped his mouth with his shirt and grabbed the phone. "Hello?"

"Who is this?"

"Brian. I'm—"

"I know who you are. Where are you?"

"We're in Queens."

"Where in Queens?"

"Who's this?"

"I work for Devon. Tell me where you are so I can come and get you."

Brian gave her the address. "It's a yellow and white house."

"We'll be there in fifteen minutes."

"We?" Brian looked at the phone. "She hung up on me."

Molina cut the thread and started cleaning up. She folded the case and zipped it back up.

"What now?" Devon asked as he sat up.

Molina disappeared into the bedroom and came back out carrying a suitcase. She looked at Brian. "You owe me one million per our agreement."

"Of course."

"I will be by your house to pick it up in three days."

She turned to Devon. "Three million in any account I choose, correct?"

"Yes, of course."

Molina stared at him for a moment. "You looked better with the dreads.

"How did—"

"Devon Carter, age 26, wanted for multiple homicides, last seen at Rosedale Station eight years ago. I read your police file at the police station. They had a picture of you they got from your grandmother."

"Police file? How were you able to read my police file?"

"Irrelevant, poppy, what you need to worry about is getting three million in this account by tomorrow." She dug in her pocket and handed him a piece of paper with a bank account number on it. "Or else that police file is going to have a lot more information in it. Like, Devon Carter AKA Devon Cartier, currently residing in London, founder of Khufu Inc… need I go on?"

Devon shook his head. "Who are you?"

"A woman you don't want to cross." Molina picked up her suitcase and headed to the front door. "Poppy," she said to Devon. "The woman on the phone sounded real hot. Tell her if I'm ever in London, I'm definitely going to look her up. Does she taste as spicy as she sounds?"

Devon cleared his throat. "I wouldn't know."

"Of course you wouldn't." She opened the door and left.

"Who in the world is that?" Devon asked Brian.

"I have no idea. I was in Crossgates mall shopping for some clothes and she just pulls right up on me and tells me that my family is in danger. I looked at her like she's a nut, but then when she mentioned you, Jason, and Jennifer, she got my attention. She told me she could take care of my problem but it would cost me a mil. I remember just walking away because I was in total shock. When I got home, I found her card with her phone number on it in my jacket."

"She didn't tell you who she was or what she does?"

"Nothing. After you left, I was lying in the bed with Arlene. I tried to convince myself that you would be all right. You know I couldn't stay away, right?"

"I told you Bee, you live for this shit."

"I called this chick, right before we left JFK. She told me to keep her posted. I called her again from the ranch and told her where everything was going down. She met me at the airport. Just as we were turning onto Ericka's street, we heard the explosion. Then we saw you tearing ass down the boulevard."

Devon began to laugh, but his cheek was killing him.

"Then we saw the Navigator fly around the corner. I was fidgeting in the seat, reaching for the door handle. And the

Spanish hottie looks at me all cool and shit and says, "relax, Poppy, I got this."

"Yeah she does look hot," Devon said.

"Don't she? She's sewing you up, blood is everywhere, I'm throwing up, and I'm still staring at her nipple prints in that tank top."

"She did have some big nipples."

"I think we're crazy, Dev."

"Nah, Bee, we're not crazy. We're rich. You never have to work another day in your life. Half of Khufu Inc. is yours."

Brian shook his head. "It sounds tempting, Dev, but I'm all right. I'm already rich. A beautiful wife and beautiful kids, what more can I ask for?"

Devon nodded. "I respect that."

They both looked up when the front door crashed open. Ginja was the first one through, pistol leading the way. Knots and Porter followed her in.

"Where is she?" Ginja asked.

"She's gone," Devon said. The side of his face was still numb, so his words came out slurred.

Ginja started to run to him but she caught herself. "The both of you okay?"

"Yeah," Devon said, waving for them to put their guns away.

"You the woman I spoke to on the phone?" Brian asked.

"Yeah."

"Help me up," Devon said to Ginja.

The anger in her face was obvious. She rolled her eyes and stormed out the house.

"She looks pretty pissed," Brian said.

"She'll be all right."

Knots pulled out his cell phone and started dialing.

"Who you calling?" Devon asked.

"Quana's hysterical. She made me promise to call her as soon as I got to you."

Brian looked at Devon. "Quana? Hysterical?"

"Ah, yeah, Bee. There's something I need to talk to you about."

Brian's mouth fell open. "You and Quana?"

"I wanted to ask your permission, because I know how Quana is like a sister to you, but there was no way for me to—"

"My permission? Man, you don't need my permission. Quana is a grown ass woman, and you're a grown ass man."

"We are aren't we?" We've come a long way, huh Youngin'?"

Brian smiled. "Yes we have... Youngin'!"

Epilogue

I looked up from my laptop. "So, it's safe to assume that you paid the Spanish mommy her three million?" I asked Devon.

"Of course I paid her. I'm a man of my word."

"And I bet she's a woman of hers." I closed my laptop. "Okay, I will send you a copy. If I left anything out or put anything in that you have a problem with—"

"I will definitely let you know, Arlene."

"Well, it's been three beautiful days. I loved the places you took me to and I'm feeling your story."

"Let's hope your readers do, as well."

"I'm sure they will."

"If it sounds boring, you can jazz it up a bit. After all, it is fiction, right? And technically I don't exist."

"Riiight, but I think it's jazzy enough."

"You sure you don't want to stay an extra day?"

"No. I wish I could, but I'm missing my baby."

Devon smiled. "Tell Brian I love him and I'm missing him, too."

"I will."

I got up from the couch. Devon stood and walked up to me. He hugged me and gave me a kiss on the cheek.

When Ginja walked into the room, she could sense I was seeing her in a whole different light.

"The car's out front," she said.

"Okay, girl from the park," Devon joked.

I could tell he wanted to hug me again, so, I hugged him first. "Take care of yourself."

"That's what I do best."

* * *

"Enjoy your flight, it was nice meeting you," Ginja said to me as I headed to the terminal. I waved at her and kept it moving.

Walter greeted me at the stairs of the jet. "Good afternoon, Mrs. Brathwaite."

"Good afternoon, Walter."

"How was your stay?"

"Wonderful." I couldn't help but look at Walter funny after knowing how he snuck those guns onboard for Devon. Devon made sure he surrounded himself with people who did whatever had to be done.

I sat down and buckled up. Within minutes, we were in the air. I was on my way back home.

I turned around when I heard the bathroom door open. A man stepped out. He kept his eyes on me as he approached.

"Can I help you?" I asked.

He didn't answer until he sat directly in front of me and placed his badge on the table in front of us. "Agent Ear Hart, CIA."

My hands started shaking.

"How's Devon?"

"I, I, who?" I didn't know what to say. All I could think about was my baby just got out of prison and I'm on my way in.

"Don't worry, Mrs. Brathwaite, I'm not going to arrest you. I know you came here to do a story on him. I'm surprised he agreed to it."

All I could do was shake my head and say, "Na, ah, no."

"I read *Youngin* and I read *Ol'Timer*, and I feel confident that you can do me some justice."

"Justice? I don't know what you mean."

Agent Ear Hart cleared his throat and spoke again. This time his voice changed. "Listen to me, Mommy."

My mouth dropped as the woman I only knew as Agent Molina removed the moustache and beard she was wearing. As she took off the wig, I was on the verge of wigging out. The last things she removed were her glasses. Something in her eyes gave me the impression that I should sit still and hear her out.

"We're going to be on this plane for the next 10 hours. So, you being a writer and me having a story to tell will make this flight all the more interesting, si?"

"Ah, Um…!" I swallowed and tried to pick my next words carefully. "What's the story about?"

"You have beautiful lips, Mommy."

I jerked back, she reached in her waist.

"Easy, Mommy. You almost made me shoot you."

Writing stories about crazy, psycho bitches is one thing, but to be sitting across from one is a whole different story.

"I… I don't know if I can write a story about you."

"You can and you will." She pulled the gun out of her waistband and placed it on the table. "After all, I did save your husband's life, didn't I?"

I nodded slowly. I opened my bag and pulled out my laptop. "So… what is the story about?"

Molina leaned back and kicked her feet up on the table. "The story's about a sixteen year old girl thrown into the streets and told to survive the best way she could. Then at the age of seventeen, she hooks up with this… special group of people who trains her to be a lethal weapon."

"Does this girl have a name?"

"Her name is… was Jamie."

"Was? What happened to her?"

"I thought you'd never ask."

* * *

When I exited the terminal and saw my husband, I ran into his arms.

"Damn, sweetheart, you missed me like that?"

I kissed my baby and hugged him even tighter.

"Maybe you should go away more often."

"Shut up and let's get the hell out of here. How are the kids?"

"They're good. I let them go to your mother's. You know how they like that pool in the backyard."

"Yeah, I know."

As we walked to the car, I kept looking around.

"You okay?" Brian asked me as we got into the car.

"I'm fine."

"So, how's my boy, Dev?"

"He's still doing his thing."

"Did you get your story?"

"Umm, hmm."

Brian turned and looked at me. "Something's wrong, and you're not telling me."

I was never the type that could hide my feelings. "I went to London to get a story, and I wind up getting two."

"Two?"

"Devon's…"

"And?"

"Molina's."

"Molina? The Psycho-sniping assassin, who calls everybody mommy and poppy?"

"Yeah."

"How in the world did that happen?"

"It's a looong story."

"Well, get to telling it."

"No. You'll read about it just like everybody else."

"You're actually going to put it out?"

"I think it's in *our* best interest not to piss this woman off. She even gave me the title.

THE DAY OF JUDGMENT

Brian shook his head. "God help us."

IN STORES NOW

ISBN: 978-1570876998

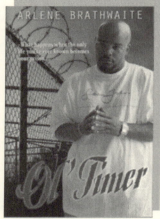

ISBN: 978-0979746208

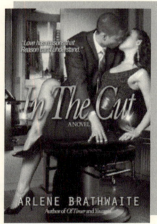

ISBN: 978-0-9797462-2-2

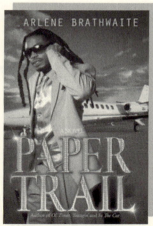

ISBN: 978-0-9797462-3-9

Brathwaite Publishing
P.O. Box 38205
Albany, NY 12203
Phone: (800) 476-1522
www.BrathwaitePublishing.com

Order Form

Title	Price	Quantity
Youngin' by Arlene Brathwaite	$15.00	_____
Ol 'Timer by Arlene Brathwaite	$15.00	_____
In the Cut by Arlene Brathwaite	$15.00	_____
Paper Trail by Arlene Brathwaite		
Shipping/handling (via U.S. Media Mail)	$ 3.95	_____
	Total:	_____

Purchaser Information

Name: _____ Reg. #:_____

Address: _____

_____

City: _____ State: _____ Zip: _____

Total Number of Books Ordered: _____

We accept Credit card payments, money orders and institutional checks.
No personal checks will be accepted.

Brathwaite Publishing in association with Oonlah Records Presents Paper Trail... The Theme music to the Novel

Written and Performed by Mr. Lee*G aka Leroy Griffith Jr.
Song Produced by: Lukas Kaiser
Recorded & Mixed at Oonlah Records in Brooklyn, NY
Publishing administered by Oonlah Publishing
Copyright Owned by Oonlah Publishing 2009
This song is available for purchase on Apple iTunes

Get your copies today!!
Available on
Apple iTunes

www.myspace.com/mrleegband

www.reverbnation.com/mrleegband

Brathwaite Publishing in association with Lil Villa Publishing Presents In the Cut... The Theme music to the Novel

Performed by the group CLESHAY
Written by: T.McClendon, R.Williams and C.Witters
Produced By: Corey "Kaboom" Blackwell and Phillip "Bang Out" Pitts
Recorded & Mixed at HillTop Studios in Bklyn, NY
Publishing administered by Lil Villa Publishing
The group CLESHAY appears courtesy of ENGR ENT LLC
Copyright Owned by Lil Villa Publishing and Brathwaite Publishing 2009
This song is available for purchase via the Engr Store at www.engrmusic.com

www.engrmusic.com

4789615R0

Made in the USA
Charleston, SC
17 March 2010